P9-BZM-323

THE REPLACEMENT WIFE

BRITNEY KING

WWW.BRITNEYKING.COM

ALSO BY BRITNEY KING

The Social Affair

Water Under The Bridge

Dead In The Water

Come Hell or High Water

Bedrock

Breaking Bedrock

Beyond Bedrock

Around The Bend

Somewhere With You

Anywhere With You

THE REPLACEMENT WIFE

BRITNEY KING

COPYRIGHT

Hot Banana Press

Cover Design by Britney King LLC

Cover Image by Nick Artnot

Copy Editing by Librum Artis Editorial Service

Proofread by Proofreading by the Page

First Edition: 2018

ISBN: 978-1985849839

britneyking.com

To Melinda.
For pure chance to have been so generous and so kind...
I was surely the lucky one.

PROLOGUE

What I'm thinking is...this isn't going to end well. At least not for me. How I'm feeling is, not ready to die. What I know is, everybody's somebody's fool. And, whoever said small things don't matter, never lit a wildfire with a single match.

Let's say you are at a stop light and in the car next to you is a girl—the words 'about to die' stamped on her forehead, the word 'doomed' written all over her—and let's pretend that girl is me.

This is the opposite of a joke. This can't be real.

If only I'd known then what I know now.

Unfortunately, rumination is useless at this point. I'm on borrowed time, so I try once again to dial out. I reposition the phone. It's not working. I have half a bar, which basically amounts to no cell service. I try 9-1-1 and wait for a connection. Then I try Tom's number. No luck there either.

It's hard to save your life when you've downed half a bottle of scotch. The wine I used as a chaser didn't help.

This reminds me, I press the button for the Instalook app. Surely, out of fifty thousand followers, one of them can help me. I'll go live when the time is right. Even without service, I can record.

I clear my throat, in search of my voice.

Testing, testing, one, two, three.

God, I hope you can hear me.

I speak low and carefully into the camera. I always forget which dot I'm supposed to focus on, so I shift until I'm sure I'm front and center on the screen. I once read it's all about the eyes. I turn and shift the phone so that it's at a good angle for selfies. Beth taught me this little trick. It's a bit cramped in here and it's dark, so I'm sure if this is actually even working, it looks all *Blair Witch Project*. You're probably thinking, how do I even know this is for real? I don't know how to answer that except to say that I once saw a thing on TV about how many people witness a crime and do nothing. It's a very real thing. I know because it happened to me too. If I ever get out of here, I'll tell you all about it. For now, it's a rather long story, and I'm afraid we haven't got time for it.

Anyway, I say into the camera. My voice comes out as a whisper. Squeaky, terrified. Meek. Not like me at all. Maybe this Instalook Live thing is working. I don't know. If you can even hear me, I don't know. But if you can, listen. And if you're listening, this is the story of everything that went wrong.

Part confession. Part last rites. My final prayer.

Hear me. See me. Remember me.

I'm trapped—on my way to my final destination, my eternal resting place. And there are so many things I'd like to change but can't.

I'm going to die. In the end, all I'll ever be is just another lie on someone's lips.

This recording is...evidence. How very hopeful I was. How very stupid. So, if you can hear me—if you're listening— it wasn't supposed to end this way. Not with me in the trunk of a car, headed for God knows where. Not with me dead.

I would have gone away quietly.

It's too late for that now.

My stomach churns. Choppy waters, this business of dying.

I feel nothing. I feel everything.

You fall to your highest level of preparation, he said that once. How prophetic.

That's the problem. Well, that's one of them. I wasn't prepared. Not for this. Probably, I should have thought to stay sober. But no, one drink turned into two, which turned into… God knows how many. *Look what you've done.* I was only trying to send a message. I should have known better.

Never let them take you to a second location. I should have forced him to kill me there. It's just—I'm not ready to die. I always thought I'd be old. I thought I'd have wrinkles and saggy skin… laugh lines well earned.

You fall to your highest level of preparation. Of all of the lines he used, this is the one that sticks out the most. It taunts me, as though it could somehow help me now. My father used to say that too. Turns out, he was right. I shouldn't have let my husband skimp on our cell service. I should have argued that these things are important. Given the *one thing* that could possibly save my life says searching…searching…searching…I should have fought harder. This thing that I'm holding, this thing that's filming me. It's useless. It's basically just a holder for apps. A façade, like everything else. The illusion of safety.

My head swims.

Regret tastes horrible, in case you're wondering.

Everything hurts.

You should have stuck to the plan. I know that now.

What I don't know is, how he plans to kill me. Will it be quick? Will the liquor dull the effects? Will he make me suffer?

You never should have gotten mixed up in this. I know that too.

I can still picture the night we met, him sitting at the bar. I can still hear the music. Jazz, I think. *Focus. Only seven percent of any given message is based on the words. Thirty-eight percent comes from the tone of voice and fifty-five percent from the speaker's body language and face.*

"Have you any interest in playing a game?" he asked over his dirty martini. Funny, I can remember his expensive suit but not the expression he wore.

"Depends on the game..." I'd said with a shrug. A playful, stupid shrug. That sums up what I was—so sure of myself, so foolish in the end.

I remember he smiled. "It's a fun one," he assured me. I can't recall his tone.

He raised his finger, and the bartender placed another drink in front of me. *Researchers have found that humans have a limited capacity for keeping focus in complex, stressful situations like negotiations. Less, if there's alcohol involved.*

I remember feeling brave. That's before I knew enough to know I'm not. I cocked my head, took him in. "Unless you're on the losing end."

"Ah, a skeptic," he said. I remember he was handsome. Not spectacularly so, but enough to take notice. Not that it mattered. "Let's start with truth or dare."

I sipped my martini. His choice. I hadn't realized it wasn't a question. *When it's important, never lead with a question, always a suggestion.* "I'm going to assume you want to go first so...truth."

Another smile. "Excellent choice," he remarked. "I've always had an affinity for the truth."

You have to feel for the truth behind the camouflage; you have to note the small pauses that suggest discomfort and lies. Don't look to verify what you expect. If you do, that's what you'll find. "Most people do."

"Now that there is a lie." He shook his head slowly when he spoke. So cool. So confident. *Breadcrumbs.* "Most people only want the truth as long as it works out in their favor."

"I can't speak for most people." Maybe it was the drink. Maybe

I was just feeding him what he wanted to hear. Maybe I was just naive. It's too late to know.

That all seems like a lifetime ago. The night we met.

He toasted me. "Shall we begin?"

I lifted my brow and then my glass. "Begin away."

That's not really where it began. I know that now.

"Do you see yourself settling down?"

I almost choked. Sometimes, but not often, I was taken by surprise. *Get on the same page at the outset. You have to clearly understand the lay of the land before you consider acting within its confines. Why are you there? What do you want? What do they want? Why?* I didn't think to ask those questions. Not of myself and certainly not of him. "Settle down? You mean with a picket fence and two point five children?"

He stuck out his bottom lip, his shoulders rose to his ears. "Something like that."

I gave it some thought. My mind was already made up. "Maybe."

"*You?*" he said, eyeing my dress. "You think you could be domesticated?"

I narrowed my eyes. Classic NLP. Neuro-Linguistic Programming. I didn't know then what I know now. *Insult them at the onset; they'll work harder to prove you wrong*. "Why not me?" I scoffed. I sat up straighter, mocking him as though I was offended. Maybe a part of me was.

He touched the rim of his glass to his lips. "You don't think you're too young?"

I laughed. "My mother often reminds me that when she was my age, she was two years married and pregnant with me."

His brow lifted. "Is your mother happy?"

I gulped my martini. "She is now."

"So, you don't think most people are living a lie?"

"Meaning what?"

"In marriage. Family. You don't think it's all a show?"

"Like I said, I can't speak for most people."

He spoke directly, affirmatively. "But you think you'd be happy under such confined conditions?"

It was a leading question. I played right into it. "I think I could be, yes."

"Not a skeptic then," he decided. "An idealist."

"Is it not the truth you are seeking?"

He leaned back, away from me. *Give them space. The further they fall.* "You're good," he'd said. "I'll give you that." I waited while he glanced around the bar before turning his attention back to me. "I don't know." I watched as he drummed his fingers on the table. "Somehow, I just don't see you as the type to be content with that sort of life."

"You don't know me."

He knew me better than I thought.

"Maybe you're right. But as the Danish folk say, 'you bake with the flour you have.'" His eyes were on my legs. I remember that.

"Are you Danish?"

"No, but that's the point. You can't be what you're not."

"I'd have to be. I'm not that good of a liar."

He half-heartedly scoffed. "Oh, I'd beg to differ."

I shook my head. "I keep the emotions real. Maybe not the rest, but the way I feel, I'm not so good at hiding that."

"In that case, how about a dare?"

"Hmmm," I said, stalling. For what, I didn't know. "Those require a lot of trust." I cocked my head studying him. "I'm not sure I know you well enough for that."

"Faith," he countered. "More than trust."

"Right."

"Is that a yes?"

I smirked. "It's a maybe."

"Have dinner with me."

"Is that your dare?"

"Not exactly."

"What is it then?"

His eyes settled on mine. There was no hesitation in what he said next. "It's an invitation to make the biggest mistake of your life."

I started to tell him he had no idea how high the bar was set. Instead, I settled on, "sounds promising."

"Oh, it is."

I sipped my drink slowly, when really I felt like downing the rest of it. I asked the bartender for a glass of water. "But who would accept an offer like that?"

His expression was serious. "I was hoping you would."

I smiled, which was in effect my answer.

Now, I realize he was wrong. That invitation wasn't the biggest mistake of my life. It wasn't any of the stuff that had happened before; it wasn't trusting the wrong person, or having one too many. Not that night. And not now, either. My biggest mistake was falling in love.

You leave me no choice. I drift back to a time when I had a choice. They say the mind goes to strange places when confronted with death.

The car accelerates, and I realize we've reached the highway. There's no turning back.

Put up a fight. How? And why, if you know you can't win? Even if I could somehow run for it, I'd always be running. Sure, I could mess with the taillights, cross my fingers we'd get pulled over. I could try and locate the emergency hatch. At least this way, I will die an internet celebrity. This way my life will have meant something.

My breath comes heavier. I feel a panic attack coming on. Not that I've ever had one, but I've never cared for small, dark places.

Frantically, I search for wires. They make it look so easy in the movies. Here, in real life, it's no use. I guess you don't always get so lucky. And anyway, I'm not the captive of an amateur.

If you can't save yourself, save someone else. Leave clues like breadcrumbs. They're more likely to find you that way.

I left my clothes. Pantyhose first, panties, and at last my bra. Like a proper drunk. And now, I leave you this. I can't be sure anyone will actually see it. I can't even make a call. But Instalook says there are eighteen thousand of you geared up, in queue, waiting to watch my demise, I say, my face centered on the screen. Many more before now. Some of you, I say into the camera, maybe *most* of you, won't believe me. You may say this is fake. It doesn't matter. If believability is what you want, then I suggest sticking to the safety of the neatly colored lines of your own life. And for God's sake, if a hero is what you're looking for, let me say this up front: you're in the wrong story.

As for the rest of you, I'm going to die. I promise a good show.

CHAPTER ONE

MELANIE

Before

No one is going to feel sorry for me. They didn't when the 'big accident' happened. They didn't when I was tormented in school. They didn't when all the other bad things happened. So why would they start now?

Someone should really take girls aside and tell them the truth: you can't be pretty *and* smart. You have to pick, one or the other. And then there's the other bigger truth, the one they really ought to chase it with: if you are both attractive and intelligent, it won't be the opposite sex that will do you in. They can make life hard, for sure. But it will be your very own kind that betrays you when it counts most. Perhaps that's the worst of it all.

I can already hear it. *Poor little rich girl,* they'll say. They would be right, of course. Under normal circumstances, I certainly look the part. Today, I confess silently to the reflection staring back at me in the mirror, not so much. If unkempt is what I'm going for, if that's what they want me to be, then I've nailed it. My hair's a mess; my roots could use a touch up. I run my hands through it, leaning in to get a better look at just how far I've fallen off the wagon. Ever so slightly, light shades of brown are beginning to peek through the baby blonde. Nothing too bad yet. But one has to be careful about these things; that's what my mother says. Like weeds in a garden, inattention to one's appearance is not the kind of thing one can stand for too long without consequence. She has a point about that. My eyes are puffy and red and without a doubt a facial is in order. I assess my complexion. *You won't be young forever.* My mother's voice again. She likes to hammer that in. Unfortunately, my pores seem to be siding with her. I roll my neck. A massage couldn't hurt. I'll get to it, to all of it, just as soon as this nightmare blows over.

For now, I force myself away from the mirror before I do something I'll regret. Almost everyone has a weak spot, otherwise known as vanity. To distract myself, I gaze longingly around my expansive closet. I guess it's now or never, sort of like ripping of the Band-Aid. I won't be able to hide out in here forever. Pride won't let me. I pull a bag off the shelf. *Too big.* I'm going to miss you, I say. I reach for another. *Too small.* I could cry just thinking about how much I'll miss that one. I let my fingers trail against the smooth, cool leather. I stop and linger for good measure. I've always had a soft spot for anything Italian. That's why I'm in this mess to begin with.

My father calls my name again, his voice loud and booming over the intercom, and I realize this is it. I can't stall any longer. The third one will have to be the charm. "Coming," I yell as I hurriedly stuff a few of my things into the chosen one. My mind is too fucked to know if I'm making the right choice. I mean, how is one supposed to choose between Givenchy and Hermes? It's like asking me to choose between my right arm and my left. I feel sick being put in this position. When I've finished shoving in what I can make fit, I realize I can't very well face my parents naked, so I throw on jeans and a t-shirt. It's the best I can do under the circumstances. My mother hates it when I 'dress down.' I'm doing this for her. For the unfairness of it all.

Everything in her life has taken a turn for the worse. It's time to cut the cord, I overheard her say to my father. Good cop, bad cop. It's always been their favorite game.

Whatever. Let them play. Once I'm out that door, I'm never coming back. I promised as much through crocodile tears.

"Melanie," my father repeats. His voice bounces through the house, through doors and walls, like an all-knowing being. "Time's up."

I fling the designer bag over my shoulder and then give the bedroom of my childhood one last look. I hesitate for a second, thinking maybe I should take more. *What we forget, we can just buy when we get there.* My mother taught me that. And anyway, who am I kidding? Of course I'll be back. I'm guessing this whole thing will be swept under the rug within a few days—my parents are experts at that—and then I'll be right back here in the only home I've ever known.

Okay, fine. That last part is a bit of an exaggeration.

Technically speaking, I have four homes, or rather, as my parents like to remind me, *they* have four homes. This one has always been my favorite. But now, thanks to a minor mishap, I'm looking at zero places to live.

"You're grown now," my father informed me. "It's time you started acting like it.

"Go," my mother agreed. "Spread your wings. We can't have you living here forever."

"I like this house," I assured them. After all, what's not to like? Ten thousand square feet all to myself. Stocked pantry. Staff of five. Parents who only fly in on occasion. The rest of the time I'm left to my own devices. And yet, here they are, kicking me out of a house they hardly ever set foot in.

My mother seemed to read my mind. "When I was your age—"

"I know." I rolled my eyes. "You were already married and knocked up."

My father started that pacing thing he does. "Why must you always be so crass, Melanie?"

I couldn't argue with that. It's what led to this situation.

"Do you realize the predicament you've put us in? The embarrassment this has caused?"

I threw my hands in the air. "Well, obviously. You keep reminding me."

The night before, I'd cost him his biggest client by getting drunk at the semi-annual charity event my parents put on. It wasn't intentional. I just glanced at the list of donors, chose the largest one, and gravitated that way. I hadn't meant to sleep with him. But I hadn't meant *not to* either. What was I supposed to do? I was bored. I didn't even want to go in the first place. But my parents insisted I "show face"— whatever that means. I certainly succeeded at that in the end, though, they would attest. A full bar and a little coercion are a bad mix for me. Someone should have warned them.

Now, he's downstairs pacing again, she's probably pinching the bridge of her nose, pleading with him to stop, and I don't know why they're acting so dramatic about the whole thing.

"How will you ever amount to anything if you keep behaving in this manner?" My mother demanded to know after the incident, or rather after hotel security was called. The way they were acting, you'd think it was the actual police or something. You'd think I murdered the guy, not just fucked him. And *they* think *they're* embarrassed? Let me tell you. He was old. Sure, to their point, he was married, and yes, I may have caused a bit of a scene when he said sleeping with me was a mistake, but that's no reason to turn your back on your flesh and blood.

Needless to say, my parents don't see it that way. They only see in dollar signs. So, here I am, Hermes bag in hand, on the verge of being homeless.

"You need to get a job or volunteer...or something," my father said. "You do nothing but sleep all day and God knows what all night."

Apparently, it wasn't a question, and seducing his biggest clients was not the response he'd been after.

"You're twenty-two years old, Melanie. It's time. Your mother and I simply can't support this behavior anymore."

My mouth gaped. I shifted from foot to foot. "Where am I supposed to go?" *Please say the Bahamas house. Please. Please. Please.* I crossed my fingers behind my back.

My mother looked like she wanted to cry, so I figured I wasn't getting my first choice. Fine. *The Aspen house?* Then she did cry, and I thought, surely that's it. She really loves that house. It was probably a compromise with my father, as a part of their good cop, bad cop routine. *If I have to kick her out, you have to give her the Aspen house.* It would take some redecorating—it's safe to say my mother and I have very different taste—and sure, I'd have to get used to the cold, but it could be workable.

Better yet, *maybe they bought me my own.* It's not like my mother to concede, and I've been pining for something that belongs to me. I told them as much, and they got me a puppy instead. I'll leave that story for another day. The short version is I'm no longer a dog owner.

When I come downstairs, bag in hand, my father hands me an envelope. I could cry. I could leap up and down and throw my arms around him. Finally. The deed to my very own home. His sudden frown at my eagerness to rip the envelope from his hands kills my excitement. I feel dead inside. "We've cancelled your credit cards," he says. "That one there," he points, "It's prepaid. I'm afraid you'll have to learn to budget."

My face drops. My stomach follows suit. It's not the deed to my own house. I break out in a cold sweat, and that's not an exaggeration. *Budget.* Who has time for that? *Prepaid?* I don't even know what this means. That word wasn't even on my radar, and I didn't think my father's either.

"How could you do this to your only daughter?"

They stare at the floor. I assume they weren't prepared for that question. It always cuts right to the heart of the matter. For all of us.

"Now I'm going to be like all of those people you think you're better than. You realize that, right? You know, the ones you look down on?" I throw up my hands. Clearly, they haven't thought this through. "What are you going to tell people?"

They look at each other. No one speaks. My parents were born into money, both of them. Their business, as successful as it might be—even with the untimely departure of their largest client—is just a front for hiding some of that good old money.

Finally, my father sighs. "Donovan is waiting in the car," he tells me, glancing at my one bag. "Have you finished packing all your things?"

Donovan is our family driver. *Look at these two.* They even outsource kicking their daughter out.

"You're serious?" I search the foyer for hidden cameras, a sign that this is all a joke. Then I pinch myself, watching as the blood pools to the surface. "Ouch."

"Please don't hurt yourself dear," my mother pleads. She wipes a fake tear from her fake eyelashes. She acts like she cares. She only cares about herself. If I off myself, it'll be on her conscience. "We know you'll make us proud."

I shake my head. "This feels like a dream."

"It's time you face reality," my father says.

"Just wait," I seethe. "I'm going to show you guys. You can't get away with treating your daughter this way and not have it come back to—"

"I've paid for two weeks at The Driskill," my father interrupts. His voice is stern. "After that, you're on your own."

My eyes widen. "You're sending me to a hotel?"

"You can't stay here," he said. And that was that.

CHAPTER TWO

TOM

Before

A clear motive is what I was looking for. In hindsight, I realize it is ridiculous. Often, you can't assign a reason to irrational acts. Oddly enough, she expected me to feel sorry for her. I didn't. Serves her right, what happened. Minus the blood. That part I do regret. I hate blood. I hate Houston. I hate that I was sent there. Even one day is too much to spend in that trash receptacle they call a city. And I really don't like hotels, or sidewalks outside of hotels. Or, for that matter, people.

She was just one among many I happened upon that day, head down, oblivious, in a rush. All of them the same in their incessant hurrying from one place to another, so unoriginal. Like insects scurrying about. Like cockroaches when you turn on the light. *Don't mess with them, Aunt Jeannie told me once, and they won't mess with you.* My aunt was a liar. But not about that. I once kicked an ant pile just to see it scatter. It landed me in the ER. Messy business if they catch ya, she said as I spent hours in an oatmeal bath that had long turned cold. Needless to say, I never tried that again.

That's what I was thinking when she bumped me, her iced coffee splattering my crisp, white shirt.

"Jesus. Look what you've done," I huffed, dabbing at the stain. At least I'd thought to have June pack me another. *Always better to be safe than sorry.* I don't know what I expected her to say, but an apology would have been nice. When I looked down, ready to meet eye to eye, that's when I saw she wasn't standing at all. All I saw was a heap of long legs, wavy blonde hair, and fair skin. I hate the unexpected.

"What *I've* done?" she quipped. "You're not the one on the ground."

"Here," I offered, extending my hand. My eyes drifted down her legs. Five, maybe six-inch heels. Nude. Not the most practical of shoes for one to wear when they aren't watching where they are going.

She refused the gesture. Part endearing, part amusing, I reveled in the time—time I didn't have, I might add— that it took her to rise to her feet.

"Easy peasy," I said.

She countered my mocking by straightening her back, causing her clear blue eyes to meet mine. They hit me right in the gut. So vibrant, so angry. I bet she's good in bed. The ones who can hide their anger, the self-contained, normally are. You just have to know how to channel it properly.

"I needed that coffee. Every bit of it. And now look—" Her voice came out smooth, direct, like music you can't help but turn up.

"Maybe you should consider putting the phone down," I offered, glancing at my watch. I frowned, realizing I wouldn't have enough time to run back into the hotel, take the elevator to my floor and make the necessary change. I'd be late, and stained shirt or not, that's a rule I couldn't break.

"Maybe you should watch where you're going." Her voice was

rougher this time. Less melodic. "Maybe you should learn to be a gentleman."

My eyes met hers. I opened my mouth to speak, but nothing came out. The words were lodged somewhere deep in the recesses of my brain. *Always be a gentleman, my father told me once. They can take a lot from you. But never that.*

She didn't try to fill the silence, she simply smoothed her navy dress. That's when I noticed the blood.

"You're bleeding," I said.

Her eyes followed mine. I expected some of her front to falter. She only shrugged. I stared into her pale eyes, awaiting a response, but her expression was blank. I was disappointed this turned me on as much as it did. I reminded myself that I am a happily married man. She smiled then, reminding me that her face is sweet, but not altogether innocent. A deadly combination, to be sure. My phone buzzed in my pocket. "I have to go."

"Aren't you going to apologize?" I detected anger in her voice. The sight of blood paralyzes me. Nothing else has that effect. Certainly not her.

"Sorry," I shifted. "About your knee." I remind her she bumped into me.

She narrowed her eyes. "You're an asshole."

`I didn't have time to argue for my limitations. Instead, I adjusted my suit jacket, turned on my heel and practically bolted in the other direction, the annoyance running through my veins propelling me toward the future. I did not come here for distractions, nor did I have time for them. *Stained shirt or not, I would sprint to that meeting if I had to. I was going to crush Watson. Get in, get out, my father always said. Make it so quick they don't know what hit 'em. Best not to let 'em see you coming. That, my son, is the art of war.*

"If I never run into you again," she called out, her voice tinged with rage, "it'll be too soon."

~

UNFORTUNATELY FOR HER, TOO SOON CAME LATER THAT EVENING IN the hotel bar. Seated at the bar, I spotted her immediately. It was the hair, half done up in waves, her slim shoulders, tanned and inviting in the backless shirt she wore. She wasn't a novice. Even I could see that.

I had six minutes and thirty seconds before Sam Watson was due to arrive, if he was on time. Thankfully, I knew he would be. I slid onto the empty barstool, leaving two seats between us. The bartender came over and pulled a napkin from the pocket of his vest. "What can I get you?"

"The lady," I motioned. "Her drink is nearly empty. How about another? Just water for me."

When the bartender placed the drink in front of her, she looked up from her phone. He nodded in my direction. Her eyes landed on me. "You."

"I hope this isn't too soon for you," I said, toasting her with my water.

Her finger trailed the rim of her glass.

"A peace offering."

Her eyes met mine. "How presumptuous of you."

"No," I told her. "Gentlemanly."

"Well, at any rate, you owe me." She twisted on her stool and brought her legs from under the bar. "My knee," she pointed. "I think you broke it."

I studied the bandage and then raised my brow. "Looks good as new to me."

"Yeah, well," she twisted back. "I guess we see what we want to see."

"That or we aren't looking at all," I said, a subtle reminder who's at fault.

"Funny." She took a sip from her glass and then held it in my direction. "Thank you for the drink. But I don't think we should talk anymore." She blushed when she said it, and I wondered if the rest of her was as flawless as her face. "I'm meeting someone."

God, she's young. "What a coincidence. I am, as well. "

"Your wife?" I followed her eyes to my left hand.

"No."

Her face fell. I was expecting the opposite effect. "Oh."

There was a lull in conversation. I knew better than to fill it.

"What's it like?" she asked, finally. "Being married."

"I thought we weren't supposed to talk anymore..."

She shrugs. "I'll never see you again..." she said. "So, I just have to know the stranger I met in a bar once upon a time was happy."

"Can I offer you a little wisdom?"

"That's why I asked."

"Most people you'll meet in bars aren't happy."

She laughed. "But you see, I wasn't asking about most people." I watched her lips as they met her glass. I felt a pang of something. Jealousy, maybe. She looked up then. "I was asking about you."

"It's everything," I answered. "It's being as happy as you've ever been..."

She cocked her head. I could see she thought I was joking. "Is that even a thing?"

"You tell me."

She gaped at me. "I wouldn't know. I'm never getting married."

"That's a shame." I checked my watch. "I guess you'll never know."

She looked away. "Are you expecting your mistress?"

"How presumptuous of you."

Her eyes narrowed. She didn't like the taste of her words on my lips.

"No," I told her, finally. "A member of my church."

She coughed, choking on her martini.

"Well, a potential member, actually."

"Here...you're meeting...in a bar?"

"They have tables and chairs." I motioned around the place. "Ambiance and...very attractive scenery." I smiled. "What more could a man want?"

Maybe she rolled her eyes. Maybe she bit her lip. I was already too far gone to pinpoint which.

I extended my hand. "I'm Tom."

She took it in hers. I wondered if she was always so accepting. "Mel."

"Nice to meet you, Mel," I said, trying out her name on my lips. Her skin was smooth and warm, her handshake soft. The kind of woman you could break and have fun doing it. The kind of woman I married.

She blushed again. *God, she was attractive.* Classically beautiful, properly so. Model perfect. A tilt of the head, a glance up and down. Curiosity, everywhere. "What?"

"Nothing." This time it was me who looked away. I forced myself to take a sip of water. Reminded myself, I'm married. Not dead. What harm could a little banter do? "Short for Melinda?"

"Huh?"

So, beautiful. But not so quick on the uptake. Guess you can't have it all.

"Your name. Is Mel short for Melinda?"

"Oh." She shook her head. "No. For Melanie."

"Hmmm," I said spotting Sam Watson across the bar. The meeting that morning hadn't gone as well as I would have liked. Not once I'd presented him with the numbers. This isn't normally my job. I'm an accountant, not a salesman. I'm here filling in for Adam, our actual sales guy—the one who supposedly has the flu and chose not to suck it up. That left Mark, our leader, with no choice but to send me. I don't like to disappoint Mark, and that is how I've found myself here, both in this town and in this bar, both of which I hate.

Sam Watson is a very close third. He wanted into New Hope, he assured me. He likes the idea of the church, of the exclusivity, the chance to invest his almighty dollars. The tax deduction is also a nice incentive. But he'd countered for a lower percentage of a tithe. A percentage I couldn't agree to even if I wanted to. In addition, he'd wanted us to waive the membership fee, and that I was for sure unwilling to concede. Which put us at a standstill. Meaning our second meeting had to work in my favor.

Melanie glanced at the clock on the wall. "I'm afraid I've been stood up."

Suddenly, I had an idea. Suddenly, I was glad for her appearance. I needed The Watsons on our books. They would be very good for business, and also, I was determined to win. I knew there would be hell to pay if I let Mark down.

"Sam," I called, motioning him over.

"Join us," I said to her.

She sat up a little straighter. "I can't."

My eyes locked on hers. "Sure you can."

For a second, she looked taken aback. But then, she downed her drink and offered a shrug. I took that as a yes.

"Tom," Sam quipped taking my hand. His eyes were on Melanie. "Sam," I said, squeezing harder than I needed to. "Always a pleasure."

He broke grip first. "And who is this?"

"Melanie," she stated, welcoming his hand. I got my answer. She's not hesitant.

Sam placed his other hand on top of hers. He held it there for two seconds too long. That's how I knew it was pretty much in the bag.

"I didn't know we were having company," he mentioned when he let go. He turned to face me. "What a lucky surprise."

"Tom and I just sort of bumped into each other," Melanie confessed shyly. I start to think maybe first impressions aren't that reliable. "Anyway," she added more candidly, "I'd best be going." I watched as she smoothed her hair. Sam Watson watched too, captivated.

"Stay," I offered. I could see that's what she wanted. Clarification. And then, "I'm sure Mr. Watson won't mind."

His brow rose. "Fine by me."

"I ordered you a scotch," I said, turning my attention to him. "I hope that's okay?" I saw the bottle in his office this morning, so I already know it is more than okay. I leave that part out.

"Perfect." His focus was on Melanie.

"You seem familiar..."

No, she doesn't.

"Everyone says that," she told him, tucking a strand of hair behind her ear. "It's my face, I think."

"So, you're not from here?"

Melanie shook her head. "Boise."

"Wow." Sam laughed boisterously. "Can't say I was expecting that."

She smiled with her eyes.

"What brings you to Houston?" Sam asked.

"A job."

"You?"

She laughed playfully. Nervously. "What is that supposed to mean?"

It means he's a pretentious prick, that's what it means.

Before he could answer, I stepped in. Marking my territory. Lying where I knew it would serve me. I didn't want to spend a second longer than necessary in this town, in this bar. I wanted to close the deal, and I'd just learned exactly the kind of bait I needed to do it. "Melanie is interviewing with New Hope."

She gave me a sideways glance. "It's just Mel."

"Forgive me," I said, lifting my water from the table. "*Just Mel* is considering a job with the church."

Watson's face offered a satisfied look. "For the project Mark has been telling me about?"

I'm not sure which one he's speaking of so I simply say, "We're not sure yet."

"Well, amen for that," he said, I assume before he realized he hadn't had enough to drink to be that brazen in front of someone he was looking to impress. "Man," he added as he straightened his back. He must have wanted to get a better look at her tits because his eyes were not where they should have been when he spoke next. "They'll be very lucky to have you."

"I haven't made any firm decisions." Thankfully, she didn't notice Watson being rude because her eyes were watching me.

Sam finished his scotch in one gulp. "Leave it to Tom to kill two birds with one stone."

He motioned the bartender for another. "I've heard about this guy..."

Melanie smiled. "Yes, I get the feeling Tom is very good at double dealing."

I downed the last of my water. "Not as good as I'd like to be."

CHAPTER THREE

MELANIE

Three months later

Be careful about the forbidden. It'll get you every time. Maybe I could get used to this place, I think, as I look out the window at the front of the house, across the street, where someone is mowing a lawn. A service person. Few people around here know much about manual labor.

In that way, it's not so different than where I came from. Somehow, although I haven't completely put my finger on exactly how, things are very different. The facades are tasteful, the lawns tidy and expansive. Here, one-or two-acre lots frame smaller, neat houses, a quaint mix of modern and old-fashioned. Sophisticated, built to look like old money, even if that's not what occupies them. To my right, there are children playing in the street. There's no absence of people. Not like back home where people have second, and even third places of residence. Often, more. That's how smart people hide money. Here, I'm the only one hiding anything. In fact, our street is particularly idyllic, an air of sleepiness, a veneer of safety. Tree-lined and shady, it reminds me of a model town constructed for no other reason than to show the way people used to live. So, I guess some things remain the same.

I watch as a mother calls her child in from the yard. Crouching so she's at eye level, she points her finger, scolding him for playing in the street. If I have children, I think, my hand instinctively going for my belly, or rather *when* I have children, I will make nothing off limits. I will let them drink their selves silly, eat themselves sick, smoke themselves into oblivion, fuck their way to heartache. And when they are at the height of their hangovers—at their worst, hurt, lonely, full of regret—I will drag them to a recovery center where we will gaze at addicts, true addicts in the throws of withdraw. I will drag them to wings of hospitals to see patients that are relatives who aren't ours just to say look, that is what you will become. It will be like a visit to the zoo, only animals of a different kind, and yet, no less trapped.

And if ever I want to show them what a person looks like who is dead inside, I can skip the strangers and the field trips. I only have to introduce them to their maternal grandmother. What is wrong with her, they might ask? They will want to know the point I am trying to make because unlike the writhing addicts and the half-dead hospital patients, she will look fine on the outside. Look closer, I will tell them. You see her eyes, notice how they are vacant? And when she wraps her arms around you, like any good grandma would, you will feel the void. That's because she is empty— a hollow shell of a woman who long ago gave all her worth to a man. Set it up like a bank account, and after years of withdrawals, one day she woke up and realized there was nothing left.

There are many kinds of love, I will teach them. And someday, when they are old enough to understand, I will tell them the truth. I did not marry for any of them. I used to see my father with his mistresses, his admirers. Don't worry, he said to me once. I do not love them. Not like I love you.

Maybe he never thought I, his own flesh, would grow up to be that. Little did he know.

I am not so different from his lovers, really. I, too, chose my partner for utility. For what he can offer me. It may not be love, but it is sufficient enough.

I do not want to end up like my mother.

I learned a few things over the years by watching her. I learned more from my father. I learned you can get away with pretty much anything so long as you're judicious about it and go about it with a smile. He started out easy with his women, matters of convenience, mostly. Secretaries— babysitters—basically the low-hanging fruit. Kind of like one might start out drinking two-buck chuck before gradually growing bored and moving on to the good, high-dollar stuff. And still, he is a kind man, well liked. That's what people who think they know him would say. You wouldn't have to twist their arm either. But appearances can be deceiving. Just ask my mother.

If one were to mention the backroom dealings or the affairs, the waves of heartbreak left in his wake, the women, so many women, those same well meaning people would mostly blame her. Well, she stays, they'd tell you, lips and palms pressed together. I guess it can't be that bad. Or more likely they'd point out a flaw. Something's missing, they'd say. She must be a prude or surely she's too controlling, too demanding. Rarely would they blame my father for being the taker, the addict that he is.

But then, nobody has a perfect heart.

That's how I landed here. In my new life, on my new lane, shiny and bright. It was simple enough in the beginning. But nothing ever stays that way, does it?

Maybe that's why short love affairs have always been my favorite kind. Abrupt, beautiful. Technicolor and surround-sound. Like a warm summer morning, when there's still so much promise to be had for the day. Before things get real. Before you see into the depths of a person. Before they see into the depths of you.

That's why I chose a starter husband. Nothing's permanent, plenty of room to move up.

Easily enough, I bumped into Tom on the street. When people ask how we met, that's how the story goes. At least that's the simple version. A drink or two for me. Zero for him. A one-night stand and, well, the truth is a little more complicated. But isn't it always? In any case, I won't bore you with the details.

Fast forward to now. He's cooking dinner. I'm cooking his kid. Or so he thinks. We've been man and wife for two weeks. Supposedly, I'll be fourteen weeks along, tomorrow. Give or take. My darling husband has been a widower for all of six weeks. It doesn't take a genius to work out the math. Simple, and yet, anything but.

"So, did you get around to reading the agreement today?" Tom asks, peering up at me once I've made my way into the kitchen. I think he must have called me three times before I could tear myself away from the front window and force myself to face him. I lean against the counter and cross my arms. Pretend I haven't heard. Maybe I haven't. I'm too focused on the butcher knife he's holding. I watch him slowly and methodically chop a head of lettuce.

"Melanie?" I realize he's going to spell it out. "The agreement. Did you read it?"

"No," I say and because I'm too lazy to come up with an excuse three weeks running, I fall back on the tried and true. My eyes meet his. "I wasn't feeling well." I sigh then long and heavy. I want him to feel my pain. "I thought they called it morning sickness... but it's all day, every day. "

He cocks an eyebrow. "That should pass soon."

"Let's hope."

He mixes the lettuce with his hands and tosses it in a bowl. "When June was pregnant—"

I suck a breath in sharply. I hold it and bend at the waist. A searing pain tears at my side. Heat rushes through me. It's fire, and it's burning me all the way down. Ligaments stretching, the internet said when I researched what I'm supposed to feel at this point. Must be the placebo effect. Or Munchausen syndrome. Who knows? It's better than the norm. At least I feel something.

When I recover, Tom says, "Maybe you should lie down."

"No," I tell him, my voice strained. My stomach flip-flops. I might be sick and not for the reason he thinks. That name—his dead wife's—it's the first four letter word, not counting work, that I actually dislike.

"Suit yourself," he says. I rise slowly, steadying myself. I fill my lungs with air and then blow out my cheeks, breathing fast in and out. Just like they do in the movies. Lamaze or whatever it's called.

The other night when I couldn't sleep, which is most nights really, I made the grave mistake of googling childbirth videos. Whoever said childbirth is a beautiful experience is a liar. All I saw was blood and gore and pain. No way am I going through that. Ever. I saw enough to know that Lamaze is something I'll never need. I'm smarter than that. I'd make a beeline for the drugs at the first twinge of pain. What's the point of suffering anyway? I'd said that to Tom once when it came up.

"I don't know," he'd said. "I guess that's the way God intended it."

"You're wrong," I told him. "If God had intended women to suffer he wouldn't have invented birth control."

He looked at me funny.

"Or narcotics," I added.

"God, I love you," he said.

I don't know why he said that. But I was relieved. I didn't say it back. Some things are too precious to lie about.

Tom meets my eye then as though he knows what I'm thinking. But he can't. I watch as he takes steaks from the refrigerator. If we're having red meat, it must be a special occasion. My husband is very particular about his health. Husband. That word didn't bother me as much as the word that is supposed to come after it. Mother. The thought sucker-punches me. Sweat beads at my temples; my knees feel weak. I might faint. I watch as Tom pulls the raw steaks from the marinade and places them on a platter. The sight reminds me of the birth video. I have to look away.

"There's something I want to discuss with you," he says catching my attention. "After dinner."

He knows.

"Which is why I was hoping you would have read the agreement."

I feel the blood rush to my cheeks. "I told you. I was sick!"

I wait for him to say something. He doesn't. He simply washes his hands carefully, soaping them twice. Then he deftly dries them. I hate the way he's so calm about everything.

I open a drawer, pretend I'm searching for something, and then slam it shut. "Aren't you going to say anything?"

Tom cocks his head. "What's there to say?"

"I don't know—how about I'm sorry you're sick? How about I'm sorry for knocking you up?"

"Here," he offers. "I think you should sit down." He walks around the bar and pulls out a chair. There's a smirk on his face. It's faint, but I see it nonetheless. I want to knock it right off.

"I don't want to sit."

"You shouldn't get so upset in your condition. You really need to take it easy."

My condition. That's one way to put it. God. My hand moves to my still-flat stomach. Instantly, I feel relieved. I'm not ready to get fat. I'm not ready to be anyone's mother. Honestly, I don't think I'll ever be ready. I can't say that's changed, and yet, I can't tell him the truth. Not yet.

"You're going to be a mother," he tells me. "That means putting what you want aside, Melanie." His tone is bitter, and I hate it when he calls me by my full name. This and the fact that he combined it with the M word makes my head spin. Just the thought of someone calling me mommy makes me dizzy. My throat tightens. I feel my organs being crushed, panic rushing to the surface. This is why I can't sleep. I can't breathe. I'm suffocating in my lies.

Tom doesn't notice. He pushes the cutting board my way. "Can you finish slicing the cucumber?"

"I thought you wanted me to take it easy?"

"Well, I have to tend to the grill." His brow lifts. "I assume you want to eat."

I roll my eyes and step toward him. He hands me the knife.

"You are so beautiful," he tells me, his hand on mine. I stare at them, our fingers intertwined, gripping the knife. Something in me melts. Or at least it wants to. I've never felt more together, more a part of something. I've never felt more alone. I read on the internet what I'm supposed to feel, what I'm supposed to think, and I try to make it come naturally. But it rarely does. It takes so much pretending to be this way. People have no idea. It's only fun sometimes. Mostly, it's exhausting.

Ask him for the money.

"I was thinking about going shopping tomorrow… Nothing fits."

He murmurs something I can't make out.

I shift from foot to foot. "Tom?"

He searches my face.

"I need money."

"I gave you money."

"I spent that."

He tilts his head. The muscle in his jaw flexes. "You spent six thousand dollars in two days?"

"I don't know," I say, rolling my shoulders. "Maybe. I guess."

"On what?"

I suck in my bottom lip and once again, I shrug. "Just because you're an accountant, doesn't mean I am."

"Well, sorry," he tells me.

"Inflation," I say. This seems like a word he will understand. "Me, too."

Then he catches me off guard. "But you should have started with the necessities."

"So, what…I'm on an allowance?"

"Not an allowance. A budget."

That word. He might as well have taken the knife and shoved it through my windpipe. Seems like that would be more pleasant.

"I can't believe this," I say throwing up my hands. "What am I supposed to wear?"

I've never felt more locked down, more trapped. I could change that. Before it's too late. When he lets go of the knife, I could decide to end this. It would be so easy. Just a short stumble forward, and I could make contact, carefully shoving his former wife's very expensive, very proper knife into his stomach. I'm fairly confident I could even make it look like an accident. He just slipped, that's what I would say. Surely it happens all the time.

"You look pale," Tom says. "Are you sure you're feeling up to this?"

"I'm fine." One tiny decision, that's all that stands between him and oblivion.

He pulls back and studies my face. "Seriously," he says. "You really are so beautiful. I don't know how I got so lucky."

Maybe next time.

"I think it's your hair," he mentions, stopping at the back door. It's like he's forgotten all about the money. "I like the way it's done up like that. Very classic looking."

I press my lips together, and then I offer a slight smile. I knew he would like it. His first wife wore her hair like this in most of the photos that still line the walls of our home. Of his home, I should say. Her home, really. Who cares if she's dead? She's everywhere.

I let the knife slide into the thick skin of the cucumber. Chop. Chop. Chop.

"I thought you might," I call out, as he's halfway out onto the covered patio. Lie. Lie. Lie. Tom might love my hair, but he doesn't love me. Three times now, he's lied. Once at our small ceremony, after our I-do's, and once after he first brought me to live here, in this shrine to his dead wife. He threw a party to show me off to his friends, his church friends, and I guess I must have passed the test. "To Melanie—I love you," he'd said as he toasted our marriage with champagne neither of us drank.

I study my reflection in the blade of the knife. I hate my hair like this. I reach up and release the pin. I don't want to look like Tom's old wife. What I want is to get a reaction out of him. I don't tell him that. And I don't tell him I wasn't actually sick or that instead of reading his agreement, I spent hours watching YouTube video tutorials to learn the updo. I don't tell him I'm thinking of starting my own channel. Or that I might name it 'the most bored housewife in the world.' He lies, so I lie. I hear that's the way this whole marriage thing works.

I watch through the window as he makes his way around the outdoor kitchen. Is his hairline thinning? God, shoot me now. All the things you notice after you marry someone. Why does no one warn you? What I wouldn't give for a drink. Tomorrow, I tell myself. Tomorrow, I'll replenish my secret stash.

Speaking of which, it's no secret what Tom sees in me. I'm young and I'm attractive, and obviously there's the tiny issue of him thinking I'm knocked up. But minus the make-believe oopsie and the ensuing shotgun wedding, the truth is, Tom could have found any number of girls just like me. He's not terribly unattractive, and more importantly, he has what most women my age want more than anything: money.

Plus, he's stable. A sure thing. He comes home every night, doesn't drink, and doesn't smoke. Apparently, the kind of husband everyone wants. I know because when we go out, women flirt with him even though he's standoffish and rude. They bend over backward for him. That says something. It's sickening, sure, but I guess I should be counting my lucky stars he chose me. And, that's not all. There's something else I'm counting: the dollar bills in my future.

I can't see this now, of course. Here in this kitchen, there is no light at the end of the tunnel. Not like before. Not like in the beginning. I think my period is coming. Hopefully that explains why I feel so down. I don't know if I can hide it another month.

But I'm not worried. Not about the hidden things or the women. They could never give Tom what I can, and that's the edge I ride in him. Unexpected and impractical, I was the kink in the tidy corners of Tom's orderly life, and now, the thing that threatens to further unravel it all. And he likes that, even if he can't see it yet, the probability of danger. But he doesn't really want to find out what I'm capable of, the damage I can do. I've only just scratched the surface, toying with the pressure. How much can he take before he realizes the truth?

CHAPTER FOUR

TOM

"Never be so sure of what you want that you wouldn't take something better," Adam says, slapping his hand on my shoulder. He rests it there. "Am I right or am I right?"

He's eyeballing my new wife from across the room. I move out from under his grip. He doesn't seem to notice. I don't answer his question, but I understand it. What he's really asking is how I managed to land a woman like that.

"Man," he sighs. "You're one lucky son of a bitch."

He's right about the latter.

The former, who's to say? All of a sudden, I've gone from invisible, which I prefer, to a man with a secret. *How'd he pull that off?* That's what Adam's thinking. That's what most men in here are thinking. What he's saying is, what everyone is saying is, look at you, Tom. You took lemons, in this case a dead wife, and made lemonade. People see what they want to see. Never mind how the lemonade tastes.

To the naked eye, Adam's evaluation is correct. I am a man who should be content with what he's got. To a more keen observer, I am equal parts man on a mission and provisional. On principle, I am not an indecisive person. That's precisely the worst thing to be. Neither here nor there. But in the proper circumstance, the waiting game is not a bad one to play. It's simple enough. Like fishing. All one has to do is stick their lure in the water and wait. Sometimes the fish bite, sometimes they don't. Fear not, they will always eat when hungry enough, which makes it more about timing than anything. In the meantime, all you have to do is sit back, fold your arms neatly behind your head, fingers clasped, kick your legs up and wait for the nibble. Eyes on the prize, you'll watch carefully as the fish circle the chum, as your enemy works its way into your web, and if one is patient enough, they always will. It matters not how long it takes, so long as one is having fun in the doing. That's the trick, you see, to make the game fun. It's about the journey. The destination is a given.

Adam doesn't notice me baiting my lure. He's more interested in small talk. "This party is really something."

I glance around the ballroom. He's right. New Hope's quarterly dinner for newcomers is a packed house. This makes him both happy and hungry.

"Just look at all of these fresh faces, would you?"

I am looking. Sam Watson and his wife are in attendance, which explains why Adam is extra chatty. He wasn't expecting me to land them. He hadn't expected me to pull it off. That and he wants to make a good impression. He wants to be seen as the guy who knows everyone. For him, it comes down to this. Everything has to go just right. First impressions and all. Not me, I say it's better to surprise them. Plus, I hate small talk.

"The ballroom looks great," I mention, feeding my line. "Very grand."

Adam grins. "Business is booming, my friend."

He means membership.

I don't disagree. "Numbers are way up and tithing is at an all time high."

"The Men's Alliance is very happy with the plans we have in place."

He means the new agenda.

Eventually, Mark comes over and joins us. "Oh, look," Adam remarks, "our fearless leader."

"Mark," I nod. It's important to show respect. Mark is one rank above me, the *only* rank above me. That means Adam comes in third place, something that bothers him more than he's willing to admit. It would bother any man, I assume. It's a long way to the top.

Mark stands silently for several moments, taking it all in. He's watching the dance floor. He too has honed in on Melanie. "Your wife," he says with a nod. "She appears to be having more fun than all of us put together."

"She likes to dance," I say.

" Maybe." Mark runs his hand along his jawline. Afterward, he meets my eye. "But you need to reign that in."

If I knew how to do that I wouldn't be in this situation. I don't say this to him, of course. It's important not to break rank and a rule for all members of New Hope. Obedience is the key that opens every door, as Mark said, who is infatuated by either/or.

"She needs to learn a thing or two about submission," he continues.

I don't disagree with that either. True strength lies in submission, said Mark. It's the backbone of the agreement.

I don't think he understands there is more than one kind of freedom.

"I'll have Beth pay you guys a visit," he suggests. "Chat about the rules. Bring her to heel. Maybe I'll even come along, too."

"Sounds like a plan," I tell him, recalling the last time we discussed the rules. God knows, if I could've reined it in, I'd still be married to my first wife. Probably June would still be alive. Alas, she isn't.

Mark signals the band. "In the meantime," he suggests. "Let me show you how to handle these things."

I look on as he strides onto the dance floor and cuts in on

Mel's dance. She's dancing with Sam Watson. Mark wants this to bother me as much as it does him. I find it amusing. He forgets the common denominator in this equation. Me. He takes her hand, nods at Sam and takes the lead. They waltz. "Handled," he mouths when he looks in my direction. He gives me a thumbs up just in case I haven't understood. I do understand. My mind flashes back to a dance of another kind, to the last time Mark and I discussed how to handle things.

~

"You mean to tell me, of all the rules, Tom—OF ALL THE RULES—you had to go and break that one?" He's already said this once. Mark likes to repeat himself. Meanwhile, he paces the length of his office. Back and forth. Back and forth. All I can do is watch. Any minute and it could all be over. That's what I was thinking.

Statistically speaking, at least seventy-two percent of men and I stand in solidarity. While I don't often compare myself to other men, by that I mean we have had at least one extramarital affair. Somehow, it didn't seem like a good time for statistics, and I didn't have to tell Mark anyhow. He already knows. That's half his mission in life. It's why he founded the church in the first place.

The irony is, there I was, his right-hand man, standing in his office telling him I'd broken a cardinal rule. I knew what this meant. I'd have to pay.

"It was a mistake," I confessed. I wanted to point out that he hadn't met Melanie, that he doesn't know her bedroom eyes or her charm, or yet understand the fact that she might very well be the devil. "Surely, we can be reasonable about this," I offered instead. I remind him of the agreement: *The strong rule the weak, but the wise rules them both.*

"Jesus, Tom," he said, running his fingers through his hair. "The church cannot afford this sort of embarrassment."

He's right. I gut-checked him. This was a dangerous thing to do. Under normal circumstances, I wouldn't be afraid. But I've seen what he can do.

He confirmed my thoughts by punching the wall. "And such a betrayal from my second in command. Of. All. People."

He threw something heavy, and he raged. "Fuck!" It was a paperweight or a Bible. I cannot recall. He was considering how to kill me. I was considering how to outrun him.

If it were only the affair he had been railing against, I realized he might let me live. It wasn't. So unless I was quick on my feet, I was about to be discreetly discarded. New Hope does not tolerate traitors. It's written into the agreement. An agreement I know better than anyone. Anyone, it turned out, except Mark.

It wasn't just the affair he was upset about. There was the other thing too. The resulting pregnancy. It wasn't a part of the plan. Neither his or mine.

"Good then," he'd said finally. I don't know how much time had passed. I was too busy plotting my escape from the building. "You can be the first member of our pilot program."

"I have no interest in being a pilot," I assured him. I realized immediately this was the wrong thing to say. I could see it in his expression. But I was eager to make light of the situation, given that he was about to order my demise. "Even though I'd be quite good at it," I said, attempting a quick recovery. "What I mean by that is... it's a completely logical endeavor." I wasn't lying. I was trying to buy time. Sometimes, occasionally, lengthy explanations help. "To fly a plane safely," I explained. "Pilots have to be aware of all the forces—such as wind and gravity—that push the plane down, lift it up, and shift it from side to side. Harnessing these forces to work in their favor makes it more likely the plane will fly the way the pilot wants." He looked at me as though I was crazy. It was a stupid analogy intended to throw him off. If your opponent has an idea what you have up your sleeve, they know how to act. Information, even useless information, forces their brain to work things out for themselves. I was making a point. Mark feels this way about the church. He wants things to work the way he wants them to work. My predicament was that he'd use any force necessary to see this happen. To him, it was life or death. Literally. To get him to make a more lenient decision, particularly one in my favor, it was imperative I channel his emotions into something constructive. I had to lead him in the right direction. I had to force his anger to subside. Sometimes you have to take the long way around.

"Tell me," he said. "What would be the logical thing to do in this situation? According to Tom?"

He wanted my opinion. This was good.

"Like all good things," I reminded him. "Take church accountants for example—honest ones—who I hear can be hard to come by— piloting is mostly science."

"So? I don't see what this has to do with anything."

"One can't be too emotional about such matters. To panic would be certain—" I paused and shifted my stance. Quickly, I decided against using the "d" word. Reminding him of death was not a point I was trying to make. "To panic in this situation would be ill-advised."

Mark scoffed nervously. "What we are not doing here is getting a pilot's license." He took a deep breath in and held it. "At New Hope," he went on, "we take vows. We have morals. *Standards,* if you will."

"I get standards. Melanie is very beautiful. I know how important excellence is to the church, and I can assure you—"

"I've heard." He waves me off. "Anyway, we've had this idea..."

My throat constricts. *I* realize he's just reminded me of the vow I took. That's always a bad sign. I've seen Mark in action. *Til death do you part. And please let it come soon.* I sit up a little straighter. "An idea. Really?" Clarification is important when the manner of your murder is up in the air.

"The Men's Alliance. We've recently disseminated some

biblical text that suggests that we as men aren't living up to our full potential."

"I'd like to hear more about that." Such calming words, those are.

"Well—the guys and I, we've had this on our minds for awhile now...when our children come of a certain age, we think it would be in our best interest to start over. Not only to further our genes but to further the mission of the church."

I have no idea where this is going but what he says makes sense. Almost. "Advanced maternal age would be of great concern."

Mark laughed. "I like how you always get straight to the point, Tom."

After several long seconds, he stood, walked over, and slapped me on the back. This is a ritual the male species repeats often, a signal of dominance. His hand comes to rest on my shoulder. *Kill or be killed. Survival of the fittest.* Mark is always saying stuff like that. He's very paranoid. Says it comes with being at the top. Perhaps paranoia can rub off on a person. My pulse quickens. I realize he could snap my neck at any moment. Thankfully, Mark likes to hear himself talk and that works in my favor. "That's where the replacement wife comes in."

I feel his grip on my shoulder. I gage each finger where it meets my skin. *Is it my imagination or is he slowly increasing the pressure?* My brow furrows. "The replacement wife?"

"Yes. Like your Melanie."

My eyes widen.

"While we would have appreciated more time for testing our theories and for laying out a plan, it seems you have beaten us to the punch."

I take this as a sign he wants to discuss specifics. "Well, you would want to be very careful in your selection process," I warned him. "In general, mathematical models have confirmed that selection builds more variation than expected from randomly combined genes."

He let go of my shoulder and moved away. "Of course," he said. I did not believe he actually knew this. Mark is smart in regard to certain things. Mostly, the lowbrow stuff. He is not, as they say, very intellectual.

"You have to take this seriously," I repeated. Also, I figured complex explanations might buy me some time. "Understanding the mathematics behind the approach is well worth the effort. In a field as mature as evolutionary genetics, it's not so frequent that someone takes an old problem, looks at it from another angle, and finds new connections."

For several long moments, he seemed to consider what I'd said. Until, all at once, his expression shifted, and he confirmed what many others before him had suggested. "You're a genius, Tom!"

"You are not the first person to make such a suggestion."

Mark's mouth fell open. His eyes were wide. He ran his fingers through his hair. He started pacing again, and I have to admit it feels rather nice when your potential is fully recognized. "You're exactly right," he said. "We have to present this as an issue of evolution versus one of morals. That's the only way we can win."

"But June will never go for me having another wife. And I don't want a divorce."

"Those are just details," he assured me. Then he smiled. "Details, my friend, which can be worked out."

CHAPTER FIVE

MELANIE

In every seduction, romantic or otherwise, there are two elements one must evaluate and understand: first, yourself and what is seductive about you; and second, your mark and what it will take to penetrate their defenses and create surrender. I learned this by watching my father.

Of course, I took his methods and refined them. There's nothing sexy about being a copycat.

For starters, if you never let anyone close, they'll have a harder time finding flaws.

People will follow a thing all the way through so long as there is a question they haven't yet answered.

Why am I so attracted to this person?

What was his motive?

What will she do next?

If he meant this, why did he say that?

But sometimes distance is impossible, and in this case, I have questions. Also, I'm dealing with the likes of Beth Jones. The leader of New Hope's wife, the *real* church founder, that's what Josie had said. Beth has just called to say she's popping by for a visit tomorrow. Apparently, according to Tom, and well, just about everyone, Beth is not the kind of woman to be refused.

I have to say, this intrigues me.

I need to see what I'm up against. I need an opponent worth playing.

The truth is, I've been feeling itchy lately, so I liked that her visit wasn't a question. I appreciate the way they say, with her, everything is a statement.

This should be fun.

I've done my homework. God knows, there's nothing else going on around here. Tom has promised he'll get me a car, but he says he wants to wait for the morning sickness to pass first. Unfortunately, I'd already played that card, and it wasn't the kind I could take back right away.

So, to say that I welcome the distraction, the opportunity for mental stimulation Beth's visit will provide, would be an understatement.

Already, I've learned a few things. Things I plan to use to my advantage. One, this meeting is important to Tom. I haven't quite figured out why, but he really seems to want these people to like him. Obviously, at least temporarily, I want what Tom wants.

Two, I'm young and pliable. This makes me attractive. Just ask Tom.

Three, for reasons I haven't yet figured out, Beth needs me more than she wants me to think she does. That's the variable. I have to find out what she wants.

Going in, I knew about Tom's affiliation with the church. He explained it in only a way Tom can, methodically and at length. To tell you the truth, details I don't care about bore me, so I tuned him out. I wasn't interested in Tom's perspective on religion, or why he was involved. I was interested in Tom. I was interested in having a place to live. Most of all, I was interested in someone footing the bill.

I do recall him explaining that new members are assigned a sponsor.

"What, like A.A.?" I'd asked.

"I don't know that acronym."

"Alcoholics Anonymous."

He apprised me carefully, his green eyes on fire with concern. "You're not one of those, are you?"

"No," I said with the flick of my wrist. "I hardly drink." *Keyword being hardly.*

"I don't know what they do at A.A. I can only explain the church."

I shrugged. He'd pretty much lost me there, but he went on. "We have rules. Sponsors help us adhere to those rules."

"Who wants that kind of life?"

"I do."

"Oh," I smiled. "Then it can't be that bad."

He didn't respond.

~

THE FIRST TIME I SEE MARK JONES, HE IS WEARING A ROBE. A LONG, red, velvety-looking robe. He enters the church, hands folded neatly in prayer, tucked under his chin, the widest grin you've ever seen. There is a processional of people behind him. My job is to take up the collection of cell phones at the door. Most people leave them at home; they are forbidden during service, Tom informs me. But sometimes members forget, and my husband assures me this assignment will serve me well. "You'll get to know everyone this way."

"Melanie," they each say, greeting me, taking my free hand into theirs. It's like they've known me all my life. I don't know what to say, so I plaster a smile on my face and freeze it there. At one point, I have to massage my jaw. I'm afraid it might be permanently stuck there.

"You must be Melanie," a couple says, holding me hostage. Service is about to start. Or at least I assume so because the music has changed, and my eyes have locked on to Mark Jones. Same as everyone else. "Who is that?" I ask as the woman shakes my hand vigorously. She refuses to let go. But eventually, she turns her head. "Oh, that, dear, is our fearless leader. That is Mr. Jones."

He stares so deeply into my eyes it feels like he's x-raying my soul.

"We're so glad to finally meet you," the woman tells me. "We'd better take our seat."

This feels like a lie because the wives were not so happy to meet me, not at first.

Here, in the church, everyone is happy. It's like a coliseum more than a church, I tell Tom later. It's like nothing I've ever seen. In the few times I've ever attended church, either for a wedding, or a funeral, or just to pretend when my father's parents were in town, it wasn't like this. In my experience with organized religion, people wore fake smiles they stretched across their face. They had to grin and bear it, but they were glad when it was over so they could get back to their judging and their sinning. So long as you made it right on Sunday, you were allowed your indiscretions on the other days of the week.

Here it is clear from the beginning: it is not that way.

I listen to Mark as he speaks, and I am fascinated. I don't fall asleep like I'd planned. Mark is too animated, too over the top, too...interesting. He is a white flag on a mountaintop, showing us we too can be saved. He also happens to speak on a topic I find fascinating. He explains DISC theory, a topic I am quite familiar with.

"People are happiest when they are submissive to a loving authority," he tells the congregation, and it is like he is speaking directly into my soul. "Compliance," he says, "only leads to resentment. Submission," he assures me and everyone, "is key."

He goes on to explain inducement. He doesn't have to tell me. I already know. Inducement is the act of seducing someone into your way of thinking and dominating them so completely that what you want is what they want. Inducement is making the other person, or other people, depending on the context, happy to give it to you. That is the secret to life, to marriage, to everything, he says.

But it's what he doesn't say that interests me most.

Women are far better at inducement than men.

"His psychology is a bit outdated," I say to Tom in the parking lot. "But it wasn't as bad as I'd expected."

He doesn't respond.

"What did you think?"

"Typical service."

"Do they always worship him like that?" It was strange. Maybe I shouldn't have been surprised. It wasn't the first time I'd seen the way people could worship other people. My father's women, the popular girls in school, my mother with my sister. But until then, I don't think I'd ever witnessed it on such a large scale. I'd never seen it like that. "How do you get that many people to just do whatever you want when you just give them the answer?"

"The answer?"

I shake my head. It's like he wasn't listening at all. "Inducement."

He keeps walking.

"It's like he's God himself or something. He's so good."

Tom halts rather abruptly. "It isn't bad or good, Melanie. There's no point in analyzing it." His expression hardens. "It just is."

"It's all very interesting, if you ask me."

Tom's grip on my hand loosens, until he drops it all together. There's a look in his eyes that I'd deleted from memory. "Well, I didn't," he says and he pulls his hand away.

~

It's hard to believe I hadn't known before Tom brought me here that this place existed. Upton Village. But then, why would I? You don't get into a place like this without an invitation and like most of the finer things in life, it's more about who you know than what you know. In this case, it's better not to know too much. They say it takes a village, and that's what they've created—an exclusive gated community just a few miles south of Austin

The church bought out the neighborhood eventually, save for a few holdouts. Gawkers, Tom called them. He said the church did things to try and force them out. Mostly it worked. He said it takes a special kind of person to stay where you're not wanted.

It seems like more of a commune to me, but instead of residents who look like hippies, the people of Upton are perfect, beautiful. Picturesque. Unmistakable.

Our street in particular is a carefully crafted, immaculately maintained mishmash of Victorians, Craftsman, and Colonials which are made to look old but actually aren't.

The streets are tree lined, mostly oaks, and I don't know how else to describe my new living quarters other than to say, it is quite literally like stepping back in time. The sun is bright, the shadows dance between the mixture of light and shade that hardly has time to blanket the ground given the cool canopy of trees. The breeze always seems to carry with it the scent of barbecue smoke and homemade bread. Things here have an exact nature, even the flowerbeds are laid out in military precision.

Here the women don't rattle on about schools, they've created their own. "They seem so insular," I told Tom after I first moved in. "All anyone wants to talk about is some new cleaning product they tried, the latest extracurricular for little Johnny, or where they plan to 'summer.'

That, he reminds me, is the opposite of insular.

One afternoon, the first week after he'd moved me in, Tom drove me around to show me what I had to look forward to when the baby came. He pointed out the baseball field, soccer fields, at least a handful of tennis courts, and the Olympic-sized swimming pool complete with three water slides. He told me not to worry about the pool being "small" as most people had their own. The playground alone was otherworldly. Swings, seesaws and slides, climbing walls, and a ropes course. All you need is a grocery store, and you'd never have to leave, I remarked.

Tom smiled and said, "That's why they have delivery, dear."

Speaking of delivery, that same week, most of the women who live in The Village (this is its nickname, I'm told) delivered what my husband called meals.

"We like to take care of our own," each of the wives say, as though it has been scripted. Like the women, the meals, they're all the same flavor. When I mention this to Tom, he says they're casseroles. What did I expect?

He has a point. Like the women here, I found them to be very unoriginal.

They probably share recipes, he told me. I thought he was joking.

This was before I realized he wasn't.

I felt terror rising. I felt like maybe I have judged things all wrong. "They don't have cooks?"

"Some of them do," he said. "But women in The Village take pride in caring for their families. Especially those who've been around a while."

I felt my stomach drop.

Tom studied me for a second. "Don't worry," he promised. "It takes some getting used to. Human beings are selfish by nature. But...I'm sure you'll fit in in no time."

It felt like a dig.

"I don't know what to do with myself," I tell Tom one evening when I find myself waiting at the door for him to come home. "It just feels so remote living out here. Maybe we should get an apartment in the city. Start over."

"Why would we do that?" he asked. His hand reached for my belly. "With the baby coming."

"Your kids are grown and away at school. Babies don't need this much space. It would be good to downsize."

He looked at me like I was crazy. "Everyone wants to live here. It's quite pricey, you know."

My husband doesn't use words like pricey. I realized he was patronizing me.

I'd come up with a solution. In the meantime, I let it be. I cross my arms and remind myself I have secured a position in what most people would consider paradise. Never mind that I had to bargain with the devil. I have arrived. I am here.

"REMEMBER BETH IS COMING BY TOMORROW," TOM REMINDS ME AS I stand at the sink applying mascara. It's Thursday, and in Tom's world, Thursday evenings are reserved for dinner club. Each week a different member of New Hope's leadership team hosts in their home. Not exactly how I want to spend my night but I guess it beats sitting around here watching Tom work. "She'll be here at 10:00 a.m."

"That should be fun," I say, eyeing him sideways. He's staring at the makeup bottles and tubes splayed out on the counter. He picks them up one by one and moves them back to my side.

"Did you really need all of this? I didn't think you wore that much makeup."

"Yes," I assure him. Best to keep it short and sweet, I'm learning, and then to change the subject, I say, "What if I have plans tomorrow?"

"I checked your calendar."

"You know I don't use that thing." I point to my head and tap my temple. "I keep everything up here."

I watch as he picks up the towel I've discarded on the floor and sets it back in its rightful place. "I thought you said you suffered from OCD."

I shrug, taking him in slowly. Meticulously. He looks good for almost fifty.

"You know for forty-eight..." I say, making sure he sees that I'm giving him the once-over. "You're surprisingly fit for someone nearly eligible for AARP."

He's changing out of the suit he wore to work into something only slightly less formal. He mumbles something that sounds like *that's nice*, but I don't think he's even listening to me. I could go on, but I can see he isn't in the mood to chat, so I stare at his abs instead. He may be twice my age, and while he's not quite youthful, he's not exactly grandpa material either. Daddy issues, they say. Something about that makes me want to reach out and place my hands on his wide shoulders. I want to look into his eyes and say something that'll make him pay attention. I want to feel his narrow hips digging into me. I want to feel something. All in time.

Instead, I slide up next to him and pout. "I don't think Beth likes me," I whine. We've only met a few times, briefly. Mostly, I want to find out if she'll be there tonight.

He fake smiles and answers my question. "You'll have a chance to show her your charm tomorrow. At 10:00 a.m."

I hold up my latest online purchase. "How's this dress?"

"Fine." He can't be bothered to look. He's too busy putting the cap back on the toothpaste and fuming inside about my incompetence. Tom likes to use that word when people don't perform in the way he expects. He nods. "Would you mind?"

"Sorry," I shrug. We're learning so much about each other. That's what happens with a shotgun wedding. Me, I'm shocked. I had no idea a person could be this clean or this boring. Not to mention this cheap. The dress I'm wearing tonight cost me my whole allowance that isn't an allowance but is instead a "budget." I don't want to start a fight so I keep this bit to myself.

"Can't I have Josie back?"

He turns and when he does he finally notices the dress. By the way he studies my face, I think he only sees dollar signs. "Josie left the church."

I know this, of course. But I like to hear him say it. Also, it takes the attention off of my perceived inadequacies. My husband is charming. He thinks I don't know what he's thinking. But Tom isn't good at hiding what few emotions he has. I can see that he's wondering why I'm bringing this up, why now. Josie was my sponsor until Josie's husband was shot dead by his mistress, and Josie could no longer stomach the church. I have to admit, at first I thought this whole thing with 'the church' was a bit over the top. More and more though, I'm finding it's good entertainment. The *only* entertainment around here, to tell the truth.

On the bright side, I get to go to parties. Like tonight, even if it is just dinner club. I'm not worried; I'll liven things up. I get nice clothes even if it means spending my whole allowance. Even if they're meant to impress people I have no interest in impressing, my husband is right—I should probably be a little more grateful. I'm working on it. It isn't easy all this make-believe. I was supposed to marry up. But I took what I could get, I had short notice after all.

Thankfully, with any luck, there's a vacation in my future. I know because that's all the other wives seem to drone on about. Well, this and yoga and pilates, and oh yeah, let's not forget about brunch. I'm twenty-two years old. My body doesn't need these things like theirs do. To me, brunch is just another meal. It's not a luxury. And vacations aren't vacations, they're a way of life. These women, they're all so bogged down with fake responsibility, and children, things they put upon themselves, that they can't see it my way. So, in time, I have to learn to love the things they love. And in the meantime, so what if there are a few "rules" I'm supposed to put up with. Big deal.

I can always find a workaround.

It's better than getting a job.

It's better than being homeless.

"I just can't understand why anyone would leave New Hope," I say.

I wonder if this is a good time to remind Tom about the car. He promised I'd get a new one soon. I'm thinking a two-seater would be nice. I decide against mentioning it just yet. Better to bide my time.

"It was too much for her without Grant," he says, reminding me I'm supposed to be discussing the Dunns, not pondering what color leather would look good with my vacation tan. Sometimes Tom is so boring I forget we're in the middle of a conversation. "Says who?"

"Says Beth."

I was hoping he might say that. The more I think about it, the more I like this Beth character, because now that I know who's in charge, now that I know who's calling the shots, I know where to focus my efforts.

CHAPTER SIX

TOM

The stuff they call music is several decibels too high to have any sort of effective communication. A fact I am quite grateful for, even if the sound offends my ears. At least it means I don't have to talk to anyone. I'm not exactly what you'd call hiding; I've just never been a fan of social affairs. That's not to say I don't understand their necessity—it's just not one I prefer. I observe on the fringes. I'm neither in nor out, but I'm here, and that counts for something.

When you rule something out, you limit your focus. My father taught me this. You can't go around parading your unconventional ways, he often reminded me. Don't fool yourself into thinking it's cute. Back then, I had no idea what he meant. I wasn't fooling myself, only him. There was nothing cute about getting pummeled every day.

When I came home with my fourth consecutive pair of broken glasses and third black eye, he sat me down and explained. "You're different than other kids, Thomas. But that doesn't mean you can't blend. You can make friends. You just have to be smart about it."

I shook my head. "They hate me." I was old enough then to

know adults lied to kids when they wanted their way. "I'm never going back."

"You are going back."

I folded my arms and dug my heels in. Already, I was smarter than my father about some things. If I tried hard enough, I could be smarter about this. "You can't make me."

"I can, and I will. You think you're powerless?"

I stared at the floor.

"No one is powerless, son."

"They call me names. They beat me up—"

"What names?"

"Know-it-all. Nerd. Four-eyes..."

He studied me earnestly. "Are you those things?"

I shrugged.

"You can beat them at their own game, you know."

"How?"

"Influence."

I knew what the word meant. I didn't yet understand how to use it.

"Help them with their school work, let them copy your papers. They'll come to depend on you."

"That's cheating."

"Maybe," he said. "But you're smarter than they are. There's no way around that. And the sad truth, Thomas, is people will always find a way to punish you for making them feel inferior."

I NEED TO REMIND MELANIE TO BE CAREFUL AT SOCIAL GATHERINGS. I thought I'd hammered this in the last time. Apparently not.

She can't help herself, I don't think. I can't help her now, so I sit complacently looking on from across the backyard. She's kicked off her heels and let down her hair. She's in her element, surrounded by admirers. I wonder if she knows what she's in for. I wonder if she knows I can't save her. Not even if I wanted to.

She throws her head back and laughs at something Cheryl has said. She and her husband Adam are hosting. It was my surprise to Melanie, not telling her where we were going for dinner club. Of all the women, I think she likes Cheryl the most.

Eventually, Melanie recovers from her laughing spell. I think she's going to excuse herself. I'm hoping she's going to find her way back to me. But then, she lightly touches the woman's arm before doubling over again. I hope whatever she is laughing at was actually funny. Melanie tends to lean toward dramatics. I hope she's smart enough to keep her energy concentrated at its strongest point. She doesn't yet know intensity beats range every time.

I have to look away. I am considering wandering into the house, down the hall, and into our host's study to see what kind of books he keeps shelved. One can always get an accurate picture of another by taking a gander at their reading tastes. After all, as my father used to say, if you only know yourself, then you're fated to lose every battle. You must know your enemy's intentions.

"So...how are things getting on?" Adam's voice asks, interrupting my thoughts and subsequently my peace. I didn't wander into the house. I felt him coming before I heard him, thanks to the shoddy music. When I look up, I'm not surprised to see he's standing over me. The glare of the patio lights forces me to shield my eyes. "It's a great party."

He moves to the right so that his head is blocking the light. "Can I get you anything?" he asks, ever the gracious host. "A beer, a whiskey...cocaine?"

I hold up my glass of water to show I'm good.

Adam grins, he can't help himself. He's rubbing it in that he's caught me red-handed not enjoying myself. I won't bother to correct him. Displaying defects on occasion is important. Only God and the deceased have the liberty to appear faultless.

He shakes his own empty glass, rattling the ice. He takes another shot. "So how are things going?"

"Sorry," I offer, rising to my feet. "Couldn't hear over the music."

He nods at Melanie and the others. "Such a great night."

I cup my ear. "What was that?"

"I asked if you're having a good time." His voice rises as he edges closer. "I asked how married life is treating you."

"Look at her," I say, following his gaze. "What do you think?"

"I think she's stunning. Young and stunning."

I swallow hard. Secondhand opinions are my least favorite kind.

He sucks in air. "Any idea where I can find one like that?" When I glance over, he shakes his head slowly from side to side. "So pure. So uninhibited. So…fresh."

"It requires luck," I assure him, which is a blanket statement to avoid having to explain the truth of the matter. First of all, not that it matters, but Adam is married. But even if he were to suddenly find himself single, or let's say if Mark's agenda were to succeed, the odds are not in Adam's favor of finding another wife. Particularly not one as "fresh" as Melanie. Adam has a few things working against him. There's his age, for starters. By the time an individual turns 40, the likelihood that he or she will ever become married, if the person is single at that point in time, is slim, as the percentage hovers around 15%, and remains relatively the same up to 60 years of age. Thankfully, not only was Melanie not married previously, not only was she for the most part pure, she is also younger than the pool of women in which Adam will likely have to choose, making the odds of his success less still. Younger women do not often fall for older men unless their income level exceeds that well beyond the average. Suffice it to say, I handle Adam's taxes.

"Remind me again." He shifts slightly. "How'd the two of you meet?"

"I thought I told you."

Adam shakes his head. "Uh-uh."

"On the street. Mel bumped into me, spilled coffee on my shirt."

His eyes widen slightly. I watch as the surprise registers in his expression. I have given him hope. I can tell by the way his bottom lip juts out. "Huh. Just like that."

I study Adam in my peripheral vision. His posture doesn't immediately tell me how to respond. When in doubt, a question is best. "Why do you ask?"

"She just seems familiar, that's all."

I press my lips to one another. "Melanie's not from here."

"I know. Boise, she said."

"Idaho, yes."

"But I don't know..." He shoves his hands in his pockets and then he turns to me. "I think I've seen her before. And I've sure as hell never been to Boise."

"No?" I say, meeting his eye. "You should visit sometime."

Adam leans back on his heel. He's looking for a change of pace. "So who's sponsoring her? Now that Josie is out?"

"Beth."

"Oh, well," Adam manages. He leans against the brick, a signal he's settling in. "That's great news for you. Beth is terrific at compliance."

The music changes. "Let's hope."

"Say, should she be dancing? In her condition?"

I scan the large yard. A conga line has formed. My wife isn't merely dancing. She's leading the pack. When the line makes its way past Adam and I, Melanie sticks her hand out and beckons me to join her. As a general rule, I don't dance. But it's hard to say no to Mel and further I want to get away from Adam. So when her fingers brush mine, I let her pull me in.

"Just close your eyes," she calls over her shoulder. "Relax. Feel the music."

I go around three times, and I never do relax, and I never do feel the music. But I do blend, and I do avoid Adam, and that's the point.

Although, nothing good lasts forever. This is evidenced as I'm waiting for Melanie by the front door. We'd already said our goodbyes and were halfway out the front door when she realized she'd left her handbag in the guest room upstairs. When I turn, Adam is there. Melanie calls for me from across the room. She mouths something I can't read. His eyes follow mine. A smile lights up her face. "Man, I swear I know her from somewhere," he sighs. "I can't place it... can't quite put my finger on it." Adam's jaw lengthens which is made more apparent by the way he rubs at it. "But don't you worry." He moves in closer, giving my shoulder a squeeze. "It'll come to me. I have a memory like an elephant."

CHAPTER SEVEN

MELANIE

When I come downstairs, Tom has fixed breakfast. Same as every morning: two eggs over easy, two pieces of bacon, one slice of toast. Butter, strawberry jam, thinly spread.

I join him at the bar, taking the high-backed stool to his right, even though I know he prefers me to his left. It's the gentlemen's way, he explained once. Something about defending a woman's honor. Swords and stuff. I forget the rest.

Right now, I couldn't care less about honor. I care about breakfast.

I stab my fork into the eggs and shove them into my mouth.

Tom glares at me. "Something wrong with the eggs darling?"

It's safe to say, I'm not a morning person.

I smile and swallow. That's what got me into this mess. "They're perfect," I assure him. He senses I'm lying, but he can't prove it because I take another bite and then another. The best kind of lie. If they're going to suspect you, might as well go the extra mile to ensure they can't prove it.

The truth is, he isn't as good a cook as the chef I had at mom and dad's. The truth is, I hate it when he's condescending. I hate it when he calls me darling. But what can you do? I guess something is better than nothing. Plus, I'm confident I can talk Tom into a chef of our own if I play my cards right. Shouldn't be too hard. I already managed a maid. Still, I'm so sick of casseroles. I don't know what I might do if I'm forced to eat another. Just the thought makes me want to pick up my plate and hurl it across the room. The rage is building like a pressure cooker. I don't know what I have to do before it's too late.

"This visit," I say, reaching for my o.j. but then opting for the toast instead. "With Beth—" I take a bite and chew. "It isn't about our sex life again, is it?"

Tom looks at me crossly. It annoys him when I talk with food in my mouth. Regardless, he knows what I mean. I've already been reprimanded once by Josie for breaking some rule in that regard. Bless her. Even I could tell her heart wasn't in it. Did I think it was a bit weird that 'the church' was involved in our sex life? Well, weird is subjective. Especially these days. But, okay, yeah, maybe a little. However, Tom is pretty inept at social stuff, so I didn't for a minute put it past him to have someone else do his bidding.

"No," he says. "It's about the dancing."

I shove the rest of the toast in my mouth and roll my eyes. Tom shifts my glass away from me slightly, so that once again it's at the perfect angle. He's explained why this is important before, but I forgot to listen. Before I know it, he has shifted his position. He is facing me full on. "With Josie gone, Beth needs someone she can rely on."

I realize he's just parroting what he's heard. His recycled ideas annoy me on account of it being so early in the day.

"I bet she does."

"Please, Melanie. This is important to me," he says, and it soothes my anger. It's my favorite aphrodisiac to hear people beg. It's nice that he cuts right to the heart of the matter. I understand what Beth wants. Tom doesn't have to tell me. She wants someone who won't quit on her. She needs someone who is compliant. She wants to believe that someone is me. All I have to do is let her think she's right. Thanks to Tom and his explaining everything, I understand how to play my role thoroughly. Nothing is more effective in seduction than letting the seduced think they are the ones doing the seducing.

"What's wrong with dancing, anyway?" I ask adjusting the juice to my liking, handle facing me. I watch my husband's jaw twitch. He hates it when I'm testy. "Is it against the rules, too?"

"You were supposed to mingle. You were supposed to be welcoming."

"What does that mean exactly, Tom—to be welcoming?"

His brow furrows. I can see he doesn't know what to say.

I scoot to the edge of the barstool. "Does it mean to have sex whenever you want?"

Suddenly, I'd like a fight to go along with my bland toast and my bland husband and my new bland life.

"Partly, yes."

I shift the nightie I'm wearing away from my thighs, pulling it up toward my hips. Slowly, I part my legs. Wide. A little wider. All the way. "Do you want sex now Tom?"

"Not when you're angry."

I roll my eyes. "You know nothing about women."

"You're right." He's not good at lying, this conventional husband of mine. It's almost like he doesn't even try. I watch as he lines up his utensils. When he's finished, he meets my eye. "But it's not good for the baby, for you to have cortisol flooding your system this way."

"You have a point," I admit. In all areas of life, never give the impression that you are angling for something—this will raise a resistance you will never lower. It's best to approach people from the side. "But I think if you were to fuck me, I'd feel better."

He glances at his wrist. "I have to be at work in a half hour. It takes me twenty-four minutes to drive there. Six minutes is not enough time."

"I thought it was in the agreement," I counter. I should have taken another angle, this gives him the chance to remind me I wouldn't know. I never read the damn thing. But it's a fight I'm looking for, and with Tom often that requires a bit of prodding. He doesn't fight directly. "I thought it says one is never to refuse their spouse."

His phone dings. He fishes it from his pocket and checks it. He knows I hate it when he does this. To make matters worse, he doesn't look at me when he speaks. "There are stipulations."

"Stipulations raise my cortisol level, Tom."

The muscle in his jaw twitches again. Something in his expression shifts. I'm pretty sure it's his resolve.

"Hypothetically speaking..." I start. He looks up briefly. And then back at the phone. "Say we were to fuck...what hormones would flood my system then?"

He likes to explain the things he thinks I don't know. It appears to be his brand of foreplay. To each their own, I say.

"Endorphins and oxytocin." He answers matter of factly. His eyes are on the phone.

I lower my voice, even my tone, arch my back and reach for his belt. "Perfect. You've got five and a half minutes."

Of course, Tom goes with it. To his credit, he is very efficient. Sure, he didn't finish his breakfast. But he seemed satisfied nonetheless. And in the end, I was too. After all, I earned equity I could later cash in on. I won this round, fair and square. Tom is no easy opponent. He doesn't think with his feelings and only on occasion with his dick.

When it was over, I was a bit shaken. Those three and a half minutes might have been the best sex of my life. Hard and rough, raw and angry, it was different than it normally is. I was concerned I felt something. Something more than the thrill of winning. There's nothing like it, but this felt like more. I guess sometimes things catch you by surprise.

CHAPTER EIGHT

TOM

I dial Beth on my way in to work. Just as soon as I'm out of the driveway, in fact.

I'm relieved when she answers on the second ring. "Howdy, friend."

"I'm afraid we need to take action," I caution. There's no time for pleasantries. "It's worse than I thought."

"What happened?"

I step on the brake. "I don't have time to go into it right now."

She sighs, and I hear the exasperation in her voice before she even speaks. "Tom."

"I'm late for work," I huff. "Just trust me when I say, this has to escalate."

A male voice says something in the background. She covers the speaker so that his voice becomes muffled. I realize it was probably a bad idea to call, but desperate times call for desperate measures.

I clear my throat. "Are you there?"

"Sorry," she tells me. I flinch at the sound of her finger moving away from the microphone. It crackles in my ear. Beth sighs again. "You men, I swear. If it isn't one thing...it's another." I don't have time for another woman complaining in my life. She doesn't seem to notice. "You have no idea how many fires I've put out just this morning."

"Nor do I care. Just do your job."

"Don't worry so much, Tom." Her upbeat tone grates in my ears. Typical Beth. "We'll make things right in no time."

~

"We'll make things right in no time," Michael assured me. I hadn't known at the time those would be the last words he would ever speak. Approximately twelve minutes later, he wrapped his Porsche around a tree.

Michael was my roommate freshman year in college, back before I was smart enough to know that living in close proximity with others doesn't work for me. Nevertheless, we developed a sort of symbiotic relationship. I kept him from flunking out of school, and he kept me from complete isolation.

By our senior year, I'd gone through six internships and three jobs in rapid succession, on account of my people skills. Or lack thereof. Everyone understands the need for change in the abstract, but on the day-to-day level, people are creatures of habit, my boss said. It was a pointless conversation. We both knew why I was sitting in his office. He was going to fire me, but thought he'd waste my time by fitting one last lecture in first. It was a ridiculous point he was trying to drill in, about my future, about making friends. About being a team player. Apparently, calling colleagues out for tardiness and inefficiency is the opposite of that. You have to make your poison sweet, he said. He informed me he was letting me go because I seemed to be incapable of doing that. When security was called to box up the few belongings I'd kept there and escort me from the building, I guess he proved his point. I learned another thing that day. People don't like being called out for being pacifists.

After that, things seemed particularly hopeless. I'd learned a valuable lesson that I wasn't sure how to apply or how to put into practice. The lesson was simple enough: employers appreciate people skills and the ability to bullshit over real knowledge. I had one but not the other. And to my detriment, it was the one that wasn't as easily faked. It was devastating to have a problem I couldn't solve. That's how Michael talked me into becoming his business partner. Though back then I can't say there was much business.

"You don't need the man," Michael assured me. "You can do it on your own."

"What? Like my own firm?"

"Yeah, just think about it. You'd be the boss, and you wouldn't have to answer to anyone."

Admittedly, I liked the sound of that. Michael was very good at sales.

"You're good with numbers. I'm good with people."

"Wait. You want to be partners?"

"Why not?" He shrugged. "I don't have anything going on."

"How will we get clients? I can't even keep a job." It hit me then. The answer. "I think my problem is...I'm too honest."

"You just let me worry about that," Michael insisted. "Let me do the talking. Repeat after me—" He motioned between the two of us. "Tom," he said, pointing in my direction. "Will focus on numbers." Then he pointed at himself. "Michael does the talking."

I didn't respond. I was mulling it over.

"Got it?"

I knew he had a point. I had seen Michael in action. Picking up women seemed effortless—how hard could finding people who needed an accountant be? I don't like to waste time, so I turned abruptly and asked directly, "Are you sure you're as good at talking as I am at numbers?"

"Equally, so. Yes." Michael had a way of speaking my language that no one had prior and no one's had since. Until I met Melanie.

He'd sold me on the idea that we could make it work, and since I needed the money to pay back my student loans, it wasn't easy to turn down an offer that made sense.

Business started out slow, but Michael knew a lot of people and before long, things began to pick up. Over the next half-decade we did all right for ourselves. Until a downturn in the economy and subsequently in Michael's personal life occurred. The ripple effect caused an upturn in his liquor consumption and seemingly overnight, we were struggling to stay afloat. Literally.

Michael made the evening news when he totaled his car and the underage company he kept died as a result. Turned out they were both indisposed at the time. Before I knew it, clients were jumping ship left and right. Legal fees caused Michael to nearly lose his house. His wife left him. I leveraged the business to keep him from being both homeless and alone.

It was a shit-show, to say the least, and we were left doing the very basic of services. Tax work, mainly.

The silver lining through it all was my wife. June and I grew closer. Thankfully, she wasn't too put off by the fact that we had to take the kids out of private school, or that we were going to have to put the house on the market.

She always said things would be fine. I didn't believe her. They looked particularly bleak that spring just after tax season ended. Michael hadn't been coming into the office, and on the rare occasion he made an appearance, he was hammered.

"Don't worry, Tom," he would assure me after each cold call. "I'm going to fix this. I have to...you're the only friend I have left."

Meanwhile, I scanned the classifieds for jobs. We couldn't keep bleeding money on operating expenses, not with so little coming in.

By the time I landed a job, Michael had officially hit rock bottom. I knew telling him was risky. Taking the job basically meant bailing on him at a time he had nothing left, a fact he liked to remind me of often.

When the day came to tell him I was closing the firm, much to my surprise, he actually showed for the meeting. He wasn't alone.

"Tom!" he exclaimed as I came out into the foyer. "I want you to meet..."

I glanced at the three men standing beside him. Michael, it appeared, had drawn a blank. He was so sloshed he couldn't pull their names from the rightful place in his limbic system.

One of the men extended his hand. "I'm Mark Jones."

I took it hesitantly. This was just like Michael to pull a stunt when I'd resolved to do something.

"This is Adam Morford. And that there," he continued, motioning with the opposite hand, "is Grant Dunn. Dr. Dunn."

"Tom Anderson, CPA."

"We've been playing golf with your business partner," he informed me. "And we had to meet you. Forgive us for being impulsive, but Michael tells us you're a savant. He says you're good with numbers."

I pressed my lips together.

"Show them Tom," Michael slurred. "Show them what you can do."

I showed them my party trick. It wasn't hard. I only knew a few.

"Listen," the guy named Mark said. He placed his arm around my shoulders. "The guys and I—" He paused to make sure everyone was listening. I moved away. Being accosted is my second least favorite thing. "We run a little church."

That's exactly what Michael needs, I thought.

"The reason we're here..." he continued, "is our accountant up and quit on us last week."

"Sorry to hear that. Good accountants are hard to come by."

Mark Jones laughed. "Well, he wasn't an honest man, so good riddance, I say."

The other men either looked away or stared at the floor. Only briefly. But long enough that I noticed.

"What about you, Tom?"

I cocked my head. I didn't know what to say, so I offered the tried and true. "What do accountants suffer from that ordinary people don't?"

Mark looked at his friends. Everyone shrugged. Everyone but Michael. He knew where I was going. He taught me himself.

"Depreciation."

Everyone laughed. Even Michael.

"This guy," Mark said to the group. "I like this one."

Next, he looked at me directly. "Could we talk for a moment?"

I nodded toward my office, and he followed me in. Neither of us sat.

"I won't beat around the bush," he said. I appreciated that. Michael looked like he was going to ruin the office carpet at any moment. Urine or vomit…with drunks one can never tell. "We have some money we need to invest, and as it turns out, we were left without anyone to handle that sort of thing. We need someone who can look out for us. Someone who has the church's best interest in mind. Someone we can trust."

"Well—" I was about to tell him I'd taken another job when he cut me off. I didn't have to.

"I know things have been tough for your firm," he said. He took a step forward, and placed his hand on my shoulder. Then he lowered his voice. "I know your family is having a bit of hardship."

I scooted from beneath his grip. "I don't like to be touched."

He glanced at me sideways. "I like that you're direct. And I get it," he said. "What I don't get," he paused and shook his head. "Is why someone with your talent is in such dire straits."

I glanced through the window at Michael. "A series of bad business decisions on my part."

Mark Jones followed my gaze. "Ah. An honest man. A rare quality, it seems."

I didn't say anything. Sometimes silence is good enough.

"Are you a religious man, Mr. Anderson? Are you a praying man?"

"No," I answered. "I'm a man of science. But I have taken to my knees a bit lately."

"You don't think beliefs play a part in making society work as a whole?"

"I didn't say that."

"Do you think you could have a come-to-Jesus meeting, so to speak, with yourself?"

"I have no interest in attending church Mr. Jones."

"Oh, but Tom," he said. "We are so much more than that."

CHAPTER NINE

MELANIE

I feel her eyes everywhere. "You look tired," Beth remarks. "Are you feeling okay?"

"Fine, thanks." I motion for her to follow me toward the living room.

"Gosh," she says pausing in the foyer. "You've certainly been busy."

I watch as she takes the place in, accessing her features closely. I want to ask who is doing her work now that Dr. Dunn is six feet under. I want to ask who is doing her bidding now that his wife is out. But I assume that's why she's here, so I simply say, "A little."

"Well, the place looks great." She is attractive for a woman her age. Whatever work she's had done, it's tasteful, not over the top, but not exactly unnoticeable either. "So…fresh," she says, turning on her heel. "Tom must be thrilled."

Sarcasm, obviously. She knows as well as I do Tom abhors change. Slowly, very slowly, with the twist of an arm and a few shallow tactics on my part, he has allowed me to replace a few of his former wife's things. Beth notices every one of them. *Oh my, I love that new mirror. Is that a new vase? Tom let you replace the rug? Is this what I think it is?*

I offer her tea with milk and a buttered croissant. Tom says she likes these things.

She declines both politely.

"I cannot believe Tom hired a housekeeper," Beth says, lowering her voice. She glances around as though our maid might pop out at any minute. "Tom hates the idea of staff. I know June tried for years, to no avail."

That name causes me to flinch. I shrug and play it off. "Really? He seems so happy now that we have Rose." June must have been weak. Come to think of it, Tom never explained why he was so against help. Had I thought—or cared—to get to the bottom of this little problem, I might have saved myself a bit of purging.

"Speaking of which, how are things working out?" I know she isn't referring to the help who has made herself scarce for our company, as I asked her to do.

I assume *trying to manage my starter husband while I'm on my way to my next,* probably isn't the answer she wants to hear. People really dislike the truth when it's delivered unexpectedly

Instead, I take a seat on the sofa and watch as she follows suit, taking the armchair adjacent to me. "So, things are going good then?" She tries again.

"Pretty good, yes. It's really nice to have help with the last minute shopping and the cleaning. Especially with so many visitors." I offer a small laugh. "You just never know who is going to pop by."

"It's impressive," she tells me, one brow lifted. "What you've done with the place." We both know she isn't talking about the decor.

Impressive is right, and I want to tell her it took faking morning sickness to get my husband to hire help. I want to tell her that desperate times call for desperate measures, and when the OCD excuses hadn't seemed to do the trick, the matter called for escalation. More so, I want this to serve as a warning. I want her to know, although I have a feeling she might already, that sticking ones finger down their throat is worse than it sounds. I have no idea how bulimics manage. Real pregnant women are lucky, their purging comes easy.

But I don't say any of that. Obviously.

I smile. "Croissant? Tea?" I offer again. One should never show their hand.

"I'm flattered, really," she tells me, eyeing the spread. "But gosh Melanie, this is just too much."

"It's just Mel." I correct her.

Beth blinks rapidly. It's clear she isn't used to being corrected.

"Only Tom calls me Melanie."

"What a shame," she says, pouring tea into her cup. "It sounds so sophisticated."

"Sugar?" I ask, nodding at the cup. Her eyes follow mine. It's June's china she's holding. She notices this too.

"No. Thank you."

She eyeballs the tray.

Pressing my lips together, suddenly I see my mistake: Just because Tom says she loves croissants does not mean she allows herself to have them. This makes me savor the moment all the more. I really take it in. Mistakes can work in ones favor that way, if you let them. Take the fake bun in my oven, if an example is what you're looking for.

I see her leaning in. She's bound to fall. "This is all very nice," she tells me, straightening her back. I can see it takes all her restraint to stop herself from reaching out. I bet if I left her alone... She clears her throat. "But you know I can't have these carbs."

"That's okay," I say. "I'm eating for two."

"If only the weight came off as easily as it comes on."

I ignore her, and then I reach for a croissant. I place it beneath my nose and inhale deeply. Closing my eyes, I can relax into the aroma. "Mmmm."

I make sure to give it the full effect before tearing a fluffy piece off and placing it on my tongue. I chew extra slowly. When I'm finished, I nod toward the tray. "So good. I hope you won't mind if I have yours."

Her mouth is open; she's about to speak. At this point, I have no intention of sharing.

I murmur something inaudible and then, "Pregnancy cravings…are very intense."

"I want to talk about the party," she says, changing the subject.

My face falls. Then I let a bit of silence settle between us. "I know," I tell her. "It didn't turn out the way I'd wanted either."

"The Men's Alliance wasn't happy with the final numbers."

"Oh, that reminds me—" I meet her eye. "I've been meaning to ask how I can join the Women's Alliance?"

Beth looks confused, although her face barely moves. Probably on account of all the filler. "There's no such thing."

I rest my hand on my chest and inhale deeply. I pretend to let what she's said sink in. "Oh. Well, I just assumed…"

"Melanie, dear," she says. She makes a clucking sound with her tongue to further convey her disappointment. Just in case I missed it. "Before you go any further, may I make a request?"

She shifts, and I see the light flicker behind her eyes. She's going to relent and ask for the damn croissant. "It's Mel," I say calmly. "Just Mel."

"Mel, right." She crosses and uncrosses her legs. Her chin dips to her chest before finally she meets my eye. "I was really hoping to get off on a good foot."

I picture her getting off. It isn't pleasant. My face twists. Beth takes this as a concession.

"I realize you're new. But we have standards to uphold."

"With the Women's Alliance?"

She doesn't miss a beat. "There is no women's alliance."

I shake my head. "Oh, that's right. You said that."

Beth glances toward the clock. It's weird how she knows

everything in this house, maybe even better than me. "Tom mentioned you haven't read the agreement."

"Yeah about that—" I pause and crack my knuckles.

She waits patiently for me to go on, but I can see I'm wearing her down. She isn't used to people taking this approach with her. "You know what they say about pregnancy brain."

"I'm afraid I don't."

My bad. It's been a long time since she's been pregnant. "Funny, how all that goes away with enough time."

I see her jaw harden. Like the rest of her. Beth Jones isn't a woman who likes to be reminded she's aging.

I toss my hands up before dropping them in my lap. Eventually, I shove them between my thighs. It's a submissive posture. "With so much to do around here…it keeps slipping my mind."

Her eyes shift. She isn't sure if I'm mocking her, or if I'm just stupid. Now that I have her properly confused, I bring it home. "Which reminds me…I was wondering…if you could…like…um… give me a refresher on the rules."

Finally, I get a smile. My question, combined with the way it is posed, has confirmed her suspicion. It's the latter. It's her mouth I watch as she works out what to say next. She has that trout pout thing going, and I'm not sure if it's work or if she's just really unhappy or if it's only temporary, like maybe she's into those lip kit things that they're always advertising on the internet.

"The rules," she says. "Of course." It's clear what she thinks of me by the way she says it. Beth thinks I suffer from a low IQ. *All beauty. No brains.* What a terrible thing for her it would be if I were blessed with both. The threat of such a travesty out of the way, she adjusts her skirt and settles in.

When she starts to speak, I interrupt her. "I love that skirt. It's such a statement piece." Her eyes follow mine and land on her legs. "You *have* to tell me where I can find one…we could be, what do they call it…" I stop myself and stare into the air between us.

Finally, I reach up and grab the thought. "Ah, matchy-matchy. I've always wanted to do that. Never had a sister... but now—"

Beth presses her perfect lips to one another. Lipstick stains her teeth when she opens her mouth. She smiles pleasantly. "I doubt they make your size."

I feign surprise. I'm not as green as my counterpart thinks.

"I mean, I doubt they come in maternity."

"You're probably right." I touch my stomach. "And I have every intention of getting as big as a house..."

She doesn't outright say so, but I can see she likes the idea of this. "Anyhow—I'm short on time so let's stay focused on the rules—"

"Yeah," I agree, shooting for eager. "I just feel like Josie was so distracted that I didn't get the full rundown." My hand moves from my stomach to my heart. This makes sense to her. She sips her tea and waits for me to go on and so I do. "I really didn't mean to upset the Men's Alliance. I guess... it's just...well, it's easy to break the rules if you don't know what they are."

Her chest heaves. It's like she's deflating. No need to worry, her implants will keep her afloat. I'm impressed by the way they're so...out there. They have to be Ds at least. I want to ask, but I don't know the proper way to tell someone you like their tits without just coming out with it. This seems like it might be breaking the rules, and anyway, she speaks before I have the chance.

"Very true," she tells me, and she seems relieved so it takes me a minute to remember what we'd been talking about. It helps when she goes on. "And, I couldn't agree more. I think we should start from the beginning."

"Wonderful," I tell her, and that's when I feel it. Unmistakable warmth, the wetness between my legs. It's subtle at first but then I'm sure, and if I stay still for a moment I know I'll get a proper gush. My period. I thank God. It's right on time.

I realize Beth is waiting for me to speak. My head spins.

I do the only thing that makes any sense. I stand. Blood runs down my legs.

"Oh, my," Beth says. And then, her face goes blank. "We'd better get you to the hospital."

I do not for a second regret forgetting to suggest grabbing a towel on the way out.

My tragedy, my forgetfulness, earned Beth a new car. But that's not all. It got rid of June's horrid couch and the armchair went with it. Small sacrifices, as they say.

CHAPTER TEN

TOM

"Is it going to hurt?" It's a ridiculous question, in retrospect. Of course, it was going to hurt. This might explain why I can't force myself to look away. As the nurse readies the instruments, my wife lays motionless on the exam table. I stand beside her and watch. When I look down at Melanie, she isn't watching. Her eyes are closed. I study the rise and fall of her chest. Her rate of breathing has increased. I can't blame her for being nervous. She doesn't want this, as much as she knows it has to happen. I think that's why she refuses to look at me.

"It smells funny in here," I mention casually. It's supposed to smell clean and sterile. Like antiseptic. Instead it smells like someone heated up their lunch—an Indian dish—and that's a real problem for me. I quite like Indian food.

This is sure to ruin it.

I let out a long and heavy sigh. When this is all over, I plan to have a word with management. It should be illegal to heat up your lunch in this kind of place, where things go to die.

"What kind of person could eat at a time like this?" I demand, as the odor grows more intense, wafting through the air like poison, doing future damage to my taste buds.

Melanie doesn't answer. She doesn't even open her eyes. The nurse pretends she hasn't heard, but later when I hear her whispering just outside the door for someone to bring a fan, and I know she has.

I take a seat in the cold, hard chair and fold my arms. Nothing in this room is made for comfort. Melanie doesn't seem to care. They have given her something for anxiety. "The meds should kick in soon," I say.

Again, she doesn't acknowledge I've spoken. Maybe they already have.

I lean forward, resting my elbows on my knees. I start to tell her this is for the best, but she knows that deep down, even if she can't see it yet.

Thankfully, the doctor comes in, saving me from further meaningless chitchat. I study his expression, his serious expression as he reads the words on the screen, notes the nurse has charted.

The baby is a boy, Melanie said. She wanted to name him Ethan. I did not have an opinion. I've always thought it bad luck to name a child before they are born.

The doctor pats my wife's knee. "Shall we proceed?"

She opens her eyes then. They meet mine. I nod slightly. Melanie looks up at the physician and nods her head in agreement.

I check my watch. This is where I'm supposed to say I wish I could take her place. The truth is, I don't. It wouldn't matter anyway. There's no point in wishful thinking. That's not how this works.

I feel the nurse watching me, watching us. I might pass out. The sight of blood, the metallic smell, it makes me dizzy. I reach over and grab my wife's hand. She doesn't pull away. But I can feel that she wants to.

"Don't worry," the doctor says. "We're just starting with an exam."

I squeeze lightly. I'm not good at these things, so I repeat the words I've practiced. "It'll all be over soon."

~

"I'M GOING TO PICK UP THE DRY CLEANING," I SAY TO MELANIE. "Then I was thinking about stopping for Indian food." I can't get that smell out of my mind. I refuse to let their incompetence ruin my favorite dish for me. "Hungry?"

"No," she tells me.

"You haven't eaten since breakfast yesterday." I can't blame her. I pretty much lost my appetite then, too.

"I'm fine."

You're not fine. You're a liar. I don't say this, of course. There's time for that.

Thankfully, Melanie let me off the hook yesterday when she asked me to step out while the doctor performed his exam. The pregnancy resolved itself, she said, and that was it. She doesn't want to talk about it, and I get it.

Needless to say, I haven't had the chance to bring up the fact that I'm aware she's been lying to me. I know about her past. I also haven't yet worked out what to do about it. When an event like this occurs, I am forced to draw on other areas of expertise. In the mathematical theory of stochastic processes, time is a stochastic process associated with diffusion processes that characterize the amount of time a particle has spent at a given level. How this relates is, Melanie's lie is not a new one. It was not random. Therefore, I decide it can wait until I've had proper sustenance. I pat her head. "I'll grab you some soup, just in case."

~

THE MORNING PRIOR AN EMAIL FROM ADAM ARRIVED INTERRUPTING

my breakfast. Adam likes to send emails during non-work hours. This one was different.

The subject line read: *Only open if you're alone.*

Never a good sign.

I wasn't alone. But I opened it anyway.

Staring at me on the screen was a picture of my wife, in a precarious position.

I remember where I know Melanie from, Adam wrote. *My kid brother's bachelor party. She was the entertainment, if you catch my drift. And let's just say...he still talks about her. You lucky duck, you.*

THE SIMPLEST ANSWER IS MOST OFTEN THE CORRECT ANSWER. Occam's razor is the process of paring down information to make finding the truth easier. According to the problem-solving principle, when presented with competing hypothetical answers to a problem, one should select the one that makes the fewest assumptions. This is how I come to my hypothesis as it relates to my wife.

Why would Melanie lie about her past?

Her sexual history, of which I did a full accounting of from the very beginning, was supposed to have included two previous partners. Not exactly ideal, as I would have preferred none, but excusable, I guess, for someone of her age and generation.

However, given the latest evidence to the contrary, which is sitting in my inbox, two was incorrect. She lied, and there can only be a handful of reasonable answers as to why that would be. I plan to force the right one.

I am thankful the bookstore has many materials on the subject from which to choose. I select the most obvious. *A Survivor's Guide to Sexual Abuse.* At checkout, I ask the clerk to gift wrap it, and she gives me a strange look. "The gift that keeps on giving," I say and then to clarify, "Closure."

She studies me for a long moment before walking away. I am

then handed off to a boy with bright blue colored hair. He offers no explanation for the delay in appropriate customer service, he only says the woman can no longer assist me. This is my fault. I should not have expected much. His eyebrows are painted on like rainbows. I can only assume his parents paid him little attention growing up, and now he is taking his revenge on the rest of society. "Very new wave," he mentions, glancing toward the book even though I haven't asked his opinion. I've never understood why people insist on making small talk at the expense of quality conversation. "With the gift wrapping," he adds. "Gotta make these things mainstream."

I shrug. I do not understand what he means. He could be speaking Portuguese for all I know. But I keep my mouth shut; I do not want to encourage him. Nor do I have time to be handed off to someone else.

Melanie is still seated on the new couch when I return. It's not really my taste, but we needed a replacement quick. At least one of us likes it. When her eyes meet mine, I hand the gift to her. The ladies from the church have been by, she tells me. To match her need for small talk, I could tell her about the rude clerk or the guy with blue eyebrows but I am not feeling particularly generous where she is concerned.

"Open it," I say.

She unwraps it carefully. "What's this?" she asks as she flips it in her hands.

"I'm sorry you suffered."

My lying wife throws the book at me. Literally.

I duck and cover.

Her brow furrows. "What is wrong with you?"

"So, you weren't abused?"

"No," she huffs. "Where would you get an idea like that?"

"But you lied."

"About what?"

It concerns me that she has to ask.

"You had more than two sexual partners."

Her eyes widen. She realizes she's trapped. "I'm— I'm—what does it matter, anyway?"

"It matters because statistically speaking, the more—" I stop myself. Clearly, she doesn't care about statistics. If she had, she would have been a little more reserved. "It matters because you lied."

She scoffs. "I can't believe you're doing this now." I recognize this as classic avoidance. In no time flat, the tears come. Soon, she has pulled out all the stops and she is full out crying. I recognize this too: A form of female manipulation.

I give her time and eventually, when I haven't caved, she wipes her nose with the back of her hand.

"Well?"

"Seriously? You want to go there now? After what I've just been through."

"What you've been through? I've just learned my whole marriage is a sham."

"Really?" She cocks her head. "Is that what you think?"

I dig my heels in. "How many, Melanie?"

She narrows her eyes, and this is war.

"How many what?" *All warfare is based on deception.*

"How many men were there?"

"I'm not doing this with you, Tom." she says. We stare at each other for a moment, waiting to see who will be the first to draw. Finally, she stands. I think for a second this is to achieve better aim. But she chooses to retreat. I listen as she climbs the stairs, goes into the guest room and locks the door. *Subdue the enemy without fighting.*

This is a poor choice on her part.

The next morning when I wake up, Melanie is gone.

CHAPTER ELEVEN

MELANIE

I had been dreaming about flirting with danger when my eyes flutter open. It's a rush, teetering on the edge like I have these past few days, and this has a way of making dreams feel more real. As I slip further from sleep, as I try to recall what the dream was all about, it dawns on me how bright the room seems. I shield my face and then twist in an attempt to pull the covers free of whatever is holding them back so I can cover my head. They refuse to budge.

I sigh at how a pleasant dream can so easily slip from your grasp, how quickly real life can thrust you head first into annoyance. It's just like Tom to open all the draperies in order to coerce me from sleep. I rub at my eyes, and then as my vision comes into focus, I shift slightly. Suddenly, I realize nothing about where I am is familiar.

A small moan forces itself from my lips as I sit up in bed with a start. I wince. My body aches. I feel it before I see it, and when I look down, there is an icepack shoved between my thighs. *This is all wrong.* I force myself out of bed. It isn't pleasant to move, but the adrenaline pulsing through my veins sees me through. I cradle my abdomen, an instinctive measure, made before it slowly dawns on me I no longer have to lie. The pretend baby has left the building. The secret remains safe with me.

"We all have our terrors, I suppose," a small voice says. Still shielding my eyes, I survey the room. Once my vision steadies enough, I settle in on the woman. I wait for her to say something further, I wait for her to explain who she is. I wait for her to tell me why I'm here. She doesn't. She stares back at me, curiously.

Edging my legs over the side of the bed, I scoot slowly until my feet reach the floor. Everything is happening so fast and so slow all the same. I tell myself it's possible I'm still dreaming.

The woman, who looks more like a girl, closes the book in her lap. She uses her fingertips to smooth her long, chestnut hair. "I'm Vanessa."

"Mel," I say, noting our surroundings. Two metal-framed twin-sized beds are situated adjacently to one another. I occupy one. Vanessa is perched on the bed opposite me. The walls are white. Bare. Florescent lights hang overhead. Other than the beds, the room is empty, save for a pair of matching nightstands. The top of mine is empty. On hers rests a stack of books.

Carefully, I push myself upward to a standing position. I waddle toward the door. Twelve steps, I count. Each one jabs worse than the one prior. When I reach the door, I desperately jiggle the handle, only to find it's locked from the outside.

I glance over my shoulder at Vanessa. She watches me carefully at first, but when I look back again in search of answers, her eyes have glazed over. It's as though I've vanished all together. I press my face against the small windowpane until I feel the cool of the glass on the tip of my nose. My knees could buckle at any moment. "Hello?" I call out. I feel eyes on me.

I clear my throat. "Hello," I call again, my voice louder this time.

"I wouldn't do that, if I were you," Vanessa says. "Screaming doesn't bring help. Quite the opposite actually."

I turn to her. "The door is locked."

She smiles wickedly. Her round, cherub-like face, her large eyes and her perfect nose, don't fit the expression she wears. Her eyes are on her book, which gives me a chance to properly study her. She's young. Maybe my age, maybe slightly younger. It's hard to say.

"Why is the door locked?"

Her eyes meet mine like a challenge she refuses to answer. I notice her eyes match her hair.

I scream this time. I scream out, asking if anyone can hear me. I pound on the door with my fists. If a challenge is what Vanessa wants, fine. You have to be good at manipulation to manipulate. You have to be meticulous in your planning and diabolical in your execution to pull it off. Judging by her simple, perfect face, I don't think she has it in her. But I plan to find out. She can either give me the answers I seek, or we can go about this the hard way. It's her call.

Nothing happens. No one comes.

"I really wish you wouldn't do that," Vanessa chides. I open my mouth to give it another go. My eyes are on her. Her voice lowers to a whisper. "We're the lucky ones."

I lean against the wall for balance. It freaks me out when strangers speak with this kind of honesty, even if I've asked for it.

"Right now, they are out of rooms," she offers. Her expression has turned serious. "That's why we're together." Finally, I think we're getting somewhere. "This never happens," she assures me, shaking her head. "You're going to ruin it."

I can't help but stare when she speaks. She's gorgeous, stunningly so, or rather she could be in another circumstance. Most people aren't beauty queens in hospital gowns. "What kind of hospital is this?"

Vanessa doesn't immediately answer, so I turn my attention back to the small window. I can see a long hallway, which is empty. "Hello?" I say to her and to anyone who will listen. I don't want to repeat the question. I realize I'm afraid of what she might say.

"Oh," she murmurs, and when I turn back, she laughs, the corners of her mouth edging more deeply as she does. "This is no hospital."

I look on as Vanessa motions grandly around the room. "This is a center for healing."

I turn the word over in my head. "Healing," I repeat aloud.

This isn't my first rodeo. She's insane.

I am rewarded with another small smile. "Many are the afflictions of the righteous, but the Lord delivers him out of them all. Psalm 34:19."

I make my way over, carefully sitting on the edge of my bed. I don't feel righteous. I feel numb. I feel weak. I feel like sleeping forever. I feel like getting the hell out of here.

"I don't understand." I look over at my roommate. She raises her brow like she expects me to say something. I rub at my eyes with the palms of my hands, willing myself to wake from this nightmare.

"Therefore confess your sins to each other and pray for each other so that you may be healed. James 5:16"

A small laugh escapes my lips. *Pray.* It makes me want to play in traffic. Prayer can't help me now.

"Okay, fine." I relent. "I get it. This is a mental institution."

"It's no such thing," she says, contradicting me. Her tone is pleasant. Sweet even. "This is The New Hope Center for Rejuvenation."

"Really." My eyes narrow. "What kind of rejuvenation are you in for?"

"Whoa, you really are new." She sets her book aside. "Like brand new."

She is legitimately crazy. I pinch the bridge of my nose. I don't know what's worse, being in here alone or being in here with someone who is of no use to me.

"Anyway," she continues, trying to change my mind. "We're not supposed to tell." I feel like I could be good with this. It's not like I'm getting anywhere anyway. Eventually, her face breaks into a full grin. "But tell you what…if you show me yours…I'll show you mine."

Her offer feels like a test and only alcohol makes me swing that way so I tell her thanks but no thanks.

She nods at my waist. "Your surgery—"

I know then to lie. It always helps in situations where one is unsure. Call it a power play. "I lost the baby."

"I heard that." She looks away, exhaling deeply. I watch as her breath comes slow and heavy. This could get me somewhere, I can see. "I'm sorry."

My mouth folds in. "It's for the best." Her sympathy feeds me. Like one of those gel packs marathoners use. A quick hit. It's something. But it's not enough.

Her face turns serious. "I didn't mean…"

I stare at the door. I pretend my mind is somewhere else, on something outside of this room. She needs space to give me what I want. I give it to her.

"My breast enhancement is tomorrow," she offers finally. "But I had vaginal rejuvenation last month, so if it's any consolation, I know what you're going through."

I feel it then. I'm not sore from the exam that confirmed my uterus is empty. It's more than that. When I look at her, I see it in her eyes. I think I'm going to be sick.

"Where's the bathroom?"

Vanessa offers a sympathetic look before nodding to the puke bucket at the foot of my bed.

I can't help myself. I hurl into the container, white-knuckling the sides. My stomach is empty. I hardly manage any bile, so mostly, I just dry-heave.

It feels like it takes forever for the waves to stop but when they finally subside, I breathe deeply. In and out. In and out.

"Don't worry," she says quietly. There is hope in her voice. "Your recovery won't be so bad. It's your head you'll have to work to get right."

I want to tell her she is wrong. There's nothing that can help me there. I bite the inside of my cheek instead.

~

A WINDOWLESS ROOM. SO THERE ARE NO DISTRACTIONS, I WOULD later learn. White walls, for purity of thought. Ten chairs in a circle, to face one another. We all wear hospital gowns like patients.

"Gather round, ladies," an old woman announces. "It's circle time."

She softly claps her hands as we file into the open room, taking our seats one by one in perfect synchronization.

"What is circle time?" I whisper to the woman to my right. She doesn't answer, so I turn to Vanessa on my left. I still haven't decided if I can trust her, but the unexpected is rarely a good thing, and I want to know what I'm walking into. Usually, she's not much help. She talks without saying anything. Still, I listen. I know that she has a young son, but that she's not in a hurry to get home. Not like the others, she says. In here she tells me she has time to think—and at least she gets to go to the bathroom on her own.

"You have to watch your back," she replies under her breath.

That much I know. I've always known.

"Don't worry," she offers as she folds her hands in prayer. I wait expectantly for her to go on until she elbows me so I do the same. "The first time is the hardest."

I have no idea what she means. I wasn't the one weeping last night. Now, I'm exhausted, which I want to tell her makes watching my back a little more difficult.

I asked the woman who escorted me to the bathroom this morning when I get to make a phone call.

She only laughed and said, this isn't jail.

"All right, ladies, take your seats," the matronly woman instructs the group. Finally, the clapping ends. The fog ends. I feel like I can think again. I count six of us.

"Yesterday there were women in those chairs," the girl next to me whispers.

I don't ask what happened to them. The old woman claps her hands, only once, and louder this time. Everyone waits. All eyes are on hers. Hands folded. Ankles crossed. I glance around and follow suit.

"Let's begin with introductions, shall we?"

There is hesitation in the room. This, a touch of loneliness, expectation, and also something I can't name.

"As some of you are new, I'll go first," the woman says. She wears a floral, full-skirted dress. The kind school teachers used to wear back in the old days. "You may call me Mrs. Elizabeth." Addressing her this way, the direction, this is the first thing anyone has said that makes any sense.

"Now," she points at Vanessa. "It's your turn."

My roommate stands. Her face is expressionless. It's her hands I watch. She picks at the cuticle on her thumb with her pointer finger as she speaks. It's the only blemish in an otherwise perfect manicure. "My name is Vanessa."

"And what brings you here to the rejuvenation center, Vanessa?"

She digs deeper. She picks harder. The skin peels back. Blood rises to the surface "I wasn't attentive enough at home."

"Elaborate please," the woman demands. "So that we may all have a better understanding." Her voice rises with each word she speaks. It bounces off the walls and sticks itself between my ears. It's a nasty sound, the kind you'd be fine with never hearing again.

Vanessa's eyes are glued to the floor. But her voice is calm and low. "Anyone who does not provide for their relatives, and especially for their own household, has denied the faith and is worse than an unbeliever."

"Well said." Mrs. Elizabeth smiles proudly. "Verse please."

Vanessa's eyes shift. "Timothy 5:8."

Finally, Mrs. Elizabeth motions for her to take her seat. "Don't forget—" she says to Vanessa but every bit as much to the rest of us. "God is in the detail."

The women nod in unison as though this is the most profound statement they've ever heard.

Next, Mrs. Elizabeth looks at me. "Your turn, dear."

I stand. The truth is, I don't know why I am here. But I do know one thing. "I am a liar," I say. And before she can ask me to expand upon that sentiment, I offer the only Bible verse I know, one my mother taught me. "All men are liars."

CHAPTER TWELVE

TOM

Everyone is replaceable— everyone. Even your grandparents who've celebrated their fiftieth wedding anniversary. If they hadn't married each other, they would have married someone else. If you can't comprehend this simple, yet profound truth, you certainly don't understand people enough to manipulate them. Your world will begin to make more sense once you grasp this lesson.

Speaking of lessons, Melanie's absence has given me a lot of time to think. It's quiet without her around. Tidier too.

It would have been bad enough had my lovely wife deceived me and me alone. But, that wasn't the case. Given Adam knows about her past, obviously other members of the leadership are aware as well. Her deception doesn't make me look good. In fact, it makes me look weak. That's why Melanie had to be reprimanded. Not only is she a liar, there was a point that demanded to be proven.

Often when one is called into battle, it is apparent that the best way to go about a thing is indirectly. Keep your hands clean, as my father liked to say. If your opponent hasn't a clue what you are up to, a defense cannot be prepared.

I haven't a clue what Melanie's defense will be. But I know how to find out. For this reason, I start with Beth for answers.

"How is she?" I say to her over the phone.

It takes her a second to respond.

"Beth?"

"Oh…um…I haven't heard much other than the surgery went well."

"Surgery?" My gut sets. "I thought she was just going in for reprogramming."

"You weren't happy with her, Tom." She sighs. "So we freshened her up a bit."

I take this for what it is. A sign. They don't think my wife's lie was big enough to extricate her, but they want her to pay for what she's done. It isn't that I don't. The church and I, we often have different ideas where retribution is concerned. "She's recovering from the loss of a pregnancy…"

"Best to get it all over with at once," Beth assures me. "This way she'll return to you good as new."

"How long will that be?" I know the statistics on single men and I have no intention of living that way.

"Hard to say."

"It's her first offense."

"Tom, you can't have it both ways. You can't ask for me to fix her and then say you want her back before the fixing is done."

"Well, I'd like to see her."

"And you will."

"When?" Specifics is what I'm after. *If the enemy is settled, make them move.*

"Give her some time, Tom." I hear the smile in Beth's voice. "You know what they say, about absence making the heart grow fonder. Melanie needs to learn her lesson. And trust me," she says. I'd be willing to bet she's broken into full grin. "It'll be a pleasant surprise for the both of you."

Beth is wrong. I hate surprises. I say nothing.

"It'll be like a whole new woman coming outta there."

I think about the other morning in the kitchen and realize maybe Beth has a point. But I can't let her think she's won entirely. "Man should not be without his wife," I tell her. "We're practically newlyweds."

My thoughts drift back to the lasagna I found this morning in the freezer. "Melanie had been preparing meals ahead of time in preparation for the baby." *A girl after my own heart.* "Maybe I exaggerated things a little."

Beth holds her resolve. Which means I must as well. "This will be good for you both. You just have to let go just a bit. Let us do our job."

"She color coordinated my canned goods." When I asked about it, she'd said she was bored. *Maybe bringing her here was too much too soon.*

"Tom." I hear the warning in Beth's tone.

"I miss her."

"I thought you preferred alphabetical order," she counters unexpectedly. I forgot she knew June.

"I thought so, too. And you know what Melanie said to that?"

"No. What?"

"She said it's important things are not only functional but that they look good."

Beth scoffs. "She's good, Tom. But she could be better. We agreed on that. That's why she's at the center. That's what we're working on."

"I like the way she looks."

"I'm sure you do," Beth tells me. "But you called me. Remember? Which means she isn't yet functional, is she?"

~

SPEAKING OF THINGS THAT WEREN'T FUNCTIONAL...MICHAEL showed up at the office one afternoon. That was the good news. I hadn't seen my business partner in three days. Thankfully, he was sober. In fact, he looked good. Clear-headed. The bad was that once again, Mark Jones was in tow.

"Tom," Michael said boisterously. "Mark has presented me with an offer I think you should take a look at."

Conveniently, he left out the part about where he'd been and why he hadn't shown up to work. A stack of papers was slid across my desk. "I would like to purchase your house," Mark Jones informed me. "You can live there rent free so long as you agree to serve as New Hope's accountant."

My eyes met his. "How did you know my house was up for sale?"

I'd expected him to say Michael had told him. He didn't say that. "We pay attention, very close attention, to people of interest."

"I can assure you I'm not that interesting."

"On the contrary, we think you would be a good fit for our team. Considering—" He turned to my business partner, "How Michael here has talked you up."

I pushed the stack of papers away, back in Mark's direction. "I'm afraid I can't accept your offer at this time."

"Tom—" Michael cleared his throat. "They're helping me get sober. You wouldn't believe it. I feel better than I have in months."

"I'm glad."

"Tom, come on. Don't be stubborn."

"I'm not interested."

Michael furrowed his brow. "I really think you ought to give this some thought."

"Mr. Anderson," Mark cut in to help him. "Is something wrong with the offer?"

"It doesn't solve my business problems."

"About that—"He opened his suit jacket and pulled from it a piece of paper. "We are prepared to pay you this…as well as offer free tuition for your children to our exceptionally rated private school."

I glanced at the floor briefly before meeting his eye. I'm aware of the cost of putting two kids through private school, and I'm aware of the cost of having to yank them out. "Your offer is very generous," I said as I leaned back in my chair and folded my arms across my chest. "But I'm afraid I can't accept this."

"I'm almost offended," Mark said.

"I *am* offended," Michael said.

"I'm sorry," I said.

~

THE FOLLOWING EVENING I ARRIVED HOME TO FIND MARK JONES and his wife Beth having coffee in my living room. Iced coffee with milk, like my father drank. June always said she hated it and yet there she sat, glass half empty.

After exchanging pleasantries, I asked my wife to meet me in the kitchen. "Have you spoken with Michael?"

"Who?" She wasn't expecting me to lead with that. Recognition passed over her face. "God, no. Why?"

I wipe at a smudge on the counter. A perfectly clean house, and still there's this, one little blemish. "No reason."

"I really think we should take them up on this offer," June said, her voice hushed. "The kids will get to go back to private school. We'd get to keep the house…"

I wiped down the rest of the counter just in case. "Define *private* school. Define *keep.*"

"Come on, Tom." She took the dishtowel from my hand. "What do we have to lose?"

"Except everything?"

"I don't think you're seeing this clearly."

"Why would I take a job with a church? I am not a religious man."

"So? It's a paycheck," she said. She placed her hands on her hips. "What does religion have to do with balancing their books and investing their money?"

"Everything, I'd be willing to bet."

She sighed heavily. This is what she did when she was defeated which wasn't often. Or, as I was learning, not often enough. She motioned with her head toward the living room. "I'll get rid of them," I said but when I turned Mark Jones was standing in the doorway of our kitchen. "Now, now." He held his palms face up. "There's no pressure, here. Really. I'm sorry if we've given the wrong impression."

I lifted the tray from the counter and handed it to June. "Excuse me," she said, looking from me to Mark and back. "I'll leave you two to talk. I promised Beth more tea."

I watched her walk out and then I turned my attention to Mark. "I hate to disappoint you, but I haven't anything left to say."

"Listen, Tom." Mark said, leaning back against the counter. "I'm not going to lie. I, myself, was not always a man of God." He glanced toward the living room, toward the sound of laughter, and then back at me. "But I think you're missing the bigger point, and I don't want you to miss the opportunity that goes along with it."

"Like I said—"

"You see, the thing is... I can relate to your position. Adam is the real fanatic where New Hope is concerned. Me...I consider it more of a social experiment. A lifestyle, if you will. Along the lines of an exclusive country club—only—and I'm sure you can understand this—with tax benefits built right in."

"I don't think—"

He cut me off again. "What I'm really looking to create within the New Hope community is something that spans time, something that exceeds all boundaries of religion. I have a vision of the way things could be. And I was hoping you could help with this."

"I don't think that is possible." I didn't explain why. I didn't think it was any of his business.

"Every religion follows a set of principles, if you will," he said, glancing around the kitchen. "I want to create our own."

I waited for him to continue. I, too, surveyed the kitchen. Everything was in order. Almost.

"Beth has already gotten started on this, but she can only see to a certain point, if you catch my drift."

I didn't catch his drift, exactly. Although, I had just briefly met his wife, and if he meant that she was a little on the unintelligent side, then yes. "Principles are not the easiest thing to create. Most of them already exist."

"Precisely," he agreed. "And you seem like a man who prides himself on excellence. I've seen what you can do. I'm aware of how meticulous you are." He motioned around my kitchen. It wasn't spotless. There was a speck of dried tomato sauce from last night's dinner just above the range. He missed that. "We do not blindly make offers like the one your family has received. The goal with New Hope has never been to create just another church. We're not interested in another run-of-the-mill Christian organization. No, we want something bigger. We want an entire community who prides itself on excellence. Just take a look around—"

I do, and it's all I can manage to contain myself. I have the need to pick up the towel and scrub the leftover sauce. But I don't. Somehow it seemed to do so would make his spiel less effective.

"Our society has lost its sense of standards. Just look at what's happening in the world. Look how many people are either broke, obese, divorced, disease-ridden, or drug and alcohol addicted."

I take account although I already know. *Me, I'm broke. The bottle owns my best friend. My neighbor eats every meal out of a sack even though he's had two heart attacks.*

"We can fix this," Mark assured me. "But it starts with us. I don't know about you and June, but Beth and I want to surround ourselves with like-minded people. People who demand success of themselves and others. People who seek mastery in all areas of life. We want that for our children."

I think of my children, the source of the laughter coming from the living room.

"Just think about it, Tom. What are we leaving for the next generation and the one after that? More of the same? The status quo?"

He has a point. "I don't know."

"Okay, fine. I'll back off," he said finally. "This is your call."

"I just—"

"I get it. But just between you and I— we don't really even follow the teachings of the Bible. Well, not the whole thing. Mainly, we focus on the important passages. You know, the ones that stand out."

"No," I said. "I don't know. I'm an atheist. "

"It's like filler."

"That seems deceptive."

"Call it what you want. You've seen our numbers. We're small —but we're growing. People want change. Like you, they want more for themselves and for their families. They want to feel safe, and they're desperate for something better."

I was in the process of thinking of a final way to say no thanks when June entered the kitchen with empty glasses. Beth followed her in, and I watched as the two of them stood next to one another, placing the dishes in the sink. It's only then I got an accurate comparison. Beth may not have seemed that intelligent, but she's aces in the looks department. Not a single hair out of place, immaculate appearance, fit and trim, even after children. She's almost perfect. "I'll talk it over with my wife," I said, looking at June.

Mark grinned. "That's a very good call."

CHAPTER THIRTEEN

MELANIE

After circle time, Mrs. Elizabeth tucks her hand inside my elbow and tells me to come with her. "When is breakfast?" I ask, toying with small talk, but also, I'm hungry.

"No breakfast for you, Mrs. Anderson," she says. "You're on a liquid diet."

I struggle to keep up with her. "When can I expect my liquid breakfast then?"

She doesn't answer me. Instead, she halts and looks down at her chart. I watch as her eyes scan the page. "A smoothie was left on your bedside table." She points and looks to see if my eyes follow. "I see here it was reported as being empty..."

Vanessa.

"Mrs. Anderson?" She turns to me and places her hands on my shoulders. The clipboard rests against my back. I wonder how useful of a weapon it might be. I wonder if I could make it to the end of the hall and if I could, how I'd get out. She searches my eyes. Her face is a mix of serious and stern and something else I can't read. "I asked you a question. Did you or did you not consume your smoothie?"

I'm not thinking straight when I answer. My mind is occupied with the thought that if I hit her just right, I could knock her out, maybe kill her, and then I could bolt. "I did."

She carefully assesses my face. "Because we take theft very seriously around here."

"There was no theft," I assure her. "I just thought there might be an actual breakfast is all," I add afterward because when you lie it's important to add a little substance. Lies should be simple. Never boring.

She takes me by the elbow, and the next thing I know we are barreling down the long corridor once again. "Not on the weight loss plan there isn't."

"The what?"

Mrs. Elizabeth doesn't answer. She walks until suddenly she stops and uses her badge to open a door. "Your advisor will explain all that," she tells me, nudging me through the doorway. It feels like she's poking a bruise, testing to see how much it hurts. She nods. "That's her there."

~

I EXPECT TO SEE BETH ON THE OTHER SIDE OF THE DESK BUT quickly learn that an advisor and a sponsor are not one and the same.

The woman gestures toward a chair on the other side of her desk. "Have a seat."

I adjust my hospital gown, which has come loose in the back, before I decide modesty in a place like this is of no use. Bracing myself on the arms of the chair, I carefully lower down into it.

As the woman writes whatever it is she writes on the notepad in front of her, I survey the small office. Behind her is a small window. The shade is down, which is disappointing since it feels like forever since I've seen the outdoors. She sits at a large wooden desk that is covered in files. There's a computer on the desk and a single painting of a meadow hangs on the wall. There's nothing personal, no artifacts from real life, which tells me she either doesn't have a personal life, or she isn't that important around here. Maybe both.

"I can assure you there's a method to the madness," she mentions, clearly noticing my eyes on the file folders that are stacked on every available surface. They aren't labeled in names, merely numbers. She isn't looking at me when she says it. She's staring at the file in front of her.

I take the opportunity to take her in. People always give more away when they don't think you're looking. Red hair, green eyes. Mid to late forties, if I had to guess. She's had work done on her face. What exactly, it's hard to tell. What I know for sure is she's strikingly beautiful, same as most of the women around here. Except for the old ones. They don't seem to care.

"Sit up straight, please."

I do as she asks. Something tells me I want to be compliant with this one. At least in the beginning. So I arch my back and bring my shoulder blades in until they touch one another.

She leans forward and folds her hands. After a moment, she lays them on the file and then meets my eye. "Do you know why you're here?"

When she looks at me, I get the feeling I want to know everything there is to know about her. At the same time, I understand. She isn't the kind of person one can ever really know. She's familiar in that way.

I shake my head slowly. *The less you say the better.*

"I'm Mrs. Ann Banks. Your advisor."

"Mel."

Her forehead crinkles to the extent that it can. "I'm aware of who you are," she tells me, sucking her bottom lip between her teeth. "And your name is Melanie."

"Only my mother calls me that."

"Well—from now on, everyone does." She cocks her head

slowly when she speaks. Her icy stare burns into me. I want to be her when I grow up.

I glance around the office. This has to be some sort of joke. "Did my parents put you up to this?"

"I don't know your parents from Adam."

My eyes widen. "Adam?"

She leans forward slightly and then pulls back. "It's just an expression."

I study the painting. It's the only thing somewhat cheery I've seen around this place. Everything else is clinical and bare. "It was a gift."

I think she expects me to say something in return, but I don't, so she fills the silence.

"I suppose you want to know why you're here."

"Yes," I reply. "And I'd like to go home."

Her fingers toy with the edge of the chart. "All in good time," she tells me.

"How much time are we talking?"

"First, we've got to get you all recovered." She glances at my waist. "I take it you've had a look?"

My brow creases. I really hate it when people make me second-guess my opinion.

"Vaginal rejuvenation has about a week-long period where minimal activity is required. In six weeks you'll be able to resume all activities."

"Six weeks? You can't keep me here for six weeks."

Her mouth forms into a thin line. "It's in the agreement you signed, Mrs. Anderson."

The words feel strange and foreign coming from her mouth. Few people call me that name. It feels personal.

"I am fast at recovering," I assure her.

"Maybe," she says. "But what matters is how efficient you are with reprogramming."

"Reprogramming?"

She slides a book across the desk. "This contains a copy of the agreement." We both stare at the cover. "I highly suggest you take a look at it." She exhales. I think she is waiting for me to say something. "It will save us both a lot of time."

I take the book from the desk and turn it over in my hands.

"You'll want to memorize it," she says. "Make sure you can recite it forward and backward, in your sleep. You'll be tested before you're released to go home."

I don't know where home is.

"Can I call my parents?"

"The answer to that question is there in that book. You should know this. It too was in the agreement you signed when you agreed to marry Mr. Anderson. Which means I can only assume you never bothered to read it."

She would be correct in her assumption. Agreements are made to be broken. I don't tell her this. Some things are worth keeping to yourself.

Her face is almost sympathetic. "Having trouble cleaving can be normal in the beginning."

"I don't know what that means."

"Leaving the nest, leaving your old life behind. It can be tough."

"Right." I stare at my hands, and when that gets old I twist my wedding ring around my finger.

"How are you feeling about the surgery?"

"Fine," I lie.

She folds her hands and places them in her lap. "Is there anything else about yourself you'd like to change?"

"So, it's a choice then?" My tone turns bitter. "Because—"

"It was a choice, yes. When you signed the agreement, you opted into this lifestyle."

"This lifestyle?"

She gives me a look that showcases her exasperation. "Read the agreement Mrs. Anderson. Please."

"How about my husband. Can I call him?"

"I'm afraid not."

My stomach sinks. "Can I call anyone?" I don't know who I'd call, even if she said yes.

"You may write letters. In time."

I look on earnestly, too eagerly, as she makes a note of something on her notepad.

"In the meantime, then what? How do I know I'm not going to just wake up with a new face? Or giant tits? You know, to go with my new vagina."

"Are you unhappy with any of those things?"

"What?" I cock my head. "No."

She nods in understanding. But I'm not sure she believes me. "We're here for you, Mrs. Anderson. To make your life better. The sooner you understand this, the easier things will be. And the sooner you get to go home." I watch as her fingers drum on her desk.

"How about lipo?" I change my mind. The drumming stops. I need to see how far this can go. "I'm not happy with my thighs. I really want that gap everyone is talking about."

"That's why you're on the weight loss program," she tells me. Then she bites her lip and raises her brow, and I realize anything is possible. "First things first."

"Body sculpting?"

"Maybe."

"What about my roots? Can I get a touch up?"

"Once you're settled, of course." She shifts. "But let's not get ahead of ourselves."

"A facial?"

She doesn't answer. Instead, she opens her laptop and turns the screen to face me, pointing a web cam in my direction. "Before we get to any of that, I want you to tell me about the first time you can remember telling a lie."

I raise my brow.

"I understand you lied to your husband about your past."

"Did he put me in here?"

She shakes her head just a touch, so it's not a flat-out denial. "You put yourself in here. It's very important you take responsibility, Melanie. That's the only way change can occur."

"Maybe I don't want change."

"You just asked me for liposuction."

"That's different."

"No," she says. "That's where you're wrong."

"Bach?"

She cocks her head. "Excuse me?"

"On your desk," I motion. "You were playing Bach."

Her eyes widen slightly. "Yes."

"A piano player?" I'm stalling, and I think she sees it. I recall years of forced lessons. Wonderful memories. All of them.

She nods her head. "Once, a long time ago, yes."

"Yeah," I say. "Me too."

She isn't one for nostalgia. I can tell by the way she redirects the conversation. "Your first lie, Mrs. Anderson. Can you remember?"

I shrug and stare at myself on the screen. It's scary how you always look different than you think. I really could use a touch up.

"I need you to speak slowly and carefully," she tells me. "Don't rush. And don't leave anything out."

~

"What if they don't like me?" I asked my nanny. My Julia, with her wide hazel eyes and big round belly. Julia, with her caring hands, creaky knees, and soft heart.

"They are going to love you, Miss Mel," she said. I can still remember her eyes glistening as she called me by my pet name. Julia was probably the only person I've ever genuinely liked.

"Look at you," she remarked, slipping my backpack on my shoulders. "A big girl."

"I'm five. And when you're five, you have to go to school," I told her, repeating my mother's words. Words I knew were supposed to mean something, but didn't.

"That's right, baby girl."

I felt empty inside. "But I want to stay here with you. Like always."

"Nah," she said, fanning the air. "You've got too many things to do yet, too many friends to make. "Here—" She held up a bottle of perfume. "How about a little something to keep us close?"

My eyes lit up. I loved Julia's magic spray. "This way you can think of me and know I'm right there with you," she said, softly jabbing her finger into my heart.

I giggled as she playfully spritzed some on my dress. For good measure, she dabbed a little behind my ears. Then she pulled me into her oversized chest and held me there. I couldn't breathe. But I never minded too much. "Now, go. Your Mama's waiting on you."

"I love you, Julia."

She smiled. "And I you."

"Jesus, Melanie," my mother said in the car. She asked the driver to crack a window. "You smell like the help."

That reminded me. "I want to stay with Julia."

My mother ignored me the first two times I'd said it. On the third she told me that was enough, it was time for the silent game. Then she turned away.

"How do I make friends?" I asked when we reached the parking lot.

My mother shrugged. She had a lot of friends. I thought she would know. "Tell them about your pony. Tell them about your vacation to Italy last summer. Teach them some Italian. "

"I was four then. I forgotted it."

She had that sad look on her face she got whenever I was around. "I thought you were a smart girl."

I stared at the lines in the pavement, so I wouldn't have to remember where the look she wore came from. "I don't like school. I don't want to be five."

"I don't have time for this, Melanie," she huffed. "I'm already missing half of aerobics, and this is how you show your appreciation?"

I don't recall what happened next. All I know is during share time we were supposed to stand and tell everyone our name. "I'm Melanie," I said. "I have a pony, and I went to Italy on vacation." The rest I said in Italian. I wanted to make Mama proud.

"Wow, Melanie," the teacher smiled. "That is very impressive."

Later at recess, the other girls crowded around me. "Ponies are stupid," a girl with red hair said. "Her dress is stupid," another said. "You stink," the redhead told me. She leaned in close to get a good whiff. "Hey," she exclaimed, pulling one of the curls Julia had given me. I stood there while they circled like sharks. "I think we should call her Smelly Melly," she chanted. "Smelly Melly!" Everyone joined in. Only one person was allowed to call me Melly. I didn't care about the rest.

At nap time, when the teacher wasn't looking, I took my scissors and cut the redheaded girl's hair. Her screams woke me from my nap.

"Did you cut that girl's hair, Melanie?" my mother demanded over dinner.

"No," I lied.

"Well, someone did it," my father said.

I shrugged and stuffed my fork in my mouth.

"It was probably that Goldsmith girl. Heaven knows her parents don't teach her any manners. Remember—"

"I'll have a talk with the teacher," my father said. "We don't want people assuming it was Melanie."

"No," my mother agreed. "We don't."

That's the first time I learned how to get away with your crimes. It was the first time I learned I liked to see people suffer.

So long as no one could prove you did it, nothing bad could happen. You were untouchable.

My mother knew the truth, though. "That is not how you win friends, Melanie," she said when she found the girl's ponytail in my backpack. But she never told anyone. Not even my father, I don't think. And no one called me names after that.

~

"Pick up the pace," Mrs. Elizabeth says as she escorts me back to my room. "I haven't got all day, Princess." I shuffle my feet, forcing her to go slowly. She guides me down long corridors. We turn left, we turn right. I try to memorize the route we've taken, but it feels pointless. This place is a maze. Plus, I'm too busy peering in small windows. From what I can see, Vanessa is right. Most women are alone. I can't see most of them—that or the rooms are empty. But the ones I do manage to get a glimpse of are basically carbon copies of the others. They're all doing the same thing. They're staring at the same book I hold in my hands, the very one my roommate was staring at when I woke up in this place.

"Move along," Mrs. Elizabeth warns.

"Sorry," I say, wincing. "It's the pain."

"There is sweetness in pain," she tells me. But she doesn't look at me when she speaks.

When we reach the doorway, she stops, turns, and faces me. "Your roommate has been moved to solitary."

I glance through the window as though I need proof.

"And Mrs. Anderson, if you ever lie to me again, you'll end up there too. For twice as long."

I keep my face neutral, which is to say, mostly blank.

"No dinner for you, I'm afraid."

"I'm on the weight loss plan."

Mrs. Elizabeth frowns. She thinks I'm mocking her, but it's

blatant enough to be debatable. I hadn't yet learned proof isn't required in places like this. She reaches for my palm, turns it over, and places two pills inside. I watch as she retrieves a paper cup from a cart across the hall. She hands it to me. "For the pain."

I pop the pills in my mouth and swallow. I have no idea what she's giving me, but I hope they make me sleep.

"Drink up," she orders. "We can't have you choking, now can we? I doubt Mr. Anderson cares to be a widower twice over."

I down the water. It does nothing to quench my thirst.

Mrs. Elizabeth unlocks the door, and with a slight shove, she forces me in.

It scares me to think I might someday go willingly.

CHAPTER FOURTEEN

TOM

Melanie had grossly misinterpreted Newton's third law. Every action has an equal and opposite reaction, for sure. But she was mistaken when she expected her push to elicit an equally forceful push back. She had not accounted for the fact that most people prefer to shove harder. She had forgotten to pick her enemies carefully because the way those enemies fight is who you become.

"This is not good," Mark says, telling me what I already know. He's here to prove a point—many points, actually—and he's started by barging into my office. Now, he's standing there, waiting for me to say something, the weight of the world on his shoulders. When I fail to come up with anything that fits, he shakes his head. "In fact, Tom, this is very, very bad."

Mark has a tendency to exaggerate. I have no idea at this point if he is talking about me. It could be any number of things. With him, it's always something. "It's not so bad," I say. "Plus, our numbers are in great shape."

"You have two options," Mark informs me bluntly. "Kill her—or see to it that her past goes away."

I take a sip of my tea. I don't have to ask who he means by her, so I say, "I've never killed anyone." I don't say that I have no idea about my wife's past—or that it is particularly extensive—or that taking that route would most certainly be the path of most resistance.

"I'm afraid I don't know what to tell you." He shoves a manila folder across my desk.

I open it.

"Jack Fielding. Gregory Hollis. Evan Burnett."

"Do you know what these men have in common?"

"What?" It's not a lie if it's a question.

"They've all had relations with Melanie. Relations that could—that will—come back to haunt us."

"How is that?"

"Never mind. I don't have time to go into it. What you need to know is this." He points to their photographs. "These are the three main players we have to be concerned about."

My eyebrows raise. "Main players?"

I'm not sure if I want to ask about the others. He's just asked me to kill three people. Who knows how far he'll go with this.

"I can't have another dead wife on my hands," I tell him. "That would look suspicious."

"Tom," Mark says. "We can't have the RWP fail."

"What's the RWP?"

"The Replacement Wife Project."

"I see."

"Melanie's past puts it in grave jeopardy."

Mark has a flair for paranoia. In his mind, something is always on the verge of failing. "How so?"

"It's in the agreement, Tom. Not to mention the fact that we need this to work. If her history comes out, as shady as it is, the whole thing will crumble. No one wants to move from a sure thing to damaged goods. No one."

He isn't exactly lying, so I say the only thing that comes to mind. "Okay."

Mark looks at me dead on. "I can trust that you'll figure this out—that you won't screw it up. Can't I?"

"Who's to say? I've never killed anyone before."

He rolls his neck. "Don't worry so much, Tom. Really, it's not so hard."

I glance down at the spreadsheet on my desk. Now doesn't seem like a good time to bring up bad news about recruitment.

"The thing is," he says, and I swear he's a mind reader. "This has to work. We cannot afford for it not to. I've made too many promises."

"What kind of promises?"

"You let me worry about that. Your job is numbers. Speaking of that, women coming in, women with children. Women seeking to join a church community…that's a given. And it's a good thing because what do we both know about women in most households?"

"They control the budget."

"Correct. But they don't earn the money. Which means we need buy in. We need a reason for the men to stick around."

"I agree," I say, hoping he'll read between the lines. Killing three of them is counterintuitive to his goal.

"What do men want, Tom?"

I shrug. "Power."

"Precisely." He claps his hands. "But you know what else they want? They want to golf. They want time alone to watch sports. They want freedom to do what men do. They don't care about parties and social standing and they especially don't care about attending church on their day off."

I know this better than anyone.

"We have to give them a reason to care," he continues. "And how do we do that?"

Again, I shrug and tell him what he wants to hear. "We offer them a replacement wife?"

"Exactly," he says. "Men are pretty basic, Tom. They only really want a few things: women, money, toys, play things. They want freedom and they want sex."

I start to mention the former leads to the other. Cause and effect. But Mark is on a roll, so I keep my mouth shut.

"Freedom and sex, Tom. Both of which they feel are inhibited by religion. We have to offer them that." He's pacing my office. He stops to glare out the window, down at the city. "This is business. We have to show them that by committing to the church, they aren't giving anything up. They have to see they're not losing anything. They're gaining a second shot at life. A do over, if you will."

I don't understand what this has to do with me killing anyone. "Why does Melanie have to die?"

"She is a liar, Tom. We cannot be associated with liars. If it gets out that her reputation is…you know…less than stellar, it'll be the death of the project."

"So by erasing her past, by killing people…what? This makes her record clean?"

"Not exactly. But at least there won't be any proof." He shoves his hands in his pockets and turns to face me. "This is why I'm hoping you'll choose the right path here… because boy, that wife of yours? She's a looker. People look at you differently for landing a woman like that, don't they?"

"I haven't noticed."

"Respectable advertising, that's what we need."

"A good accountant too," I remind him. I glare at the numbers.

"Yes, that too," he agrees.

When I look up, Mark glances down at his watch. "I gotta run. That file there," he points. "It has everything you need on your marks."

"Of course."

In two short strides he's halfway out the door. Finally, I exhale.

Mark stops abruptly and pauses just inside the doorway. He

turns and leans against the doorframe. "David will pay you a visit later, should you have any questions on specifics."

I expected as much. Mark rarely does his own bidding.

"Oh—and Tom?"

I raise my brow.

"Please don't force my hand on this. I'd hate to have to handle this matter myself."

I salute him.

Mark smiles. "Been there and done that, remember?"

I nod. I remember, all right.

I'D ONLY STEPPED AWAY FROM THE HOSPITAL TO TAKE CARE OF A FEW things at the office. Work was piling up, and certain things had to be dealt with. Already, I'd been out quite a bit with June following her surgery. The infection on top of it all was unexpected. She hadn't recovered well from the beginning, and now that she was back in the hospital, she didn't want me to leave. June swore they were out to get her. She was never very specific about who "they" were, unfortunately, and I was too preoccupied to dig very deep. But the doctors all agreed, the infection combined with the medications was enough to cause paranoia.

"It's okay, Tom. Just go," Dr. Dunn advised me when he made his rounds. "I've given her something to make her sleep." I looked on as he checked my wife's chart. "I'd say you have a few hours at least."

"I don't know. If she wakes up—"

"She'll never even know you left."

"It's good to see a familiar face among so many," I told him. Grant Dunn was second in command at New Hope and our resident plastic surgeon. One rank above me, we weren't exactly close friends—I don't have many of those—but as experts in our respective fields, you could say, we regarded one another with a professional affinity. In other words, we stayed in our lanes. Which is exactly why when he told me to go, I trusted that I could.

"You don't think she'll wake up?" I asked again. I knew what he would say, which is at least half of the reason I asked the question. I was looking for reassurance. I hate hospitals, and I was looking for any reason possible to get out of there. I couldn't put off things at the office any longer. That, and Melanie was blowing up my phone. She'd started to get antsy with me spending so much time with June. The truth was, I wasn't good at juggling multiple women. It was never my intention. In reality, I got mixed up in something I was having a hard time getting out of. In reality, a one-night stand turned out to be something else and that something else was more than I'd bargained for. Really, I just wanted her to go away. But she had other plans.

"It's good stuff we've given her," Dr. Dunn assured me. "Trust me, she'll hardly know you're gone."

I stood and quietly stretched. "The infection is improving, Dr. Comey says."

"Comey?" Dunn cocked his head. "The infectious disease doctor?"

I nodded. "That's how he introduced himself."

Grant Dunn scratched at his jaw. "He's not supposed to be on this case."

I didn't ask what he meant. All I could think about was the work back at the office that had piled up. The work that was continuing to pile up. And the mistress I needed to get off my back before she did something stupid.

He walked to the door, opened it, and motioned for me to follow. "Yes, Comey is right," he told me as he led me out of the room. We walked down the hall. "Her numbers look good. Very good."

Dr. Dunn walked me all the way to the end of the corridor. I was grateful when we came to the entrance of normal life, to life outside those hospital walls where time stood still. "Don't worry," he assured me. "I've got things handled here."

That was all I needed to hear. I hadn't even bothered to tell her goodbye. I hadn't wanted to disturb her. Work was waiting, and I had other things on my mind.

The next time I saw my wife she was dead.

CHAPTER FIFTEEN

MELANIE

The next time I see Vanessa, her chest is bandaged, and her eyes are vacant. We're seated in a small room with a clear glass wall separating us. A man in a white coat stands to my right. He explains that it's his lab assistant I see sitting with Vanessa. I watch the two of them until Vanessa's eyes meet mine. I don't know what I was expecting—a smile maybe, the finger, I don't know. But definitely something more along the lines of our first encounter. What I got was indifference. So not even close.

"Is she all right?"

He assures me Vanessa is fine.

The first lesson in *The Good Book*—that is literally what it is called—is: Seek mastery in all areas. The man in the lab coat opens to it, and points. "That's our ethos," he says. "Mastery."

I watch as his assistant places wires on Vanessa's arms.

"That's the lesson we are focusing on today."

"What's the difference between *The Good Book* and the agreement?"

He cocks his head. "You don't know?"

I could lie. But I'm hungry, and it feels like too much effort. "I want to make sure."

"The agreement is a part of *The Good Book*. It's an admission saying you adhere to it."

"Right."

"Any other questions before we get started?"

"Can she hear you in there?"

"Same as you can." He reaches out to shake my hand. "I'm Dr. Mueller."

I don't introduce myself. I take it he knows who I am. Otherwise I wouldn't be here. Instead, I stare at the switchboard in front of me. I count thirty buttons.

"Shock therapy," he tells me.

"Seriously?" I could be in a movie. I could be in a book. I could be anywhere. All my life, I wanted it to be interesting, and now it is.

"That there," he motions, "is a shock generator. Each switch," he points to them one by one, "renders anywhere from 10 to 50 milliamps."

I lean forward and touch one of the switches lightly. "Does it hurt?"

"On the low end, not so much. On the high end…well, it's no picnic."

I glance at Vanessa. She doesn't look at me.

"We're going to work on mastering our emotions this morning."

I decide right now might not be the best time to tell him I don't have emotions.

"I understand Mrs. Bolton stole from you."

I shrug.

"Well," he says. "Did she or did she not?" Dr. Mueller gives me the once-over, as though he's accessing my intelligence. "It's a very simple question, Mrs. Anderson. We only make things complicated with our answers."

"She did."

"And you lied."

I press my lips together. Guilty people hate it when accusations are thrown around. We're wrong often enough to know when we aren't, and often enough to know how little it matters. You screw up enough and everyone just assumes you've screwed up again because that's who you are.

Of course, his accusation is correct. What bothers me is it wasn't that I lied to save my roommate. That's what he's thinking. I just never cared for smoothies. I've never understood why anyone wants to drink their calories? Of course, this was before I understood what true hunger felt like. Now, I know better. Now, I know what leads to such nonsense. Starvation. It's a gnawing, awful feeling. It's like something invisible trying to tear its way out of you. And until you feed that something, the clawing never stops.

Whatever. They can starve me all they want. But I will not let them break me. I will play their games for as long as it takes. I will play them until I learn how to win. There is simply no alternative. This is who I am.

The man in the white coat repeats his statement. "You lied, Mrs. Anderson. The question is...why?"

"I take it that's not considered mastery?"

He huffs. "You might think you're being cute, but that won't help you now, not in here. And especially not with me."

"I don't know what you want me to say."

"I want you to say you understand why you're here, and why we're doing this."

I glance down at the book and scan the code of honor written into the agreement.

1. Seek mastery in all areas.
2. Never ignore a friend in need, in danger, or in trouble.
3. Submit to a cause greater than oneself.
4. Remain obedient to furthering the mission.

5. Never abandon a group to which you owe your success.
6. Serve your leaders with unwavering devotion.
7. Your honor is more important than your life.
8. Never deny your spouse what is rightfully theirs. Strength is found in submission.
9. Family is the cornerstone of everything. Care for them faithfully.
10. The world is governed by appearances. Act accordingly.
11. Cleanse your home. Purify your heart.
12. Your body is your temple. Treat it as such.
13. Keep counsel. Guard your reputation with your life.
14. Never fear harming another with just cause.
15. Seek like-minded individuals to walk the path of greatness.
16. Strive for excellence at all costs.

"It's all written," I tell him. "That's why I'm here." I don't say it's because I was only looking for a meal ticket and failed to read the fine print. Sometimes less is more.

"Ready?"

When I nod, he rattles off instructions. "Okay," he says. "We're going to ask Mrs. Bolton a series of questions in regard to the agreement. How this works is…if she answers correctly nothing happens, and we move on to the next question. However, if she answers incorrectly, I will signal to you, and you will press the appropriate switch that will deliver a shock. Once I signal that the shock is complete, you will then offer her the correct answer and move on to the next question."

I study his face. He thinks I am going to argue, so I give him what he wants. "This is crazy. I'm not shocking her."

"Would you prefer to switch places, Mrs. Anderson?"

I give his question some thought briefly. Very briefly, to be honest. I haven't studied the agreement enough. I haven't really read the book. So to offer to switch places, even if I were an altruistic person, which I am not, would be a dumb move on my part.

On the flip side, I saw Vanessa reading, so she should be okay to answer a few questions.

Also, she really should not have taken my smoothie, whether I wanted it or not.

She has to learn. You don't get in a boat with holes.

~

TEARS STREAM DOWN VANESSA'S FACE. I'VE ADMINISTERED THREE shocks. It's one of the most interesting things I've ever seen, watching electricity course through a person like that. I've asked her seven questions. There are three to go. She has missed nearly half. I think she is doing this on purpose. Why, I don't know.

"In our code of honor, Mrs. Anderson," Dr. Mueller says. "What is law number four?"

I repeat the question into the mic for Vanessa. Her head hangs. She mumbles something. It's inaudible. But that doesn't make it wrong.

I finger the switch. I'm ready to get this over with. I feel like the walls are closing in on me. I feel like I could be next. "Give her a moment longer," Dr. Mueller insists.

After several moments, he instructs me to repeat the question.

"Law number four," I say. "What is it?"

Vanessa meets my eye. She seems to find her voice again. "I said. I. Don't. Know."

I wait for Dr. Mueller. When he gives the nod, I flip the switch. Vanessa shakes violently.

After several seconds that feel like forever, Dr. Mueller tells me to kill the switch. When I look up again, Vanessa is slumped over.

"Law number four," I say, reading straight from the handbook as Dr. Mueller has instructed me to do. "Remain obedient to furthering the mission."

The room is silent and still after that. There's a calmness about it I've never felt before.

Minutes pass. It's no time at all. I feel more alive than I've ever felt.

"Law number seven," I repeat after Dr. Mueller. "Please explain it."

I wait. And wait. Vanessa appears to have lost consciousness. "She can't answer," I tell him. "I think she's had enough."

"Please continue," Dr. Mueller insists.

"She's just had surgery."

"The process requires you to continue."

"Look at her," I say.

His eyes watch me closely. They never leave me. "It is absolutely essential that you continue."

I administer the shock. I hate his face. I hate his brown eyes with the hazel specks. I want to make him go away.

There are screams. I'm floating above my body. Vanessa has wet herself. That I can see.

"The answer," Dr. Mueller says. "Read her the correct answer, please." His voice is monotone. Succinct and clear.

I sigh and read the words that are blurred on the page. Maybe I am crying, I don't know. I hear myself speak but is it even me? "Always remain obedient to furthering the mission."

"Final question," Dr. Mueller announces, pulling the mic in his direction. He nods to me.

I take a deep breath in and hold it. When I can manage, I exhale slowly. Dr. Mueller motions me forward. I lean in and speak into the mic. "State law fourteen please."

I see Vanessa's lips move, but nothing comes out. I will the words into her mind. I plead silently with her to say them. I feel numb. I feel on the edge of something I can't stop.

"Go ahead with the shock please," Dr. Mueller instructs.

"She's too tired," I tell him, pointing. "Look, she's mumbling."

"Please continue with the treatment."

I shake my head. "She has a baby."

"You are required to continue."

"I don't want to." It's not fun anymore.

"You have no other choice but to continue."

"You do it," I say.

Crossing my arms, I wait him out.

When he speaks, his voice is stern. "We are not leaving this room until you complete the task."

I look up at Vanessa. She's passed out. I'm hungry and I'm tired. I want out of here. "Fine," I seethe. I flick the switch. Vanessa comes to life. I've never seen that much agony on a person's face.

"Enough," Dr. Mueller says, finally. "Now, law fourteen. Give her the answer."

I can't look at Vanessa. Maybe I've killed her. I don't want to know. I bring the mic to my mouth, and I speak slowly, so she hears it. I speak so slowly that neither of us will ever forget it again. I make sure it is drilled into my very core. "Never fear harming another with just cause."

CHAPTER SIXTEEN

TOM

To make a fair decision, I made a list of the things I like about my new wife. Criteria having to do with her appearance filled numbers one through fourteen. The fact that she was willing to marry me was number fifteen, and beyond that I was stumped. It's no secret I hadn't really known Melanie outside of between the sheets when I proposed. She was pregnant with my child, which put her in a vulnerable position. With June dead, I was without a wife. Marriage appeared to be a solution that would fit both our needs.

What I had failed to consider was the fact that I was not in love with her. I covered for this with the notion that arranged marriages have a greater success rate than do those who come by way of natural selection. This is due to many factors, including but not limited to cultural beliefs and stigma around divorce, as well as the financial status of the females in the partnership.

But I was not making the list to determine whether or not to divorce Melanie. Now that A) the pregnancy and resulting child were no longer factors in staying together and B) she had proven herself to be untrustworthy, I was determining whether or not to kill her.

To get a few things straight: I am not a murderer. While I have contemplated the act on many occasions, I have yet to act on the compulsion. And although I assume the skill involved would not be too difficult to acquire, there is one major problem: I would not be a good candidate for prison. I do not read social cues well enough to survive in that type of environment.

So, as one can imagine, given the choice between killing one person (my wife), or killing three (her previous lovers), the situation seems like a no-brainer. Killing one person is certainly less labor intensive than killing three. On the flip side, it's easier to kill a person you haven't had sex with. Generally speaking. Particularly, if you're a fan of the sex, which I am, very much. My wife is incredibly cunning, and this creativity spills over, if you know what I mean.

In addition, the risk involved with killing Melanie and getting caught is far greater than killing men I have lesser or no ties to. Everyone knows when a woman is murdered, it's always the husband. This doesn't even take in to consideration that killing Melanie would mean having to replace her. The cost of acquiring a new wife would be substantial. Not only would I need to find a suitable candidate, which can be quite labor intensive, I'd have to find one with equal or greater looks who would be willing to accept my proposal.

This makes finding a solution to the dilemma I face rather difficult. It's important I ensure all factors are examined and analyzed before making a determination.

Which means I need more time. Time is not something Mark is particularly lenient about. He will kill Melanie—or rather, he will have her killed, just to prove a point. Problem solved. On one hand, that would make my decision easier. But who do you think the cops will come looking for when I'm presented with a second dead wife on my hands? It won't be Mark.

As the saying goes, when you meet a swordsman, draw your sword. Do not recite poetry to one who is not a poet. In short, in order to buy time, I have to go around Mark, directly to the only source capable of stalling him. His wife.

~

I END UP WHERE MOST PEOPLE GO TO RESEARCH SOMETHING WHEN the internet isn't safe. The library. I need to know the most efficient method to murder a person without getting caught, preferably without having to handle the clean up. As I mentioned, I do not do well where blood is concerned. I like things neat and tidy, and blood is the opposite of that.

While there is no shortage of ways to end a life, humans are quite fragile when it comes right down to it. I learn that hit and runs, strangulation, drive-by shootings, or poisoning a person fit well with what I am looking to do. The problem with hitting someone with your car and drive-by shooting them are that you need weapons, namely a car and a gun. I don't even own a sword. I'm living on borrowed time. Plus, these items will always link you to the crime, particularly so if there are witnesses involved. Those only lead to further complications and more people to kill. As I've come to find, silence has a price, and often that price is murder.

The third option, to poison a person, would mean either acquiring or manufacturing the substance to handle the job. And while I know enough about chemistry that this shouldn't be too big of an obstacle, I'd have to get close to them. I'm not sure I want to look my wife's past in the eye. Self-awareness just so happens to be a strong suit of mine. And I know that to do so would only provide inspiration for the final method: strangulation. After all, nothing is safer than dead.

~

BETH HOSTS BOOK CLUB ON MONDAY EVENINGS IN THE GARDEN AT

church, which makes it easy to schedule a run-in of sorts. Basically, this is what less intelligent people like to call coincidences.

Predictability can almost always work in one's favor. First, you have to set things up by creating patterns. Routine makes others comfortable. The more familiar with you they become, the easier time you'll have lulling them to sleep. Then, once you have them where you want them, you can allow preconceived notions they hold about you to act as a smoke screen, a pleasant front from behind which you can carry out your deceptions. Patterns are extremely powerful, and you can easily terrify people by disrupting them.

"Tom," she says, her brows raised, eyes wide, proof of my success. "I wasn't expecting to see you here."

"I wanted to discuss something with you."

"Oh," she says, glancing at me sideways. "Sorry, now isn't the best time." She pulls out her phone, if only to prove a point. "I'm meeting Mark for a late dinner."

"That's perfect." She walks, I walk. "Because I have a meeting upstairs in five minutes." And because I understand Beth lacks intelligence, I provide clarification. "I don't have long."

She picks up the pace and I match her stride. "I noticed the numbers are down for incoming couples in the 20-34 age groups."

"Yes," she says without looking at me. "We're working on that."

"Well, I think I know why."

We've reached the parking lot. She is searching for her car. I don't have much time. Less than I thought. "Why?"

"People are getting married older."

"Ok." She's digging for her key.

"That means unless their parents are members, people in that age range aren't seeking out the opportunities a church community can give them."

"That's too bad." She's not even listening.

"You're right. It is bad. Very. That demographic doesn't join because they don't think they'll find a life partner here. And the truth is, it's a catch-22. Unless we bring numbers up, they won't."

Finally, she is successful with the key. "You have a point."

"So that's what I was wondering…how are you recruiting in that age bracket?"

She turns to me then. I may not be good at reading social cues, but I have known Beth long enough to understand that she's curious as to why I want to know. "Well…" she starts. "Same as the others. Social media. Ads in strategic places. Word of mouth…"

"What you need are influencers."

Her face twists. Women like Beth do not appreciate it when you try to do their job for them. She's not good at hiding it, either. It's clear in her tone. "And where do you suggest I find those?"

"You could start with my wife."

I know that my idea will mean releasing Melanie sooner rather than later. And in order for me to make a determination about how to move forward with Mark's demands, frankly, I need this to happen.

Her head cocks to the side. "Melanie."

"Yeah." I shrug like it's no big deal, when it's a very big deal. If Mark makes his move before I make a final decision as to which way to go, I'll be out a wife and a job as well, and under investigation for murder. My house is in the church's name. I really like that house. Without time to put a proper plan in place, I'll end up with nothing. No one wants to live like that.

She's still looking at me quizzically. "You've seen her at parties," I add, and I leave it at that. Few women like to see another woman admired.

Beth folds her arms. "We've considered that," she lies. "But we're working on the reprogramming first."

"With the reprogramming—there's something you aren't taking into consideration."

She rolls her eyes. "And what would that be?"

"The reprograming makes her like you."

Her mouth falls open. Prior experience with her type tells me she's offended. I have to make a quick recovery. But not too quick. "Is that so bad?"

"No. Not at all," I promise like a confession. "Unless you're wanting millennials to join the church." I take a deep breath and hold it. This is going to hurt. Logic often does. "When is the last time you wanted to be like your parents?"

Her eyes narrow. "Um, never."

"According to my research, the last thing millennials want is to be like the generation that came before. Which means we have to lure them in with something different. Melanie is different. Before we change her, we should use her."

I watch as she does a double-take. People often first balk at solutions before they accept them. "Well, it certainly seems to have worked on you, hasn't it?"

"Just talk to Mark about it, would you? See what he thinks."

I know Beth will never let on that a good idea wasn't hers.

"I will," she promises. I open the car door for her. Once she's in, she pauses and looks up at me. "In the meantime, you have any other grand ideas?"

"Nope," I force a smile. "Now that we know how to increase the numbers, I'm fresh out."

CHAPTER SEVENTEEN

MELANIE

Mrs. Elizabeth assures me I didn't kill Vanessa. And yet, I haven't seen her, so there's really no proof. I haven't killed anyone before, but I've not ruled it out either. Interestingly enough, this religion, if that's what you want to call it, allows for it in their doctrine. *Never fear harming another with just cause.*

They won't let us room together. I asked. Which is a good thing probably. I'm afraid I would rectify the situation. Given the chance, I might murder Vanessa with my own bare hands for what she made me do. In fact, I've been busy contemplating the ways I might go about it. In here there's not much else to do but think.

If only she wouldn't have been so self-sacrificing.

There's pleasure in being taken beyond our limits. That's what Mrs. Elizabeth says. Maybe Vanessa already knows this. Whatever the case, without a doubt, I know she knew the answers to those questions.

She wanted to make me suffer.

She wanted to test my limits.

Sure, I could waste my abundance of time asking myself why. But I don't care enough for that. People do what they do.

Everyone else spends so much time on the cause. They want a motive. They want answers. Pick any of the twelve billion news outlets and tune in. All they talk about is why. Name the latest tragedy and watch how much time they spend dissecting it. It's insane. But it's simple: sometimes people do bad things because it makes them feel good. Sometimes they do them to make themselves feel better. Sometimes they are just plain evil. It's not rocket science. Too many people believe that just because they're good, everyone else is.

But that's not the way the world works. There's too much history to prove otherwise.

People forget how good humans are at rationalizing their behavior.

I may be young by some standards, but I've seen enough to know. The real horrors of this world are other people.

To prove a point, after the shock therapy, I was given an assignment to write a letter to someone to show the pain I have caused. I could have chosen Tom. But he's the one who put me in this place, and I wasn't feeling particularly charitable where he is concerned. So, I chose my parents instead. I will be in need of a place to go once they let me out of here.

Dear Mother and Dad: Since you forced me from the nest, I have been remiss in writing, and I am sorry for my thoughtlessness in not having written sooner. I will bring you up to date now, but before you read on, please sit down. You are not to read any further unless you are sitting down, okay?

Well, then, I am getting along pretty well now. The skull fracture and the horrible burns I sustained when I jumped out of the window of my hotel when it caught on fire shortly after my arrival are pretty well healed. I only spent two weeks in the hospital, my vision has almost returned to normal, and thankfully, I'm only getting those terrible headaches once a day.

Fortunately, the fire in the hotel and my jump was witnessed by a man on the street near the hotel, and he was the one who called 9-1-1. He visited me in the hospital, and since I had nowhere to live because of the burned-out hotel, he was kind enough to invite me to share his home with him. In actuality, it's a shrine to his dead wife, but it's kind of endearing. He is a very fine man, and we have fallen deeply in love and are now married. I realize you might have appreciated an invite to your only daughter's wedding, but it had to take place before the pregnancy began to show. Yes, Mother and Dad, a real shotgun wedding in the family. I could hardly believe it myself. At any rate, I know how much you are looking forward to being grandparents, and I know you will welcome the baby and give it the same love and devotion and tender care you gave me when I was a child.

The reason for the delay in contacting you is your biggest client, the one who fired you, apparently had a minor skin infection, which I carelessly caught from him. In addition, unbeknownst to me, my new husband is involved in a massive cult, and they have placed me in a mental asylum. They call it a 'rejuvenation center' so it sounds better, and I am assured it's all on the up and up. Here I have undergone surgery to my nether regions to 'make me whole again.' I have also learned the sixteen levels of mastery and had a fancy introduction into shock therapy. It's my understanding there are future surgeries coming, and I guess the other stuff kind of makes up for not having to pay out of pocket for bettering yourself. No matter that my husband's first wife died after a botched surgery. I figure it's kind of like all that bad stuff you had to say about those people in favor of the Affordable Care Act. Who cares if they kill you off in the end or manage your care to death with denials, so long as it's free, right?

Now that I have brought you up to date, I want to tell you that there was no hotel fire, I did not have any burns or skull fracture, I am not pregnant, I am not infected. However, I will soon be homeless once again, and I want you to see this in its proper perspective. Now, can I come home? Your loving daughter, Melanie

~

I DON'T KNOW HOW MANY DAYS I'VE BEEN HERE. THEY ALL RUN together like a string of bad dreams. I'm fed a healthy dose of pills, which are supposed to help me sleep but really don't. The sounds in here when the lights go out aren't the falling asleep kind. People go mad in the dark. We all have our terrors, Vanessa said, and it turns out she was right. The woman two doors down is convinced her bed is covered in spiders. It may be, for all I know.

On the other side, a woman weeps for her children. Robert and Catherine. I've learned their names. Everyone on this wing has.

And somewhere at the end is "Screaming Sheila." You don't want to know what they do when she won't stop. I beg them to put her in solitary so I can sleep. So we can all sleep.

Mrs. Elizabeth says there's no lesson in that.

Speaking of lessons, I didn't meet my weigh-in yesterday. I haven't a clue as to why. I'm still on a liquid diet, and sometimes I can't stomach even that. I haven't earned cafeteria privileges yet on account of being on the diet plan.

"I'm not overweight," I said to my advisor.

She only smiled and said, "You're not under, either."

Mrs. Elizabeth said I have to cut weight this week. "If I lose a few pounds, do I get to go home?"

She shook her head. "You have to recover."

"I feel very recovered."

"You can't be sexually active yet." I could see that she doesn't like having to spell things out, which is exactly why I make her do it.

"That's fine."

Mrs. Elizabeth looked at me crossly. "What good are you, if you can't perform your wifely duties? Your husband doesn't deserve a broken woman. That's why you're here."

Bingo. I got my answer. Not only did Tom not want to put up with me after I lost our fake child, after he found out I wasn't as flawless as he'd thought, but he was callous enough to send me here. "How can I get unbroken?"

She glared at me with her squinty eyes. "This is a large organization, Mrs. Anderson. People get lost in bureaucracies like this. Trust me, you don't want that to be the case where you're concerned... "

"I meant... what do I have to do to go home?"

"You can start by cutting weight." In order to make this happen, I am told an aide will retrieve me from my room.

"Let's get you thinned out," the woman says when she finally comes. I'm relieved to get out of there. I'm relieved to finally see another face, and I don't even like people.

I ask the aide if I am getting lipo.

The woman doesn't answer. She leads me to the shower instead.

The bathrooms here are quite nice, actually. If sparsely decorated and plain white happens to be your thing, then everything is nice.

Usually, I am allowed one private shower once a day. I had mine this morning. Normally, the aide stands outside like the bathroom attendants at my favorite bars. Only different. But sometimes I pretend.

"Undress, please," the aide orders. She is an older frail looking woman, with thinning gray hair and deep-set green eyes. I imagine she might have been pretty once.

"I've already showered today." I choose my words carefully. The aides in this place don't like to be corrected.

"Undress, please."

"What for?"

"For your shower."

"I already had a shower."

She points to the door. "This is a bath."

"I'll just undress in there."

"This isn't the spa," she tells me, and then I watch as she pulls a small device from the belt around her waist. "Have you ever been tased, Mrs. Anderson?"

I shake my head.

"Well, I assure you, it's far less pleasant than taking off your clothes. Something I've heard your quite good at."

So, I guess not that frail at all. I hate to be wrong.

"Welcome to your first ice bath."

"I'm not allowed baths on account of the surgery."

She smiles widely. "Your physician has okayed it."

I peel my hospital gown off and let it fall to the floor.

"I see they haven't helped you out up top." She laughs. "Don't you worry, love. I'm sure that will be next."

We stand there for a long time, waiting. For what, I haven't a clue, but eventually the door opens. It's a tiled room with nothing but a round porcelain tub in the middle. "Well, go on," she says.

I walk slowly into the room. The chill hits my bare skin immediately. There are few things I dislike worse than being cold.

"In you go," the woman says, ushering me into the full tub. The water is frigid. "It's temperature controlled," she tells me. "Good for inflammation. Good for healing."

I bring my knees into my chest and huddle into a ball.

They will not break me. They will not break me. They will not break me.

Buckets of ice are lined against the wall. One by one, she pours them over my head. I could put up a fight, protest even a little. But

I've heard the cracking that takes place down the hall where "Screaming Shelia" resides. I've seen her in casts. In circle time, I've studied the patterns of her bruises. Suddenly, an ice bath doesn't seem so bad. There are seven buckets total. I count each one as it's poured over my head. The cubes pelt my body. I force my eyes to focus on the red welts they leave up and down my arms and in places I can feel but can't see.

"Your body is your temple," the woman whispers. She shakes her finger at me. "You young ones, you never learn."

~

THE NEXT TIME THERE'S A WEIGH-IN, I COME IN UNDER. I'M rewarded with a day at the rejuvenation center spa. I get my hair done, a massage, facial, mani-pedi, body wrap...I pretty much get it all.

The following morning after circle time, my advisor calls me in her office. I'm not surprised. I assume they've read the letter to my parents. I was looking for trouble, after all. Anything to ease the boredom. I figured they'd read it. This place is enough like prison, so it would make sense they'd read all outgoing mail. That was at least half the point. I just wish they'd found it sooner. I assume there's a lesson in this. The ability to delay satisfaction is important in all manners of seduction. Make no mistake, this is why I'm here. And this is how I'll get out.

"Good news," she tells me. My worries went unfounded. "You've performed very well lately."

I nod.

"With the shock therapy. With your weight loss." Her smile widens. "Your latest scores are excellent."

She's referring to our daily tests on the agreement and the code of honor. "In fact, yesterday you earned a perfect score..."

"That was only yesterday?"

She cocks her head. "Are you having trouble keeping track of your days?"

"No, I've just been busy…reading and studying…you know how time can get away from you."

She seems as pleased with my response as I knew she would be. "Guess what else?"

I eye her expectantly. At this point it could be anything.

"You earned yourself a ticket home early."

All of a sudden I feel like one of those pageant queens whose name has just been called and now I'm forced to act surprised when really I saw it coming all along. I knew my parents would come through. My eyes widen. "I'm going home?"

"That's right. Now go pack your things."

I practically hurl myself out of the chair.

"See you soon, Melanie."

I don't ask what she means. I probably should have. But revenge comes to us all, eventually. I slap a smile on my face. "Not if I see you first."

It isn't Tom who comes to pick me up. It's Beth. Mrs. Elizabeth sees me out. When she opens the door to Beth's brand new SUV, the first thing I noticed is she has seat covers.

"Hello." I scoot into the passenger seat. "Long time no see."

"Good to see you, Melanie," she tells me. She sounds like a robot.

"I'm all good down there now. You wouldn't believe it."

She sort of does this thing where she half deadpans, half flinches. "That's great."

"Really, my vagina looks brand new. They work wonders in that place."

Beth looks over and offers a small smile, but I can see she doesn't think it's funny.

Mrs. Elizabeth touches my hand before closing the door. "Serve your leaders with unwavering devotion," she says, which I now know is law number six in the code of honor.

"Of course," I nod.

She puts her hands in the prayer position and bows her head. "See you soon."

She should really hope not.

"I would like to go to the airport, please."

Beth puts the car in gear. We drive without speaking. I'm surprised to see we're actually in Austin. Having been heavily medicated when I was brought in, I had no idea. None of the other women in there did either.

As it turns out, the rejuvenation center is smack dab in the middle of the city.

"I am taking you home," Beth tells me. "Your husband is anxious to see you."

"Is he tied up?" I ask as I stare out the window. It's good to see sunlight and clouds, normal things. Things like traffic and people in clothes that aren't hospital gowns.

Beth looks over at me. "No. But I wanted a chance to speak with you. How are you feeling?"

"Fine."

"I hear you did well in there," she says. When I glance to my left, I notice her expression has turned sympathetic. "I know you feel like everything is up in the air."

"Not up in the air," I say. "A mistake."

She presses her lips together. "It's normal to think that. With the miscarriage, I'm sure your hormones are all over the place. Don't worry. These things take time. I know Tom isn't great at communicating his feelings. But I wanted you to know, he's still very much committed to making this work."

"And if I'm not?"

"There are things we can do."

"Things?"

"It's in the agreement."

I'm just testing her. I know what's written in that agreement. None of it is in my favor.

"The truth is, Melanie, you're one of us now. You've proven yourself." She glances over and eyes me from head to toe. "And you look amazing. Really."

"Proven myself how?"

"With what you've endured, you've proven you can be a leader. Tom needs you. We need you."

"Who is *we*?"

She white-knuckles the steering wheel and grins all the while. "The church, of course."

CHAPTER EIGHTEEN

TOM

I'm on my way home from my run, just two streets over from the house when a car pulls up beside me. I know it immediately. It's Mark's. "Get in," he says when the window is half down. "I'll give you a lift home."

"This makes no sense." I motion toward my running shoes. "The point of this," I say, "is to exercise."

"It's about Melanie," he tells me, and that's all it takes. I know I'm getting in that car.

The next thing I know, we're sitting in my kitchen. "Have you been working out?" he asks, nodding at my upper body.

"A little." It's a lie. I've been working out every spare moment I have. I want to win Melanie's affection. I want her to forgive me for sending her away. I want to show her I have rejuvenated myself, too.

"Melanie will be pleased. In fact, the reason I'm here is to tell you that she is on her way home."

I don't know what I'd expected, but it wasn't this. I need to shower. I need appropriate attire. Mark has to go.

"I hope you'll excuse me," I say to him.

He takes the hint. "I'll get out of your hair in just a moment. First, there's something I want to discuss."

I check my watch and calculate the time it takes to drive from downtown at this time of day.

"The women are not responding to plastic surgery well after June's death. Plus, with Grant not around…they need someone they can trust."

I don't see what this has to do with me; I am not a physician.

"What makes older women feel inferior more than anything?"

I have forty-five minutes. Max. Mark doesn't notice I haven't responded and he doesn't wait either. Thankfully. "The answer is, a younger, more attractive woman thrown in the mix."

I still don't offer anything up. I want him to keep talking, which he does. "I have a plan for Melanie."

"A plan?"

"A recruitment plan."

"Hmmm."

"We need more young women in her demographic."

"Was this your idea?" I have to know.

"Of course." He lies, which can only mean Beth didn't tell him it was mine.

"I see." It's nice to have reassurance the game you're playing is going the way you want it to.

"Well," he says, throwing up his hands. "What do you think?"

"If it keeps us in the black, what do I care?"

"Ah, Tom." He stands, finally. "You're always such a good sport."

I walk Mark to the foyer, where much to my annoyance he pauses. "Now, listen," he says, his expression turning serious. "I need you to fix this with her."

"And if I can't? I don't know what they did in there. I don't know how far they took it…with the reprogramming."

I'm fishing for answers, but he doesn't take the bait. "Whatever you did the first time…do it again."

"It was illicit then. That made it more appealing."

He shrugs. "So, make it that way again."

I have no idea what he means.

"Oh and the other reason I came—I need an update. How's the plan to take care of your wife's past coming?"

I take a step toward the door. "I'm working on it."

He smiles and holds my gaze. "Work harder."

~

MARK TELLS ME TO MAKE IT ILLICIT, AND SO I DO. FIRST, I HOP ON the internet and buy Melanie the car I knew from her browser history she had been eyeing. A Maserati. With her life more or less still on the line, I went with the lease option. I'm all for practicality.

Then, as the church accountant, I set up an expense account in her name, which I plan to call a recruitment fund. Surely, Mark will understand. I've seen his wife's, so I have a healthy understanding what she spends on upkeep. Melanie will need money for a new wardrobe, a personal trainer, and a chef, all things I know Melanie has had her eye on. I assume these are the kinds of things all women have their eye on.

Next, I book us round-trip tickets. I email Mark and tell him he's right. When you mirror your enemies, doing exactly as they do, they cannot figure out your strategy. This mocks and humiliates them, which causes them to overreact. By essentially holding a mirror up to their psyches, you seduce them with the illusion that you share their values; by mimicking their actions, you teach them a lesson.

I write that I plan to "make it illicit" with a second honeymoon. I explain that Melanie and I will be gone a week. Everything is in order on my end. He can take that to mean whatever he wants.

This leaves just enough time for a quick two-minute shower.

Then I sit back and wait for my bride to come through the door.

~

When Melanie comes barreling through the door, I'm not at all surprised that she immediately begins packing her bags. She doesn't know what I know. "What are you doing?"

"I never signed up for this." I look on as she grabs as much as she can muster from the closet and tosses it all onto the bed. "This is crazy."

"You look amazing," I tell her, and she does. She looks more like June than I thought possible. A younger, slimmer, more beautiful version, yes. But a transformation has taken place, and it's visible.

"I lost our child, and you sent me to…you sent me away!"

"In many cultures," I say, "women go away when they are menstruating. Historically, it has proven they have been highly successful in their relationships."

"I wasn't on my period," she tells me as she throws her stuff into a bag. "I lost our baby, you fucking asshole."

I back away and give her some space. "I read anger can be good for grief. It shows you've moved into the second stage."

"You're insane."

To prove her wrong, I explain further. "Understanding anger as a natural but volatile stage in the grieving process can lead to better methods of coping, healing, and support after loss or death."

"I don't even have words…"

The doorbell rings. Her eyes meet mine.

"That's probably your car."

"My car?"

"The Maserati. The one you've been looking at online."

Her head tilts slightly. "You bought me a car?"

Leasing something isn't exactly the same thing as buying it, so I say, "You needed something to drive, so we don't have to downsize and move downtown."

Melanie's eyes grow wide. It takes a split second before she makes a beeline for the door. I am pleased to see she is healing well.

"Mom?" Her voice is shrill. "What are you doing here?"

This is unexpected. I have yet to meet my in-laws. Melanie has assured me we won't like each other and judging by the look on her mother's face when I go to the door, it seems she was right.

We exchange pleasantries. "I had to see for myself," her mother says. "My daughter. Married." Her eyes light up. I see a bit of my wife in them. "I can hardly believe it."

"And to an accountant," Melanie adds, which is ridiculous. I don't know a more respectable profession.

I invite her in. Melanie looks at me funny. Her mother gives me a similar look as she takes a seat on the new couch. I can tell it isn't her taste, either.

The doorbell rings again. I look to my wife. "Your father? Third cousin? Best friend from high school?"

Melanie rolls her eyes.

I open the door. It's the car delivery people.

A clipboard is passed my way. I sign to show I am taking possession. I haven't even finished half my last name before Melanie is grabbing me. She plants a kiss on my mouth. And they say it's just men who have a thing for cars.

"What a lovely gift," her mother says.

"Tom is the best." Melanie is beaming. How easily she has forgotten she was trying to walk out on me.

"I hate to cut this short," I say, glancing at my watch. "But our ride will be here in half an hour."

Melanie's brow furrows. "Our ride?"

"Yes, to take us to the airport."

"Airport?" she and her mother say in unison.

"A honeymoon. I wanted to surprise you," I tell her, feigning disappointment.

Melanie's mother crosses her arms. "You had me really worried."

"About that—" she says. It's clear she's hiding something.

Her mother turns to me and places her hand on my forearm. "Melanie wrote me this crazy letter. She gave this address and said she was being held against her will. Scared the daylights out of me. So here I am."

I glare at my wife.

"I should have known better. My daughter has always had a very vivid imagination."

Melanie's eyes are locked on mine.

"She said some nonsense about being in a cult, and I rushed all the way here...only to find she's done quite well for herself."

Melanie laughs playfully and then she throws her hands up. "Surprise!"

I laugh too.

Melanie's mother looks from her daughter toward me and then back. She's not sure what to think.

"Looks like I'd better get packed," Melanie says.

"Good thing you got a head start."

Her mother's expression is expectant. "Okay, then. But you'll have me for dinner when you return."

"Maybe—" Melanie starts.

"Of course," I say. "We'd love to."

Her mother looks practically giddy. She's glowing. "Your father is going to be so happy."

I wave as she backs out of the drive.

She lets down her window and waves back. "You two be good."

~

"YOU BE GOOD," MY FATHER SAID.

I was none of it. I shook my head, stomped my feet, and clung to his leg. I was only five, so he still tolerated small acts of defiance. "Why do you have to leave again?"

"It's my job, son. A soldier can't bail on his duties."

I hadn't thought to ask him why he couldn't say the same for his duties as a father. It was what it was. "Plus," he added, patting my head. "It puts food on the table."

That part was a lie. I don't think I told him that either. At least not then.

When my father was deployed, which was most of the time, he left me in the care of his sister, my Aunt Jeanie. Jeanie was a dreadful woman. She was addicted to men and booze, and was emphatically not addicted to raising a child that wasn't hers.

I'm not your mother, she used to say. As though I could forget.

My mother died a few years after I was born.

At least that was the story I was told. Another lie in a long string of them.

Later, I would learn some truths are better left unknown.

Take, for example, the fact that cockroaches littered our house. Ants crawled up the wall. I was young and inexperienced. I thought everyone had them. I assumed everyone lived like that. Aunt Jeanie used to say the roaches would outlive us. They could outlast a nuclear explosion. I read it in a book, so it made sense. Until the first and only time I brought a classmate home, and I learned other people did not, in fact, live in filth. Jeanie had a very unique housekeeping schedule, which usually picked up right before my father was due home on leave. This was back before I learned how.

"I'll send you something special when I send the money for the month," my father said each time he walked out the door. Maybe it absolved his guilt, maybe he really meant it. I'll never know.

My eyes met Jeanie's. By that point, we both knew any money my father would send would be blown on liquor, unemployed men, and other stuff I was still too young to know about. Real food, sustenance, was an after thought. "Sorry, it's pasta again," she would say. "And, yes, without meat. Have you seen the price of ground beef these days?" she'd ask, taking a long pull on her cigarette. That's what I remember most. To this day, pasta still tastes like Marlboro Reds to me. You'd think I'd hate it. They say you never really get away from that which you know.

When I was older, I brought her the grocery store flyer. I pointed out the price of ground beef. Then the price of her beloved Jack Daniel's. I surmised that if we cut her consumption in half, we could afford meat a third of the time she cooked. She thanked me with a broken nose.

It wasn't always bad. We did have meat and other food that consisted of more than noodles right before my father was due home. Jeanie made sure of that. I was so happy during those times, I'd mark the days on my calendar. Often, I'd eat so much I'd throw up. The rest of the time, it was NoodleO's. That is unless one of Jeanie's men was joining us, and then she'd go the extra mile and boil the pasta herself.

"Sorry, kid," she liked to remind me. "Money's tight again this month." She'd look at the man sitting at our table. "They send our men over there to fight and pay them diddly squat."

I got tired of Aunt Jeanie saying that, so I wrote a letter to the president once. When a response came, I was awarded with two black eyes. I had to miss school. After that, I stopped writing letters.

It was probably for the best. One day when I was home sick I found all the letters I'd written my father in a stack in my aunt's nightstand. It hit me why she hadn't sent them. There was too much truth inked on those pages. All of a sudden, it made sense why my father never answered my questions or wrote about any of the things I was interested in. He had no idea. He didn't know me at all.

Not long after that, I vowed I would never be poor again. I learned everything I could about money.

Senior year, when the money I'd stashed away went missing, I intercepted the check my father sent that month, cashed it, and took what was mine. Maybe I should have let it go. But this was important. I was taking a girl to the prom, and even though it wasn't a real date—she made it clear she just didn't want to go alone—I couldn't exactly let her down at the last minute.

When Aunt Jeanie realized what had happened, she showed up to the gymnasium drunk, railing. "You think a girl like that could ever want you?" she yelled. She walked right on the dance floor and accosted a poor kid that wasn't even me. That's how drunk she was. "You're fooling yourself. Look at her. She pities you. There's a difference, Thomas." Everyone knew who my aunt was. She didn't have to say my name. "And someday," she slurred. "Someday you'll learn what that is."

It wouldn't have been so bad if that had been the worst of it. It wasn't. A few weeks later, I came home from school to find Aunt Jeanie on the couch staring at the ceiling. Her eyes were glazed over. I thought she was dead. The doctors said she'd had a stroke. Eventually, she woke up, but she wasn't the same person. She was worse. Combative and angry, even more so than before. The doctors diagnosed her with dementia, likely brought on by the excessive alcohol use. She did get better after a few weeks in the hospital. But not much.

We didn't have money to keep her there, or anywhere else for that matter, so I brought her home. My father was supposed to come home on leave, but then some conflict broke out somewhere and he couldn't.

Every day Aunt Jeanie would make my father a cake in preparation for his arrival. Every day, the conflict was not resolved. After two weeks, I explained there could be no more cakes. But Jeanie insisted. She cried like a small child. She reverted into herself. Dementia is a horrible disease. Eventually, I gave in. This time Jeanie was convinced it was my father's birthday, so I stocked the house with cakes until her use of the oven became a concern. It was the least I could do. I'd come home from school and a cake would be waiting. It was the same day, every day. At least to her. I would celebrate with her and she would insist that I blow out candles. At first, I wished for my father to come home. Then I wished for Aunt Jeanie to die.

She called me Anthony when she sang. My father's name.

In the beginning, I cared to correct her. I'd say, "No, I'm Tommie, remember?"

"That's right. You're Thomas."

I'd tell her stories to help her remember. It's the only thing that keeps you sane when there's no one left to remember everything you thought you knew.

"Anthony," she'd say in the next breath. "Why don't you get a job here in town? Surely the lumberyard would hire you."

"No, Aunt Jeanie. I'm Thomas."

"But that boy needs you," she said. "You know I don't like kids."

When I left for college, my father put her in a home run by the state. Even after he was discharged, he never came back from wherever he'd been, not really. She couldn't be alone, he'd said, and I couldn't stay. I'd drive sixty miles one way on Sundays, after work, to see her. She always called me Anthony when I walked in the door.

Eventually, when she forgot both of our names, I stopped going all together.

Not long after that, my wish finally came true.

CHAPTER NINETEEN

MELANIE

How well can you really ever know a person? I ask myself this, looking over at Tom. I consider asking his opinion. But I won't. We're backing out of the drive, and this could be a mistake. Mom left. Maybe I should have stopped her. Was I wrong to send her on her way? I don't know. I don't know much of anything right now. I don't know where we're going or how long we'll be gone. I don't even know if I have packed the proper attire. I do know it was the first time I'd ever seen my mother look proud of something I accomplished, and even if that something was landing a man, I couldn't bear to let her down. Sometimes you take what you can get.

Speaking of which, what I didn't get is a chance to drive my new car. Maybe I should have insisted. But Tom was adamant. Planes don't wait. Before I knew it, he was hurling me out the door.

Maybe I should tell the driver to pull over and let me out. I don't know.

If I keep my eyes focused straight ahead, I'll come up with a plan. I'll figure it out.

Tom briefly glances over at me. Then he looks down at the

phone in his hand. "Just have to tie up a few loose ends real quick."

We're seated in the backseat adjacent to one another. I study the back of the driver's head. If we're going to have a fight, and we are, I realize now is the best time to have it.

"Are we even going to talk about what happened?"

My husband's eyes shift in the direction of the driver.

"Of course we are."

I widen my eyes. I'm expecting more.

He holds up his phone. "First, the loose ends. They need tying."

"Where are we going?"

"I told you. Our honeymoon."

I lean the back of my head against the cool glass. "Yes, but where?"

"It's a surprise," he huffs, his fingers typing furiously.

"Did you grab my passport?"

He smiles when his eyes meet mine. He's aware I'm digging for information. He couldn't have packed my passport because in my haste, I left it at mom and dad's. "Don't worry," he assures me. "I have everything covered."

Eventually, when he doesn't say anything else, I shrug and stare out the window at the blur of scenery whizzing by. Just once, momentarily, I glance over my shoulder and look over at my husband. He seems harmless enough. But even I know bad things exist to show people where their vulnerabilities are.

~

WE BOARD A PRIVATE PLANE. AT TAKE-OFF, I SAY, "I DON'T EVEN know who you are."

"Touché."

I look toward the cockpit and lower my voice slightly. "You put me in an institution and had them perform surgery on me without my consent."

"And yet you're here."

He makes a good point.

"Why?" I ask.

"You know," he says, and he's staring out the window as the wheels lift. Suddenly, we're airborne. "I've asked myself the same thing. Why would she lie to you, Tom? Why?"

"What? Hold on. We're talking about me. About the fact that you had my vagina reconstructed."

"For the record," he counters, "that was not my doing."

I close my eyes. I just want him to say something that makes sense. "I don't understand."

"Do you want this marriage to work, Melanie?"

"We don't even know each other."

"No," he agrees. "We don't. The only thing I really know for sure is that you're a liar."

"So I know everything there is to know about you then? That's what you're saying?"

He juts out his bottom lip while he mulls it over in no time flat. "Pretty much."

I find myself wishing for a parachute. Jumping without one might be better than this. At least that way, I'd know where I was headed. "That's interesting because I hardly know anything."

He swivels in his seat. He looks different. "Have you been working out?"

"Don't change the subject."

"Your arms look bigger."

"Why would you lie to me about who you were?"

"I didn't lie."

"You are a stripper."

I laugh. I can't help myself. I've never met anyone more matter of fact in my life. If I wasn't so angry, I might find it refreshing.

"What's funny?"

"I'm not a stripper, Tom. Just a girl who likes to have a little fun."

"Show me," he says. And then I do.

~

"I CAN'T STOP THINKING ABOUT YOU," HE SAID. I COULD SEE FROM the moment we met he wanted me to show him what I was made of. And that's just what I intended when I'd invited him to my hotel room under the guise that I wanted to know more about his church. This and the job he'd hinted at down in the hotel bar. Mostly, it was him I want to know more about.

"Show me."

"I'm here, aren't I?" I could see that he wasn't completely sure of his next move. I didn't think this was something he normally did, but then, you can never be certain.

"Yeah, well. About that—you're married," I reminded him. Sometimes it's good to get to the heart of a matter. "And by being here, you're asking for trouble." Bait with the promise of reward. It's an important key to winning.

His brows rose like a challenge. "I'm aware."

"Why are you here then, Tom?" Using his name was supposed to make it real for him. It was important to know what I was dealing with. Only then could I decide which route to take.

I made a move to remove his suit jacket. He did the work for me.

"To talk about New Hope."

"Don't lie, Tom."

"I'm not. Like I said, I can't stop thinking about you."

"And your wife?"

"I can assure you she isn't thinking about you at all."

"So matter of fact. Such a dry sense of humor. I like that about you."

He leaned back against the dresser and crossed his arms. "How many men have you been with?"

"Excuse me?" I sat back on the bed and crossed my legs.

"Your sexual history. If we are going to do this, I need to know."

"Whoa. Wait just a minute." I held up my hands. "You're very presumptuous, aren't you?" It was a rhetorical question, so I didn't stop there. "I only invited you for a drink. And, to learn more about your religion."

"I don't drink," he said. "I'm sure I mentioned that. In fact, I'm certain I did."

"So?"

"So— we could have conversed down in the bar. So—unless, I'm mistaken, which this is your chance to clear that up, you invited me here for sex."

I leaned back, propping myself on my hands. His eyes drifted to my tits. No doubt about it, I told myself. This was happening. "How many women have you been with?" I apprised him carefully

"Two."

"What? Seriously? No way." I can see by looking at him that this could be true. Nevertheless, it astounds me.

"Seriously."

"And men?"

He gave me a look.

"What? I have to ask. One should never make assumptions."

He offered a look of recognition. "You're right about that. Now, answer the question."

"Same."

"You? Two partners." He cocked his head like he was waiting for the punch line.

"Yes. Me." I feigned offense. "My parents are very religious. But my father had a lot of affairs. So I guess you could say I learned early not to throw that part of myself around freely."

"How early? You're so young."

I laughed. "I'm twenty-two. That's not that young."

He didn't say anything. I don't think he knew what to say.

"Okay, maybe I'm a little young. But I know what I want when I see it."

"And what is it that you want?"

"A little fun, a little distraction with someone I can trust."

"So, not much."

I acted like I was giving it some thought, when really, I had it all figured out. I knew I had to make myself Tom's ideal. I had to create an illusion for him. I had to find out what was missing in his life and become that. Doing that for a person may not be love, but I wasn't looking for love.

Quite the opposite, actually.

Love is common. But being someone's ideal is rare in today's world. It takes effort, and time, and most of all, patience. It requires attention to detail. Why go through all this when these days all you have to do to find a lover is swipe right?

I'd been there and done that. I'd had my fun. And now, I wanted more.

Tom had the means to be the more I was looking for. He had the means to fulfill those desires. Tom was a safe bet. Smart, boring. Looking to win, as was showcased in the meeting down in the bar. Basically, Tom was easy prey. But don't get me wrong. The seduction started well before I got him up to my hotel room. In fact, it started down on the street. I looked for subtleties, and I found them. I made a point of reading what was said between the lines. "No," I told him finally. "Not too much at all."

"SCOTTSDALE? YOU THOUGHT ARIZONA WAS AN IDEAL PLACE FOR A honeymoon?"

He shifted. "Have you been here before?"

"No."

"Well then, you wouldn't know, would you?"

It's familiar, though, this place. I remember my former sponsor, Josie, posted photos of a trip she took to Scottsdale not long before things went south for her. "What are we going to do here?"

"Whatever you want?"

He doesn't actually mean whatever I want. But I intend to make him mean it.

When we arrive at the hotel, the man unloading our bags makes a comment to our driver. "Could be his daughter…could be his whore," he laughs. "Who's to say?"

Before I realize what's happening, Tom has the guy pinned to the ground by his throat. "She's my wife," he says.

"Tom," I say. "Let go. His face is turning blue."

He isn't looking at me and he doesn't let go. "Apologize."

I'm afraid he is going to kill the guy. His lips are purple. "Tom," I say. "You're choking him."

My husband shakes his head slightly. "This is grappling. It's a simple submission hold."

"Oh my God." The dude's eyes are bulging. "Tom, you have to let go." I reach for his arm.

"Right now, I have control," he says. "But if he doesn't apologize soon, he has approx— "

I remove my hand from my husband's forearm. This is all very sexy.

I hear the guy mutter something that sounds like an apology. Tom lets go.

"Say it again," he tells the guy. "Clearly, please."

"I'm sorry," he stutters. I watch as he backs away, holding his neck and looking at Tom like he has lost his mind. "It was just a joke."

"Jokes can get a person killed," Tom warns. It isn't a threat exactly. But now I can see my husband is smart that way.

As we stand in line to check in, Tom's breathing finally returns to normal. "You know karate?"

"Jujitsu."

My eyes widen. "Anything else I should know?"

He doesn't have to think about his answer. He leans forward and kisses my cheek. "I hope we can make this marriage work." Afterward, he pulls away and meets my eye. "I really hate liars."

CHAPTER TWENTY

TOM

Melanie thinks we're here honeymooning. Someone should have told her, honeymoons aren't supposed to be based on a bed of lies.

What we're really doing here is not honeymooning. It's business. If I can keep Mark happy, and Melanie away from things that might put her in immediate danger, then I can work behind the scenes to carry out my plan. Part of that plan is saving my own ass. In the process, I have to make the determination of whether or not to keep my lovely bride around. You could say there's something about a betrayal that leaves a bad taste in a person's mouth. On the other hand, I have to say, while there are some kinks to be worked out, so far, so good. My wife is good entertainment if you're looking for that sort of thing, and right now I could use a bit of levity in my life. Which is why I was pleased to receive confirmation from a mile high that all is nearly in working order. They really put her into shape. Where I thought things were perfect, they made them better.

Nonetheless, I'm aware the ultimate warfare is the understanding that the moment one feels secure is the moment you have to change things up. God knows, aiming low is seductive.

Personally, I aim high. Around the throat region, generally. That's why I paid the guy to let me prove a point to Melanie. It still amazes me how far people are willing to go in pursuit of the almighty dollar. I could have killed that guy. It's risky, to say the least, when the only thing standing between him living and dying was a few seconds and a little control on my part. Seems like a lot to risk for fifty bucks, if you ask me. But then, it's a proven fact that once people make a decision or a commitment to something, they are likely to follow through for no other sake than they don't want to be seen as inconsistent. If compliance is what you're looking for, it's best to start small and build. Works like a charm. In this case, as soon as I got him to say yes to helping me impress a girl, I knew the rest was pretty much in the bag. The devil is in the detail. Who cares that I left out the part where I'd choke him into submission when it was only meant to be a shove? He'd already agreed to the deal.

"Fancy a swim?" I ask Melanie after lunch.

"I don't swim."

That's good to know. Drowning is the third leading cause of unintentional injury death worldwide, accounting for 7% of all injury-related deaths. "Fine," I say. "You can lay out. I'll swim."

We'll start small and build.

"Perfect," she quips. "I'll bring the agreement. I've been reading up on it, and this will give me a chance to ask a few questions…."

"What kind of questions?"

She yawns loudly, and after a second or two, she holds a finger up. "First a nap."

~

While Melanie is sleeping I check my phone. I'd purposely left it in the room when we went to lunch, and I was pretty sure what I'd missed. Three calls from Mark. I step out of the room to call him back.

He answers on the first ring. "How's the honeymoon going?"

"Very well."

"Good," he says. There's a pause. "Listen, I have a bad connection. I'll ring you right back."

I don't think much of it. Mark has always been suspicious of being recorded. He likes to be the one initiating calls. He thinks this matters.

Three seconds later, he rings me back. "I have to ask…is there a reason you chose Scottsdale?"

I hadn't told him where we were going, but I'm not surprised by the question in the least. Mark knows everything. "It's sunny here."

"So then it doesn't have anything to do with the flagship location Grant Dunn had in the works?"

"No," I tell him "But while I'm in the area if you need—"

"Do you know why Michael is dead, Tom?"

His question catches me off guard. I don't like to think about Michael's death. But I never forget either. "I know speed was definitely a factor."

"Michael was a drunk, Tom."

"Yes," I say. People like Mark need all the reassurance one can give. "I'm aware."

"Do you know how long we had been trying to rehabilitate your friend?"

"No." The truth is a fickle and vindictive mistress.

"Ten months," he tells me. "We gave him ten long months."

I find myself pacing the length of the hall. "I see." I don't see. I have no idea what this has to do with anything.

"Rehabilitating Michael was a social experiment for the church."

"I see."

"And you know the interesting thing about experiments Tom?"

No, but I have a feeling he's about to tell me.

"He couldn't mess up our rate of success if he were dead."

"Like June," I say.

Mark inhales deeply. "You are very good with your deductive reasoning Tom. Very good."

"What did you need?"

"Huh?"

"You called. I assume it wasn't to tell me how smart I am."

"Oh." There's a brief pause and then he says, "You're right about that Tom. You're my favorite accountant. But that you already knew."

I hear a door open down the hall. I assume it's Melanie looking for me. I walk around the corner so I'm out of sight.

"Tom?"

"I'm here..."

"We need to move our latest experiment along. The men's alliance is getting antsy."

"How can I help?" I want to make him spell it out.

"Stick to the plan," he says. "You have the portfolio. Make a choice in the direction we should take. One way or the other. Something has to be done."

"What do you mean one way or the other?" I want clarification.

"I trust you'll make the right decision." He doesn't give an inch.

"I'm working on it," I assure him.

"Great. Now, go enjoy yourself. You know what they say about being all business and no pleasure..."

"No, I don't."

"It makes Tom a dull boy."

CHAPTER TWENTY-ONE

MELANIE

Tom is in the pool. I sit on the side. I half-watch as he swims several laps and half-study the agreement. If I'd known it was this fascinating, I wouldn't have put it off so long. I'm glad I did.

No doubt, if I'd read it, I wouldn't be sitting here now. I would have found an easier route to get what I want. Sometimes you can't see where the path will take you, and sometimes you realize it's where you want to go, but that you wouldn't have started out in that direction, if only you'd known what was ahead.

Tom takes a break and swims over to where I am. I can feel his eyes on everything as he examines my body. Thankfully, I've already ordered a drink. When it arrives, he gives me a look that conveys his disappointment.

"What?" I shrug. "We're on our honeymoon."

He doesn't offer a response. He's too busy running his hands along my thighs. "Have you ever thought about getting lipo?"

"Only every other day."

He splashes some water on my legs and watches as it drips off. "We should schedule that when we get back."

"Sounds like a plan," I say, and then Tom kicks off on the side of the pool. He backstrokes his way to the other side. I hold the agreement where he'll see it when he looks my way. Eventually, he swims over.

"I have some questions for you..."

My husband raises his brow, and then he glances around to see who might be listening. It's late afternoon, and the pool area is starting to fill up. I follow his gaze. So many people in this town, I've noticed. With a little lipo, I tell Tom, I could probably live here.

"So you like it here then?"

"I do." It isn't a lie. You can smell the money coming off the patrons. Perpetual vacationers. I guess one never really ventures that far from what one knows.

"How much money does the church make anyway?"

He puts on his surprised look. "Why do you ask?"

"Just curious," I say. I lick the sugar on the rim of my daiquiri. "I'd like to learn more about our finances."

Tom doesn't respond for several moments. He's stretching, and I can see he really has been working out. Finally, he says, "I'm not here to talk shop."

"Fine." I stuff the agreement in my bag. "What do you take home?"

"Enough." Tom likes his double entendres.

I silently seethe as he props himself on his elbows. He rests against the side of the pool. After several minutes, he glances over his shoulder and gives me the once-over. I take this as a sign to continue the conversation. "Well, as your wife, I'd like to know." He stares at my bottom lip as I chew on it. "It just seems like for the amount of work you do, they should give you a bigger piece of the pie, is all."

"Like I said, I do well."

"If you insist on being vague...whatever. But I think I could help."

He looks at me for a moment. I can see he's pondering his next move. We both know he wants to go deeper.

"If you want to talk numbers…I can tell you about your new clothing allowance."

"My allowance," I laugh, choking on my own spit. "You make it sound like I'm a child."

His silence hangs in the air for a bit too long.

"It's a business expense, the clothes," he tells me, finally. "There's money for other stuff too. The church wants you to take a more active role. Obviously, you really proved yourself at the center."

"How much?" I have to ask.

"Plenty."

"What do they want me to do?"

"That much I don't know." He shakes his head, and then gazes off into the distance. "Not for certain."

"Well, what do you know?"

"I know they're setting up social media accounts for you."

"I don't do social media."

"You do now."

"So basically what they want is a replacement for Josie?"

He furrows his brow. "Josie?"

For someone so smart, sometimes he can be really dumb. "Yeah, that was her job. Remember how she was always posting on Instalook?"

"Not particularly."

"Well, I do. I watched her. She couldn't put that damned phone down. Checking, always checking."

"I never paid attention."

"Have you ever thought about leaving the church?"

"No," he tells me, meeting my eyes. "Why do you ask?"

I sip my drink and say, "I'm just not sure I understand the appeal." This, of course, is a lie. Free clothes. A nice lifestyle. A community of like-minded people. It's all about image. Everything is. I get it. I do. People want to see themselves a certain way, every bit as much as they want others to see them that way. Offer them the chance, shine a mirror on what they think it is they see, and they'll be putty in your hands. Ripe for the picking, or however the saying goes.

"The church owns me, Melanie."

I didn't expect him to say that. I feel like we've gotten to the point of oversharing.

"Own you? How?"

"Never mind," he says kicking back. "You said you had a question about the agreement?"

"You know what?" I down the last of my drink. "I've forgotten."

He doesn't believe me. "Must be the alcohol. It feels like forever since I've had a drink..."

"Twelve weeks tomorrow," he says.

I raise my brow. I'm impressed. "Yeah, something like that."

At dinner I get drunk. Like properly drunk. I don't know how, but I have to make myself fall in love with this man. The writing is on the wall. We could be good together. We could stage a coup. We could have it all. I don't recall what I ate. My appetite is diminished by my memories of ice baths and liquid diets, only now I've exchanged smoothies for rum. I could probably make it a combo deal if it came down to it. Mrs. Elizabeth would be proud. I guess I'm coming around to the idea of drinking my calories. This explains why the evening is kind of hazy.

But I do intend to remember what happens when we go back to our room. I have a plan. Clearly.

"Let's fuck," I tell Tom, stripping out of my clothes. Sometimes sex can lead to love.

"We can't."

"Sure we can." I can hear my own slur. I need to slow down. We need to speed up. "It'll be fine," I assure him.

"I don't want to hurt you."

Tom is a liar.

He walks over to me and takes the glass from my hand. "I don't like to see you like this."

"What? Happy?"

My eyes meet his as he takes my chin in his hand. I don't have a choice. He forces me to look at him. "Do I make you unhappy, Melanie?"

I shake my head slightly. It's as far as Tom's grip will allow. "I make myself unhappy," I say. "I am not a nice person." It's one of the only truthful things I've ever really told him.

"How so?"

"I destroy everything in my wake."

Tom offers a tight smile. I am too drunk to realize it's not an appropriate response. "You won't destroy me."

"I might try." This is the first time I come to understand that alcohol and Tom Anderson don't mix well. There's chemistry here. Maybe not love. But the chemistry is unmistakable. Without it, this would not have been a successful seduction to begin with.

He leans in and plants a quick peck on my lips. "Melanie," he says as he pulls away and meets my eye. His expression is serious. More serious than I've ever seen. "Don't take me to the deep end, if you know you can't swim."

~

WHEN MY HUSBAND EXITS THE BATHROOM, HE'S STILL IN THE process of toweling off. "There's something I've been meaning to ask you," he says, but in a way that it seems as though he's just thought of it.

The room is spinning. I can't recall the last time I was this drunk.

"Can you tell me a little about your previous lovers?"

"Why would you ask that?" My hand reaches for the wall. I have to steady myself otherwise I am going to be sick.

"You really shouldn't drink," he says. "Look what it does to you."

I feel the weight of him as he sits down on the edge of the bed.

"Tell me what they liked."

My eyes meet his.

I stare at him curiously. "You want to know what they were into?"

"I want to know everything about you."

My breath catches.

Tom leans in and touches my face with the back of his hand. "I think we should do a little role playing."

"You're fucked in the head," I say. "Seriously sick."

His face is unreadable. "You have no idea."

"Who raised you?"

"My aunt."

"Really?" I realize I know nothing about this man or his past. Not really.

"But none of that is the issue."

My head tilts. "What is the issue?"

"I want to know what they were like. The men in your past…"

"Why?"

"Because I want to be the best lover you've ever had. Which requires a little research on my part. Most things can be explained by digging at the past, right?"

I pull at the towel he has around his waist. Suddenly, I've got a second wind. "I think I just fell in love with you."

"Hot and cold? You wanna play?"

I don't answer. I'm headed south. It's possible I might puke all over him. But who cares? I've just realized I've met my match. Someone who gets me. I feel something. And that something is pleasantly surprised. In this moment, this is all that matters.

Tom pulls my hair, forcing me to look at him. "Well—are you going to make me guess what they were into? Or would you just spell it out? Personally, I prefer the latter."

Little does he know, that's not nearly as much fun, which is why I roll my eyes. I get back to business, pushing against his grip. Tom seems like the kind of guy who likes a little resistance. "Can't you see?" I smile up at him ruefully. "I'm working on it."

CHAPTER TWENTY-TWO

TOM

I can't begin to tell you the things I discovered while I was looking for something else. I shouldn't have been surprised. Most of science works this way. The obvious answers usually come indirectly. After Melanie's confessions last night, I know enough to know I have to delay killing her. At least for a little while.

I realize it's cliché to insinuate that a man should make a decision with his appendage. But I am, after all, a man and I am finding there is apparently something to that cliché.

If I'd rather not kill Melanie, on account of the sex—and the fact that I've pretty much solved the problem of her being expensive to keep around—and I am forced to make a move on one of Mark's targets, at least there's a silver lining in the whole thing. My lovely wife gave me another clue last night when she mentioned Josie Dunn.

A clue that deserves an in-person visit.

After three days, we fly home. Being with Melanie no longer grates on my nerves the way it used to. Well, not most of the time. She makes me think things could be different. I'm concerned I might actually be starting to like her.

This is a problem when determining whether or not she lives or dies. It's akin to naming a puppy you know you can't keep.

I know I shouldn't let a prick like Mark determine the course of my life. But he holds all the keys.

Even if he didn't kill me— say if I left the church and made a run for it—he'd have leverage. I'm not exactly an innocent bystander in the acts the church has committed. I know what goes on. I know how they manipulate and control, the allegations of abuse. I know about the payouts, the bribes, and the hush money. I'm their accountant, after all. Half of my job is seeing that funds are disguised as other things.

Unfortunately, that's not all he has on me. Mark has hours and hours of video straight from the deepest recesses of my mind. The cover for Mark, his idea, a valid front for New Hope is that it's in the business of rehabilitation. He started it when he wanted to rehabilitate Michael from his alcoholism. Well, let me assure you, this makes for good business. Everybody has a vice. Everyone. Some are worse than others. But a crutch is a crutch. And most people are running from something. From the get-go, I wasn't willing to give up much. But I was wise enough to know I had to give something. If Mark's goal was to rehabilitate me, the best I could offer him was my past.

Back then, New Hope wasn't that sophisticated. Back then, Mark liked to do his bidding himself. He hadn't yet learned who he could trust. So, he saw to my 'healing sessions' personally.

They always began and ended the same way. First, we would sit in a room adjacent to one another. He would start by asking me a single question. It got worse from there. His goal: to free me from my painful past. I'm an introvert. Up until that point, most of my life had not been that exciting.

Mark thought by talking through painful memories, it would help.

And you know what? To my amazement, it did. For a while.

Those sessions were the only time, except when June was

killed, that I've ever cried. I cried for Michael and for Aunt Jeanie and for the father I hardly knew. He himself always said it was better not to feel. Logic runs low when emotion runs high. I didn't see the truth in that. Not then.

At the time, I'd hit a low point. It felt like I had a friend again.

The sad part is that's not the main reason I gave Mark what he wanted. I did it because I wanted to keep my job and my house. Most importantly, I wanted to keep my family intact. June would have left. Eventually, if not right off the bat. And I would have let her go. I knew the kind of life she wanted for herself and the kids. I had been working twenty-hour days just to provide it. The ability to keep it up was quickly slipping through my fingers. There was always more, and I knew she would have found some excuse to get it, and I knew it wouldn't have included me. It wasn't that she didn't love me. It was that we both knew she deserved better. After all, it wasn't her that had changed the unspoken rules of our agreement. It was me. I'm the one who let Michael fool me. I'm the one who nearly caused us to lose everything.

"Do you miss June?" Melanie asks one afternoon out of the blue. Sometimes I think she's clairvoyant.

"Yes," I say. I should lie. I've read enough to know that women don't like to know you're thinking of another woman. It doesn't matter if that woman is dead.

But I don't lie. I don't want to betray June more than I already have.

"I thought so."

Her eyes lit up. To say this reaction is unexpected would be an understatement. "I think we should do a little role playing."

"That's not funny."

She comes closer. "I hadn't meant it to be."

I swallow hard.

"I want to learn everything about you," she says in that sultry way of hers. "I want to be the best lover you've ever had."

I take a step back. God, she's good. Already, just the way she is. With slight tweaking, I can't imagine. Which brings me to my biggest problem yet—I really think I could love this one.

~

"Do you miss it?" I ask Josie.

I'm seated on her new sofa in her new condo downtown. It overlooks the city, and I should be surprised she'd trade the suburbs in for this, but I'm not. Josie has the illusion of safety here. She likes being at the top, looking down at others.

"Me? Miss the church?" She thinks about my question for a long while. I realize, glancing down at my watch, that I should have called and asked for a visit. I can see she's in shock. Everything is taking longer than it needs to. It's rude to show up unannounced, and I abhor rudeness. But I knew she wouldn't have agreed to see me. So, I apologize once again.

"Sometimes," she tells me finally. She sucks in a breath and holds it. At some point, she lets go. "Under different circumstances, maybe I could have made it work." She pauses and then turns to meet my eye. "But I assume you aren't here to learn about my regrets."

I don't respond. Not at first. I tell her I like her place.

She crosses the living area and comes to a stop by the window. "Who sent you to spy on me?"

"I'm not here to spy."

"Let me guess...Beth? Mark?"

"No one."

She rolls her neck. "Adam? Cheryl?"

I see her point. People work as teams at New Hope. Usually husband and wife. But not always. That's part of the reason I'm here.

"No," I tell her. "No one sent me."

"How are Adam and Cheryl these days?"

"Fine." I haven't a clue.

"I do miss them," she offers, looking over her shoulder at me. "They were a fun couple. You know, the kind that's for real."

I know what she's talking about. I didn't come here for fun or for gossip.

Josie looks away again, out at the expanse of the city. "And Melanie? How is she?"

"She's great."

"Adjusting, then."

I nod. She can see this is not why I've come either.

"Those old neighbors of yours..." I start. I pause to pull my phone from my pocket. I need time to gage her reaction. "Do you have any way of getting in touch with them?"

She turns on her heel. "The Becks?"

"No." I shake my head. "The other ones. Jude, I think his name was. And her name was—"

"Kate." She finishes my sentence.

"That's right." I hold up my finger. "It's coming to me now... Kate. Kate Anderson. Same as mine."

"It's a common name," she tells me. Her expression gives nothing away.

"Yes. And you know...I always liked them. They say people like things that are familiar."

Her brow raises.

"Remember they had that party that time, and that woman OD'd in the bathroom?"

"Yes," she says.

Her memory makes me smile. It means success in getting what I've come for. "Man, they were interesting."

"Trust me," she tells me, heaving out a sigh. "They wouldn't be good candidates for your church."

"So you're still in touch with them, then?"

"No, not really." Her voice cracks.

"Do you have an address or a phone number? I remember Jude…didn't he work for Maxicorp?"

"I don't recall."

"Well," I sigh as I stand. Sometimes it's important to get on eye level. This way she'll know I'm as eager to get the hell out of here, as she is to see me go. "I'm in need of a contact there. And I thought of him."

She seems to understand. Finally, she retrieves a number from her phone.

I look on, taking care not to appear too eager, as she scribbles it on a piece of paper. When she hands it to me I can see we both know I'm lying about the reason for needing it.

"Be careful," she advises. I smile then. We have a secret, a bond.

"Thank you," I say, and then I start for the door.

"Oh, and Tom…" Her voice stops me in my tracks. "Jude is a good guy. I bet he can help you out."

I turn back. I know what she means. Her old neighbor is a contract killer. In effect, she's saying with different words, that she knew all along. She wants me to know she understands why I've come.

"But you know the saying…never wrestle with a pig. You just get dirty, and the pig enjoys it."

"Yes," I tell her. "I'm familiar with it."

A tight smile plays across her face. "Just wanted to make sure."

CHAPTER TWENTY-THREE

MELANIE

New Hope is having its annual Spring Fling tonight. I have no idea exactly what this means nor do I know what to expect. I only know what it means for me: a new dress, shoes, and jewelry to match. I'm also aware that my purchases in preparation for the event will mean having to ask Tom for more money, as I have depleted my "expense account."

I have a feeling this news won't go down easily because as good as my husband is with numbers, he is clueless when it comes to inflation, not to mention what it takes to look good. Being the kind of woman he wants me to be, looking the way he wants me to look, isn't cheap.

I plan to break it to him at the actual black-tie charity thing. He should be in the mood to receive this kind of information, given the nature of the event. It's a fair assumption. I know because when I asked what the party was all about, he told me it's where members go to feel important, and more importantly, to look altruistic.

I'd meant to grill Beth on the dollar amount of her expense account at our sponsor meeting this morning. But as it turned out, she had other more pressing matters to discuss.

"We're on such a tight deadline for enrollment," she cautioned over coffee. "We really need to end the quarter strong. Tom has told you, no?"

My husband has not, in fact, explained this.

As I tried to determine why he would have kept this information to himself, Beth retrieved a cell phone from her purse. "This is yours," she said handing it to me.

"Nice." I pressed the button to power it on. "Thanks."

She leaned over until she was practically on my side of the table and pointed at the screen. "I've set up all of your social media accounts for you. Your church email address is in the notes. I've listed your new phone number, too."

"I'm not really a fan of social media. Everyone just seems...I don't know...narcissistic."

Beth gave me a patronizing look. "I doubt millions of people all suffer the same disorder, Melanie." She cocked her head and glared at me like I'd just reached over the table and backhanded her. "Well," she said. "Personally, I don't feel that way at all."

"I mean—"

"Listen, Melanie. Let me explain how this works, okay?"

It's not a question, and she doesn't wait for me to answer. "You take photos of the things you're proud of. That new car in the drive...pretend you just got it. Those new earrings, they were a gift from your adoring husband. June's china: a gift from your new best friend."

"I don't have a best friend."

She grinned wryly. "You do now."

"Wow," I said as my hand clutched my throat. "I'm honored."

Beth shifted proudly. "We're all in this together."

"June's china is old...maybe I need new."

"No," she countered. "Old is good. It's very fashionable these days. Caption your photo with the hashtag #antiques. That sort of thing always gets a ton of likes."

"Is that the goal...likes?"

"The goal is to sell. Sell yourself. Sell the church. Sell products. Get money." Beth laughed. "Get it?"

"So...basically...Sell. Sell. Sell."

"Well, yes. But you'll want to be interesting. You have to increase your followers. It's like anything, a numbers game."

I crossed my legs and settled in for the long haul. "A numbers game..."

Beth pointed at the phone. "I put some sample captions in the notes too...just in case. It's easier if you plan your content out," she said, and then she waved me off. "But you're young. You'll figure it out in no time."

I made a play at uncertainty. "This feels a bit like curating my life."

"Maybe," she relented. "But everyone loves a good story, don't they?"

As Beth rattled on, I scanned through the notes. She went on and on about me going to spin class. She's scheduled it out on my phone. I'm supposed to post that I'm there with "the girls." This, I'm told, is for community building. After spin, I'm supposed to have coffee, but not just any coffee. Per Beth's instructions, it has to be designer coffee. She explained how I'm supposed to take a picture of my designer coffee with my designer sunglasses, next to my key displaying the Maserati symbol, and a copy of the latest New Hope Book—penned by her of course—*Ten Ways To Live a Top Shelf Life.* She tells me how I have to make it all look natural, and then asked me if I knew what a flat lay is. Of course, I lied. She's very intense, Beth, when she sets her mind on something. This intensity had me thinking about other top shelf things, and thankfully, it too is on the list. In order to show we are non-judgmental at New Hope, I'm supposed to post photos of champagne and strawberries with the caption #datenight.

"But Tom doesn't drink," I remind her.

She laughed. "No one needs to know that."

"They don't?"

"This is about creating a fantasy, Melanie. This is about making your life better. You have to be more interesting, more fun, and more beautiful. You have to outdo the average girl your age who is sitting behind some screen in her two-day-old pajamas, with her unwashed hair, wishing she had half the life you have. All the while, she's wondering: will the boy call? Maybe if I had this or that, maybe if I was a member of that church, maybe if I was more like Melanie. She'll think of you when it comes to getting what she wants because—you— you have it all. And she's going to want to know what you're doing. That's where New Hope comes in."

I press my lips together like I'm shocked. I really want to be. I do.

Beth shook her head and tossed up her hands. "Fake it till you make it, right?"

"No, I get it," I said, making my eyes light up. "I have to live a top shelf life."

She pressed her palms together and brought them into the praying position. "Exactly."

~

When I was eight, my wrist snapped in two during a soccer game. I kept playing; I ran the ball all the way down the field and straight into our opponent's goal. This was a pretty easy thing to do, given the other players. Everyone stopped and took a knee. They looked on as I gloriously ran toward the goal, my wrist flapping like a flag on a windy day. It hung proudly from my arm like jelly. All the while I felt nothing.

Early on, I learned to mimic social cues on my parents' faces in regard to what I should be feeling. I would fall down, and their faces would be wide-eyed and cautious, and this showed me the correct emotion in which to draw upon. This time I was too distracted. That's how I was found out.

Not long after, I was finally diagnosed with congenital analgesia. Basically, that's a fancy term to say I have an inability to feel pain. It's a rare disorder but I wasn't surprised. I had always been rougher than other kids. Braver. More audacious. The sort of things that don't earn you a ton of friends. No one likes to be reminded of their inadequacies. No matter that I was the one with the faulty genetics.

It's not your genes, Melanie, my mother liked to say. *It's just no one likes a show-off.*

I didn't know what she meant. I was missing any markers on what I should feel. There was no reference to show me how far I could take things, and so I went all the way.

This didn't last long. My peers ended up hurt as they tried to keep up until I was left with few kids willing to play with me. Slowly, but surely, parents pulled their kids away, as if I was doing the hurting on purpose. It's tough to have empathy for other people's pain when you have no personal reference.

It was okay. I was dead on the inside, too.

Eventually, this was proven when the NPD diagnosis arrived. Narcissistic Personality Disorder. Who's to say what came first. The chicken or the egg. Maybe it was cause and effect. It's easier to push people away as opposed to watching them leave on their own accord. All I know is at some point it became a game. Win people over. Hurt them slowly.

TOM SAYS I LOOK STUNNING WHEN HE SEES ME IN THE NEW GOWN. I assume this means he won't pick apart the price. Accountants. Man. I guess because they spend so much time around numbers they have a hard time seeing them for what they are. Fake. Just like my new life, there's really nothing tangible to back all those zeros up. It's not like we're on the gold standard anymore. So who cares?

My husband, obviously. He's been working overtime, he explains, trying to make all the numbers fit. I tried to help by explaining that money is infinite. You can literally create it from nothing. Banks do it all the time. He said, I am not a bank.

At any rate, absence apparently does make the heart grow fonder. He's happy tonight. At least as happy as a man like Tom can get.

It's okay. With a little salt, he'll go down easier. And, if that doesn't work, I'll try a chaser.

I'm not that surprised when we arrive at the charity fling or whatever it's called, only to find it's like all the other charity functions my parents dragged me to over the years. Actually, I thought of inviting them, just to show off. *Look, the apple doesn't fall far from the tree.* But then I came to my senses when I realized I'm not ready for that level of personal involvement yet. So I made it a point to send my mother an invite to Instalook. This way she can see all the photos of my new life.

I know it'll make her and my father proud. There's only one problem. One I've just realized. I only have eight hundred and two followers. It doesn't matter that I haven't a clue who these people are. I need more. When I remember Beth said some people have millions, I set out to find her. It isn't hard. She's positioned herself by the door, the best way to be seen.

I mosey up to her, and in a hushed tone, I say to her, "I have a huge problem."

"I'm in the middle of something right now, Melanie," she replies in her usual pissy, shrill tone. "Can you give me a moment?"

"No," I inform her. "It can't wait." I want to remind her that we're besties, and besties are there for one another. I don't think she'd either get or appreciate my sarcasm. Most people don't.

"Excuse me," she motions to the couple. I can't help but notice she doesn't use that tone with them. Then I see their nametags, the label 'donor' proudly displayed. She smiles neatly. "I'll be right back."

Beth takes me by the elbow. "Melanie," she chides. "We don't have problems. Not in public. It's unbecoming." She gives me the side eye. "Jesus. Who raised you?"

"But I do have a problem." I hold up my phone. "I only have eight hundred and two followers. I need to have more."

"Have you been posting?"

I show her my feed. I feel a wicked rage for recognition building.

She studies my photos and then says, "You probably need to reconsider your filters. Remember I said sunny and bright?"

"But how do I get followers?"

"My God," she huffs. She crosses the ballroom. I follow on her heel. "Give me the phone."

I hand it to her and watch as her fingers work their magic. "Here," she says. "I just bought you ten thousand."

"That's it? Ten thousand? You said some people have millions."

Beth looks at me softly, and this is how I know I've learned her love language. This is how I know I'm in. "Yes," she says. "But you'll want to take things slowly. You don't want too much too soon. People will notice."

It's like she's speaking directly to my heart.

"Right," I murmur. We stand there watching the number of followers as it ticks upwards. "Are these even real people?"

"Some of them."

My face breaks out into a grin. It feels good to be liked. "When can I buy more?"

"Give it a few days. Now, if you'll excuse me, I have to get back to our guests."

I nod, and I can't wait to tell Tom about this. He'll be amused to know followers are the same as those numbers he's been poring over. Unsubstantial. And yet they offer the promise of so much.

~

I stand in the corner, checking out the profiles of some of my new followers. It's amazing what you can learn about people. If Tom doesn't shape up, this seems like a totally viable way to meet a second husband. How great will it be not to have to wait to find out what they're worth? What a time saver this is. It's right there at my fingertips.

At one point, Beth comes over and reminds me I'm supposed to be mingling. I really have no idea how I'm supposed to fulfill the obligations of my new online life and the real one. I don't know how she expects me to get followers and likes if I'm not online. And I found out the hard way that people in real life really do not appreciate it if they're trying to have a conversation with you, and you're staring at your phone. I feel like I can't win. Talk about a rock and a hard place.

Anyway, it's not like I'm missing much. In real life, there's a band and dancing and lots of boring people. I haven't had enough to drink to feel like partaking in either. But on Instalook, Beth is right. I do need to change my filters up. Everything is bright and beautiful.

Eventually, my battery dies, and this seems like as good a sign as any to go and find that husband of mine. I come up behind him and palm his backside. "We should sneak away," I whisper in his ear.

"Melanie, there you are," he says, which makes no sense because he moves away from me. This is probably because he's standing with Adam, another church leader. Adam is not a fan of mine. I blame his wife. She's always giving me dirty looks. In fact, she's wearing one now.

"Why would we do that?" Tom asks out in the open.

"Why do you think?" I say. "There's nothing so intimate as a large party." I smile sweetly and sidle up close to him. Tom hates to be touched outside of the bedroom. But he's good at pretending. "Fitzgerald said that."

This is probably why Cheryl hates me. She seems like the kind of person who dislikes anything intimate. I can tell by the way her husband gawks at me. He's practically salivating. She takes an awful lot of care not to notice.

"Excuse me," Tom tells our company. "I think my lady wants to dance."

"Horizontally," I confess. Then I lean in close to Adam and Cheryl, and just so there's no confusion, I say, "the tango."

Tom frowns in my direction. He really hates it when I embarrass him in front of his highbrow friends.

~

On my way out of the ladies room, someone grabs me by my forearm. "Mel?" I turn to see it's Vanessa. I stare for a moment. I hardly recognize her. She looks completely different.

"Vanessa?"

"It's me." She smiles excitedly as though there's no bad blood between us. As though she didn't stick a knife in my back.

"Wow—" I say. "Your hair—and your—"

"I know. My husband wanted a redhead." She points to her face. "With freckles."

"Wait, you have fake freckles?" I'd just been reading about those on Instalook. I want to ask if it hurts. But then, what do I care?

Vanessa cocks her head. "It's amazing the ways in which one can change."

This feels really deep. Like Beth said. *Too much, too soon.*

"I saw you're on Instalook now..." she tells me. "That's how I knew you'd be here."

"And you? You live in Austin?"

"No. Not yet." She shakes her head. "Well, not permanently. But we'll see."

I don't know what to say to that, so I say nothing.

"Sean is positioning himself for leadership," she continues. "We're in a rental now." She crosses her fingers and holds them up. "But hopefully soon, we'll find something a little more permanent."

I take a step back and take her in. She's just so completely different. Everything about her. She seems to read my mind.

"About what happened. I figure you must hate me." *Please say yes. Please let this be the case.* Vanessa seems like the type to cling. She has nothing to offer me, and for the entire forty-five seconds we've been standing here she's only talked about herself. News-flash, I want to tell her. No one wants to stand around and listen to your life story. These days people go online for that.

But she surprises me when she says, "No. Exactly the opposite. I know you just wanted better for me. I should have wanted it for myself."

"Oh," I say. I never felt more disappointed in my life.

Her face lights up. "These days I spend most of my time caring for Daniel. It's nice to want a little something for myself."

I assume Daniel is her son. I have no idea what she's talking about. But then I remember Beth said I'm due for a coffee post tomorrow, and I don't have a partner. I think I'm supposed to have a partner.

Vanessa drones on. "Especially with everything else…you know…the cooking and cleaning…it's never-ending…the things us women manage."

She's wrong. I don't know. I don't say this. I offer a smile instead. This is like permission for her to never shut up. "I have to get back."

She practically blocks me in. "But I also spend a lot of time up at the church. Cleaning and straightening things. Making sure everything is in order."

"I remember you hated cleaning."

"Yeah, well..." She glances away. "All that's changed. I realize I'm meant to serve. It brings me joy."

When she says she spends a lot of time at the church, something in me stirs. I could use eyes there. And Vanessa is very open. A great combination. "Maybe we can meet for spin class. Or coffee..."

"Gee, I wish I could," she tells me. "But I have so much to do at home."

God, shoot me now. "Yoga? Brunch?" I purposely list things on Beth's agenda. I have not yet determined that Vanessa is the kind of person I actually want to spend my free time with. But if she has information I need, then I guess I can maybe suck it up.

"I really wish I could." She sighs heavily. "But there's vacuuming and waxing, and I really need to take down the drapes this week."

I give my best *what the fuck* face. I have to recover quickly when a man who I assume is her husband walks up.

"I've been looking all over for you," he says, planting a kiss on her cheek.

Vanessa smiles and leans into him.

My mouth hangs open, and I have to force myself to shut it. This guy could legitimately be her grandpa.

"I'm Sean." He extends his hand.

"I'm sorry," Vanessa says. "How rude of me."

"Mel," I say, sizing him up. It makes sense why he wants her barefoot and in the kitchen. He hails from the Ice Age.

"I know who you are," he tells me, and the way he says it, and the way his eyes look right through me, set off alarm bells. "Tom's wife."

I exhale and he smiles. It's so icy my stomach turns.

~

I NEED A PHOTO FOR INSTALOOK, AND I'M PART BORED AND PART curious, so I decide on the fly to pay Vanessa a visit. When she opens the door, surprise registers on her face. There's a toddler on her hip.

"I'm sorry to just show up," I tell her. "I was in the neighborhood." It's not even a good lie. Most everyone from the church lives here.

Vanessa comes out from behind the door. She steps outside and closes the door. "I hate to seem rude. But Sean isn't golfing today. And I was in the process of mopping."

"Dressed like that?" She's wearing Dior. I know because I tried that very top on myself. I decided it made me look too matronly. On her, it just fits.

She shrugs. The baby pulls at her earrings. He's drooling. He looks like an alien with his enlarged head and huge eyes. "This is Daniel," she says when she notices me looking.

He drops his toy. I lean down to pick it up and notice her Manolo's. "Those are terrible shoes for mopping."

She offers a pleasant smile. But she does not acknowledge her lie. Which means she's either smarter than I thought or she's hiding something really interesting. Maybe both. She half-turns to open the door. "Thanks for stopping by...but I gotta get this little guy down for his nap."

Her body is different. Everything about her is different.

"And get back to mopping," I say.

"That too. Plus, it's Wednesday, and Wednesdays are for dusting."

I don't know if she's fucking with me or if this is for real, but I don't like to be blown off. "You should get Grandpa—I mean Sean—to get you a cleaning lady."

"No, I love it." She adjusts the kid higher on her hip. "It's a great workout. Means I get to skip leg day. And Sean appreciates it when he's home. Having someone take care of him."

"Right." At first I think she's talking about the kid. Then I realize she's referring to her husband. I turn to go. I don't know what kind of fetish thing these two have going on, but who am I to interrupt it?

"I've been following you on Instalook," she says, watching me go. Her voice is so low, I have to really pick the words apart in my mind to decipher them. "You've taken to things very well."

I turn back to her. "Have I?"

"I was like you once," she says nostalgically. "But then I had Daniel..." She motions toward the baby or toddler or whatever you call children these days and she smiles. "And well, then life changed, as life has a way of doing."

"Do you ever visit that park?" I ask. I point. "The one I passed on my way in."

"Every day at three o'clock."

"Great," I say as I fish for my key. And then, I let her get back to it.

~

THE FOLLOWING AFTERNOON AT THREE O'CLOCK SHARP I FIND myself seated on a park bench, two coffees beside me. I hate coffee. When Vanessa comes down the street pushing one of those baby things, she is surprised to see me and it shows.

"Fancy running into you here," she says. She shifts as though she's voice-activated.

"Here," I say, handing her a coffee. "Maybe this will help with all the cleaning."

She doesn't get the joke. Suddenly, I resent her meek face.

"Actually, I don't drink coffee anymore. But thanks."

She's dressed to the nines. "Do you always come to the park in Prada?" It's not even fancy yoga clothes the mom's all wear these days.

She narrows her eyes. "Where else would I wear it?"

Her kid lets out a squeal, so she lifts him from the stroller.

"Would you mind?" she asks, handing him to me.

I'm allergic to children, so immediately I set him down. I don't know for sure, but he looks old enough to walk.

I watch as he takes a handful of dirt and shoves it in his mouth. *Shit.*

Vanessa is digging through a bag. It looks like she's packed for an overnighter. I know I should brush the dirt away from the kid's mouth but he's really got it in there. I'd have to dig, and yeah, no thank you. Hopefully, he swallows before she turns around.

"Oh," Vanessa gasps when she sees him on the ground. "He likes to eat dirt. And whatever he can find, really. "

She retrieves wet wipes, and I wonder if there's a school where they teach you these things.

"Sorry," I tell her. "It's still hard for me. After…you know."

"Oh my gosh. I am so sorry!"

"It's okay." I shrug. "He's just so cute…and my baby was a boy."

She looks like she might cry. "I'm sorry."

We sit in silence for a long while. Vanessa lets the kid half-toddle half-crawl out into the playground and then she glances around the park. "I was looking for my water bottle so I could take my pills, but I can't find it anywhere. Sean says I'm so forgetful." She smiles. "Sure enough, I'll go home, and there it'll be, waiting on the table in the entryway."

"A sip of coffee won't hurt."

She massages her temples.

"Headache?" I ask. I feel one coming on too and I hope she has the good stuff.

"No, these are our daily vitamins. New Hope branded them. Isn't that funny?"

"Our daily vitamins?"

"Well… yours will be different, since you're trying for a little one."

This is news to me.

"What kind of vitamins?"

She searches for the bottle and puts them back in on account of not having the water and the coffee being forbidden. I take it from her. "Do you even know what's in these?"

She shrugs. "Who cares? They give me so much energy."

I almost want to pop a few. Her stupidity is draining mine. I shift on the bench and get a good look at Vanessa. She's hardly older than I am. I shudder to think that could have been me. That this could have been my version of escape, too. That coming here could be my best shot at a break. I take my phone from my pocket and snap a picture of the ingredients.

"They really help with the postpartum depression."

"The what?"

"It's a real thing. I didn't believe in it either…but then moving here…and dealing with being a second wife and all. I guess it wasn't as easy as I thought it was going to be."

"Your husband. Where's his first wife?"

"She died."

I cock my head. "How'd you meet?"

Vanessa's eyes light up. "Online, actually. Then I ran into him in person, and we figured out he was the person I had been chatting with all along. Like that movie. What's it called?"

"I hate movies." I know exactly the one. This version seems a little different. I can't yet tell Vanessa that.

"But after Daniel was born, Sean saw me differently. Less like an object of desire. More like a…well, more like a mother, I guess." She's looking far off. I don't know why I'm still here.

"I know having a child was supposed to make me happy. But it didn't. Quite the opposite actually. And the saddest part of all is, it's not his fault."

She takes a deep breath. I'm just about to make a run for it when she says, "Do you know what it's like to hate yourself, Melanie?"

"No. I'm a surface level kind of person, to tell you the truth."

Of course, I don't tell her the real truth. That I don't know because I don't have real feelings.

She meets my eye. "Well, I do. My son, he deserves better. I know what it must look like to someone like you. But I clean, and I take these pills, and that's enough for me. It has to be."

I nod. She really should know better than to offer up this kind of honesty. Someone should warn her; it'll only get her into trouble.

CHAPTER TWENTY-FOUR

TOM

When I add it all up, ten grand and some change is what it takes to make Melanie happy. A car lease, clothing items no doubt made by slave laborers in horrific conditions, in addition to visits to the rejuvenation center for spa treatments, laser hair removal, and body sculpting. Who knew it could be so easy on someone else's dime?

She looks good. Life is grand. We're on an upswing. Nothing can stop us now. But it only leaves one question...what will it take to keep her happy?

When I was in junior high we participated in the Million Dollar Project. Now, I'm not exactly a young guy, but I start by saying that it is far, far easier these days than it was back then to blow a million bucks.

Back then, I thought it would be a dream, all those dollars. So many zeros. I literally dreamed about all the stuff I would buy. Being a poor kid, I assure you, it was a lot.

In the end though, there was a bigger lesson than getting rid of all those zeros. I was surprised to find that having the fake money hadn't made me as happy as I thought it would. I was surprised to find it was a burden trying to spend it all.

I wanted more to manage it than see it fly out the window on fleeting happiness. What I learned is it took very little to actually make me happy. I realized then my threshold was lower than a lot of people's. It was lower than June's, and it's certainly lower than Melanie's. This adds up to a compatibility issue.

Clearly, I know my part in the problem: I have expensive taste in women. One I've managed to solve in the short-term by throwing off expenses onto the church's back. But it's only a matter of time before someone finds out. Not everyone gets to be Mark Jones. My work is to see how long I can.

Basically, you could say I'm testing his tolerance threshold. He hasn't yet realized this. But he will. What Mark needs is something to worry about other than the killing spree he wants me to embark upon. It's exhausting, this business of murder. Add in trying to maintain a job, and a home, and deal with a needy wife, and well, I have no idea who has the time for this. It's time-consuming interviewing contract killers, trying to nab the proper one for the job while managing everyday life and trying to keep one's hands clean in the process. It requires speaking in code, secret meetings, and a transfer of funds. I know enough to know you're guilty the moment money exchanges hands. No one even has to die. Suffice it to say, I'm still not convinced I shouldn't handle matters myself. Get my feet wet, so to speak.

In the meantime, as I weigh my options, life goes on as normal. I mostly work. It's big business shuffling digits around, hiding some, bringing others to light. This is an art, crafting things the way you want them to be. Even numbers. Especially numbers.

Speaking of art, Melanie's spending is out of control. She appears to be consumed with improving herself. She's obsessed with what the other wives are up to. Lunching or brunching or whatever is popular these days. I'm too busy making it all work to dig too deep. It's tough to stay caught up on the trends with so many balls in the air.

One morning over breakfast Melanie says to me, "You'll be happy to know I scheduled my rhinoplasty for next week."

This is news to me. "Your nose is fine."

"Beth doesn't think so." She points. "And I've always had this little bump..."

I squint. "I have twenty-twenty vision, and I see nothing."

"Don't worry. It's outpatient. So, I'll be home in time for dinner."

"Do you know how they perform rhinoplasty? They literally chisel your bone. With a chisel and a hammer."

"I watched YouTube videos," she says.

"Your eyes will be black...I've heard it's quite painful."

"Did you try and talk June out of the boob job?"

I deadpan. "No. Why?"

"Nothing," she tells me. "I just thought you might be worried that the same thing might happen to me."

"Anesthesia is relatively safe," I inform her. "In most cases."

I watch as she crosses the kitchen.

"I was wondering something..."

I hope it leads to sex.

"How many men at New Hope have younger wives?"

Talking about other women rarely leads to sex. "Why do you ask?"

She twists her mouth. "Just curious."

"I really like this one," I mention, stabbing at my french toast. If she's going to blow off my desire for a morning quickie by talking about other women, I'll join her.

Melanie tilts her head. "This chef," I say. "I think this one can stay awhile."

"Tom?" She repeats my name, which is her way of reminding me of her question. "How many?"

"I don't know."

She softens. "Like, what percentage would you say?"

I spin the bread around in the syrup and watch it pool

together. Same as blood, I tell myself. Call it conditioning, if you will.

"Tom!" I meet my wife's eye. For a second, I consider killing her now. At least then I could enjoy my breakfast in peace. But she looks so good in that new nightie, and I haven't yet found a replacement, so I keep it simple instead. "It's fairly common in this tax bracket."

~

Another email from Adam arrives. This time thankfully I'm already on my way into the office.

The subject line reads: *Only open if you're alone.*

Not again.

I am alone. But I would have opened it anyway.

Staring at me on the screen are words that change everything.

Melanie uploaded a photo of New Hope vitamins to Instalook. Mark is livid. That's proprietary information, Tom. Surely, you had to have warned her. But brace yourself...that's not the worst of it...not for you. I'm sorry, man. You need to be careful. Not only that, you won't want to hear what I'm about to say. Melanie's been visiting Vanessa Bolton. Sean's wife. Which I guess isn't such a bad thing considering the rest of it...

Fine, I'll bite. I write back. *The rest of it?*

Adam responds immediately. *Supposedly, Melanie told her she was never really pregnant—that she tricked you into marrying her.*

Everyone knows Sean Bolton's wife is crazy, I type. *We've sent her for reprogramming, what like six times? And, what's wrong with posting the vitamins? I'm sure she thought it was branding. That's what Beth wants...*

My notification chimes. I scan Adam's response. *It was the ingredients she posted. Pretty telling, don't you think?*

I don't write back. I call Mark.

"Don't worry," I tell him. "It'll be taken care of tonight."

CHAPTER TWENTY-FIVE

MELANIE

Planned obsolescence. I can see what's happening here. What a surprise to realize my husband is not the first man in the church to bring home a new young wife shortly after being recently widowed. I've learned about seven cases in the neighborhood so far. One of the wives died like June, two have committed suicide and the other four simply disappeared.

What I intend to find out for sure, before my gravy train runs out, is just how much Tom knows. As soon as the time is right, I have every intention of a confrontation. In the meantime, I need to safe guard my future. More than anything, I'd like a taste of the settled in, married life, I'm always hearing about.

When Tom calls me from work a few days later, and I detect blatant anger in his voice, I think the time has come to go toe-to-toe. "Pack a bag," he tells me. Those three words put the brakes on things.

"Why?"

"Melanie," he says with a heavy sigh. I hear the exhaustion in his voice. It's the opposite of what a vacation is supposed to feel like. This doesn't sound like the Tom I know, so calm, so sure of himself. "I'm going to give you a set of instructions and I need you to listen to me. This is serious."

"How serious?"

"Don't leave the house, serious."

I wait for him to go on.

"We're taking a trip, serious."

For Tom to do anything spur of the moment, I know he's right. To him, this is serious. To me, it sounds like an adventure. "What should I pack?"

"Lightly. That's all that matters. We don't want to raise any red flags."

All of a sudden, this is starting to sound like a bad movie.

"Can you at least give me a clue? What can I expect— temperature-wise?"

"I haven't decided."

I think he's lying. With my husband, everything is decided. "What if I need to go shopping?"

"You can shop when we get there. In the meantime, don't pay anyone any visits, don't answer the door, close the blinds, make it look like no one is home, and whatever you do, do not leave the house."

"Jesus. You're not—"

"I have some things to take care of here at the office," he says cutting me off. "And then I'll be home."

I stare out the window. I think he's lost his mind.

"Oh, and Melanie—"

"Yeah?"

"For God's sake, don't post anything to social media."

~

When I hang up the phone, I realize this must have something to do with Instalook. Tom hates social media so I'm not surprised. I open the app and scan my profile to see what could have pissed him off. Sometimes Beth posts for me. She says I'm still getting the hang of it, and when you're building something, momentum is important.

Sure enough, Beth has posted three photos on my account. One of new shoes, a photo of some weird looking food that only a tiny bird could find appetizing, and a photo of me in a yoga pose she snapped last week. She isn't all wrong. My profile has grown by twelve hundred followers in three days. She assures me this is good. I say there should be more. I'm half-dressed in most of the shots. She says this helps with the momentum of things.

That's when I see it. The shot I took of Vanessa's "vitamins." My breath catches in my throat. A lump forms around it. I hadn't meant to post that, as Beth would say, I'm still getting the hang of it. This reminds me I never did look up the ingredients.

First things first—I delete the photo from Instalook. It doesn't match with my theme or color scheme. Beth is always getting onto me about this. She drones on and on about aesthetics and how important they are to my target demographic. I bet she finally mentioned this to Tom, and that's why he's insisted on the trip. She must have convinced him I need something interesting. Probably something to match my color scheme. You're selling an image, she's always saying. I hope for my sake the image she's going for now happens to be exotic. I could really do for a turquoise beach. I mentioned this to Tom. But he only knows work. That's why it's nice to have someone else do your bidding. Someone like Beth. Surely, my husband will understand. It feels nice to use a trick from his playbook.

I scan my phone for a photo to upload so Beth can see I'm doing my job. If it needs to be on the teal side of the color chart, then so be it. Maybe this will help Tom with his destination decision. I know how much my husband wants Beth's approval. As I'm scrolling through the photos in my album the shot of Vanessa's vitamins catches my eye.

I must know. I open Google and type in the first ingredient into the search bar: sodium fluoride.

What I come up with is a whole host of articles. Apparently, especially in large quantities, sodium fluoride is a neurotoxin. I don't know what constitutes as large but I know Vanessa mentioned she takes three capsules, three times a day. I could barely remember to take my birth control pill, I'd said. She told me she lives and dies by her alarm.

Crazy, I'd said.

But the more I read, the more I realize it could have something to do with what she's taking. According to the internet, sodium fluoride effects memory, IQ and a whole host of other things. Several articles cite that it causes calmness and complacency. Who knows what's fake news these days and yet this could explain why Vanessa acts dumbed-down, more like a robot than a person. Surely, this has to explain why she cooks and cleans and child-rears to her heart's content. I don't know anyone in their right mind who would sign up for that kind of boring life.

~

I SPEND THE MORNING PACKING MY SUITCASE AND ORGANIZING many of my new things. I don't want to bring along too much, otherwise my husband will think I don't have a reason to shop. Things have been good between us lately; the last thing I want is a fight. Especially since I can't be sure he won't replace me. There's a lot riding on this. I haven't yet secured an upgrade, nor do I have a significant enough investment to warrant the kind of divorce settlement I'd need to sustain this kind of lifestyle. Plus, I like it here. I finally have something I've wanted my whole life. Friends. I haven't managed to mess it up yet, and I don't plan to anytime soon. I have a bestie now, thanks to Beth, and the other women are starting to look up to me. But there's another issue too. A bigger one. I think I might actually feel something for Tom.

I've been practicing. I've been praying about it. There's a method to my madness.

By the early afternoon, after I've packed and internet researched Vanessa's problems, and Tom still isn't home, I dig out his and June's wedding album. He keeps it at the top of his closet. I flip through the photos just as I do most every day. This one is no different. I realize I want that. Then I pray. I breathe in and out. I do what they call meditation. Then I pause and pray some more. I tell myself, if I can love him for one minute, then I can make myself love him for two, and if I can love him for two, I can love him for three, and if I can love him for three, I can love him forever. I tell myself I can feel something. Something for real, something like love, and in this moment, even that seems insurmountable.

~

IT GOES LIKE THIS: ME. A BOTTLE. GHOSTS. REMINDERS. Mementos. Truth. This is how the majority of my days unfold in this house, in this stupid neighborhood, on this stupid idyllic street. I shuffle my way through the wedding album. This causes me to pull from my secret stash of scotch. Sometimes I only go for wine. Scotch is what I reach for when I'm not messing around. This feels like the good old days. Then I get this itch, I can't stop. It helps if I do another shot and then another. I keep trying to satisfy it, trying to make it go away. But eventually, it gets so bad I have to scratch it, and this is when I log in to June's computer, still in its place, like so many other artifacts. I click on the icon she had on her desktop, the one with all their family photos. I don't stop until I get to their wedding video. It looks nothing like ours. It's like picking a scab. I never feel the pain. I just want it to scar so I have proof. This is why I keep going back.

Who am I kidding? *Tom will never love me the way he loved you,* I say to the screen. I say this to her, her in his heart, her with her eyes wide and full of glee. Her on the walls. Her everywhere. In the video, she throws her head back and laughs. She's taunting me. She knows.

This makes me know too. I'll be the first to admit, I don't know my husband that well. But I know a few things. He could never have killed June himself. He wasn't looking for a replacement when he found me— he was making a mistake. He was looking for a distraction.

I know enough to know that he'll never love me like he should. He'll never love me the way I want to love him.

BY LATE AFTERNOON, I'M PASSED OUT ON THE COUCH. I AWAKEN TO the robot vacuum powering itself on. I sit up slowly. My mouth is dry and I'm in proper need of a glass of water. Brushing the hair from my eyes, I glance out the front window, trying to assess how long I've been out. I notice there's something in the street and then as I lean closer toward the window, I see it isn't something, but rather someone. A little boy on a tricycle. In the middle of the street. Surely, his mother is nearby. I move toward the window. The street is mostly deserted. No one seems to notice there's a child in the street. I realize I'm either still dreaming, or I'm more inebriated than I thought.

I force myself from the sofa and make my way to the door, where I pause to check my disheveled appearance in the mirror that hangs in the entryway. I know Tom asked me to stay in. But there's the kid. I look terrible, and I can't very well let the neighbors see me like this. I go back to the window to check again. The kid is still there. Damn it.

What if Tom hits him on his way in the drive? He's low enough to the ground that he may not even see him. If this happens, we'll have to cancel our trip. I walk to the door and place my hand on the knob. I check myself in the mirror once more, leaning in to wipe away the mascara that's smudged under my eyes. I straighten my top. At least I'm wearing the workout gear Beth suggested. This way if I get to be on the news for saving a kid, she'll be extra happy to see I'm promoting her favorite brand. I'm an influencer now, she says. If we want the other women of New Hope to look and feel their best, it's up to us to set an example. God forbid, they should think for themselves.

Whatever. Maybe I could even get a good selfie with the kid and the sunset in the background. Everything is about lighting, Beth assures me. Imagine the likes I could get for saving someone's life.

"Hey," I call to the kid when I'm halfway across the yard. "You're in the street."

He looks at me, his big brown eyes wide.

"What's your name?" I don't recognize him. I ask where he lives. He points. His nose is snotty. "What's your name?" I ask again.

This time he answers, but it's gibberish. I assume this means he's not old enough to talk. At least not coherently. I'm having a hard time myself. "How old are you?"

I shield my eyes from the sun. He holds up two fingers. Proudly.

"Where do you live?"

He looks one way and then another.

Finally, he points to a wooded area down the lane. "Deer," he says.

He has no idea.

"Don't worry, kid," I tell him. "You and I, we're in the same boat."

"Here," I say lifting his tricycle and pointing it in the other direction. "Let's get you out of the street."

I ask him once again where he lives. He points. I ask him to take me there. "Take me to your toys," I plead. I have a plane to catch and planes don't wait. Tom will be home soon, and I know how much he hates tardiness. The last thing I want is to fight on vacation. So this has to work. If it doesn't, I'm going to be forced to set him on someone's doorstep, where I'll ring the bell and run. Except everyone has cameras these days, and I can't have the neighbors thinking I'm irresponsible. I don't know much about kids, but I know he's a male one and nothing stands between men and their toys. "Your toys, "I say. "Where are they?'

It takes forty-five minutes, but he finally proves my point when we find his home a block over. He waltzes right up and rings the bell. His father, or who I presume to be his father answers. Like mine, his hair is disheveled. The kid caught him by surprise too.

"You," he says, rubbing his face. "How'd you get out there?"

"He was in the street," I say and suddenly, I'm angry. His child was in the street, and he was sleeping. The boy could have been killed or kidnapped, and he was sleeping. Everyone knows parents don't get to sleep. "You might want to keep an eye on your kid."

The guy opens the door wider, and I watch as the little boy toddles in. His father looks at me, yawns and says, "thanks" before promptly slamming the door in my face.

~

I WALK THROUGH THE FRONT DOOR TO FIND I HAVE FIVE MISSED calls from Tom, one from Beth, and two from an unknown number.

I set the phone down. I can't deal with either of them right now. The search and rescue mission has worn me out. I fill a glass with water. The little boy's face flashes in my mind. I have to admit, he was kind of cute. For a split second, I wonder what it would have been like to have kept him. You know, like finders, keepers. It must be the liquor talking. That or all of the family photos. It must be the nostalgia of Tom and June's stupid memories that's causing my sudden neediness. Whatever the case, his parents really should be more careful. If you ask me, it seems like a simple way of going about getting a kid. All you have to do is find one whose parents aren't looking, and bam, just like that, you get to skip out on the whole morning sickness, weight gain, and pushing them out of your vagina part. Lucky for them, I am not in the market for a kid. Not today. Not ever.

Just the thought sobers me up. The phone rings. It's Tom again. "You'll never believe —"

"I've called six times." I hear neatly concealed rage on the other end of the line.

"I found a kid."

"What?"

"A kid. In the street. I found him."

"I told you not to go outside."

"He was out there alone."

"Where is he now?"

"I took him home."

"Good, listen...I'm almost done here." I hear him moving about. The speaker rustles. "Are you packed?"

"Have been for hours."

There's more rustling. "Perfect. Eat something. I'll be home shortly."

"Don't we have a plane to catch?"

I listen as he clears his throat. He hates it when I fish for information he doesn't want to give. "Not right away."

We hang up. I decide to make Tom dinner. I want to clear the air between us. I want to make amends. I want to show him what he's done to me. I want to know if there's a future between us. I want to know if he could ever love me the way he loved her. I want to burn this house to the ground. We could start over.

I begin by opening one of the bottles of wine we received after we married. Cooking is hard work, it turns out. One glass turns into two, and two turns into three, until before I know it, I'm watching the wedding video again, and I have to open a new bottle just so he won't know I've finished off the first.

When dinner is ready, which happens to be Tom's favorite, lasagna, and the only thing I really know how to make, I finish off another glass of red. Then I put on a nice dress, and heels. I want to show Tom I can be like his old wife. But better. I straighten up, the way he likes it. I don't stop there. For good measure, I don't just hide the bottle like I usually would. I go around back so I can bury the wine bottle deep in the trash. The hard stuff, I put in the neighbors. I've heaved the lid halfway up when I feel something hard shoved in my back. I stumble forward. The wind is knocked out of me. "You really shouldn't be out here."

~

WHAT I'M THINKING IS...THIS ISN'T GOING TO END WELL. AT LEAST not for me. How I'm feeling is, not ready to die. What I know is, everybody's somebody's fool. And, whoever said small things don't matter, never lit a wildfire with a single match.

I finish the recording. But I'm not holding out false hope. No one is coming to save me. I'm naked in a trunk. How much worse can it get? It's like Mark Twain said, it's no wonder that truth is stranger than fiction. Fiction has to make sense.

Even if the recording uploads, they'll say I'm a liar. It's been this way my whole life. I tried to tell my sister not to make that leap. No one believed me. I tried to tell my parents about my first boyfriend, the only one they ever actually liked, and the wicked games he liked to play. I tried to save the animals. I couldn't even save my sister.

They didn't believe me about him either. He comes from a great family, they said. They were almost right about that. Except that great family meant he had so much money that to entertain himself he told me he had to go deeper and deeper. For a while he was into dog fighting. He said it beat hookers and blow. Anyway, he took me once. To a fight. There were a lot of people there. Big money maker, he said. Two dogs went into the pen. I watched intently. How much money, I asked. He told me to watch. It was not a time for talking, he said. One must respect the fight. It wasn't much of a fight, I said. One dog was reluctant. He's just standing there, I said. He should be doing something, I said.

Sometimes they don't, my boyfriend said.

So, yeah, if you're watching this, I understand what you're going through. I know you'll probably think it wasn't a match. I thought that, too.

My girlfriend expected a fight, he told the guy heading it up after the reluctant dog bled out onto the pavement. His blood was practically black, his tongue hanging out the side of his mouth. My boyfriend punched him in the face. The guy, not the dog. Blood squirted from his nose like how those firemen go around letting the water out of hydrants. That's how it looked. Like a waterfall you couldn't stop because it was too fast. And it kept coming. I thought he might bleed out right there. Like the dog, only his blood was bright red. His nose hung all funny too. It was like his bones had just collapsed into his face. This, he said to the gusher, with a nod, was not a fight. This was a suicide mission.

He nearly beat the guy to death. All I could do was watch. I will say he was good in bed, that one. Always up for something new. Always one to keep you on your toes. One never knew quite what to expect. Let me tell you. But they say exes are that way for a reason and you don't want to know what he does for fun these days. Trust me.

I hit the front of the trunk with a thud as the car comes to an abrupt stop. My grip on the phone slips and it goes flying. I fish around desperately in the dark. The driver kills the engine. Finally, my fingers land on it. The screen lights up. I have bars. I press upload on the video and hope it works. I start to dial 9-1-1.

The trunk is popped. There isn't time. I stuff the phone under the carpeting. For this, I need to be hands-free. I shouldn't have stripped out of my clothes, I realize now. Not only were they designer, I've practically offered up an invitation for what's to come. My future is bleak. My final moments on this earth will not be pleasant. The trunk lifts. It's show time.

CHAPTER TWENTY-SIX

TOM

I'm seated at my desk, poring over the numbers from last quarter. I really need to get home. But I can't. Not until I complete this transaction. Something is missing. Something is off.

I'm concentrating so hard on finding the missing link that it startles me when the phone rings, the sound thrusting me hard and violently back into the real world. It's not that I'm jumpy. I just thought I'd had the ringer switched off.

I pick up the receiver and shove it back down in its cradle. I'm in a hurry as it is. As a matter of principle, I keep the ringer switched off to avoid such disturbances, so whoever was calling shouldn't have expected to reach me anyhow. That's what my secretary is for. I silence the ringer and turn my attention back to the balance sheet. I sigh in relief, not because what I'm seeing makes me happy. It should. But it doesn't. And it won't make New Hope leaders very happy either. The accounts are nearly emptied. A parting gift, I guess you could say.

Still, the problem is, there should be more, in excess of two million dollars more if we're being exact and trust me, I am. For hours now I've racked my brain. I've meticulously combed the bank statements trying to find out how and more importantly *when* the transfer could have taken place. Two million dollars does not just disappear into thin air. I'll find it eventually. I have to. It is not in my nature to leave things undone. But then, this is why I've always liked numbers. They tell the truth, even when people don't. In reality, it's not the money I'm in search of. It's the truth.

At some point, Martha comes in, a cup of hot tea in one hand, a stack of mail in the other. She places the tea on the corner of my desk and the mail in its rightful spot. "You've had a message," she says.

I adjust the handle on my mug to the perfect 45-degree angle. Martha is pretty good. But on occasion even she gets it wrong. This feels like a betrayal. "Did you switch my ringer on?"

Her eyes narrow. I nod toward the phone to make myself clear.

"Of course not." Clearly, she's offended. In part about my calling her out, but also because I'm working late, and she would like to be dismissed. "Why would I do such a thing?"

Why would you get the angle wrong after all these years, I want to ask. But to do so would only cost me more time, and there's no point in wasting it when I still have a little work ahead of me yet. To rectify the situation, I answer her question indirectly by taking the ruler from my desk drawer, shifting the mug to the original position in which it was placed on my desk. Then I lean forward at eye level and measure it. I meet Martha's gaze and smile.

"See," I motion. "Numbers don't lie." My imperfect secretary shakes her head and sees herself out without another word. Women don't like it when you call them on their imperfections. Explicitly or implicitly.

I open my browser and type out an email letting my secretary know she's dismissed for the evening. It's easier to keep communication to a minimum with people like Martha, but in this case, my reasoning is two-fold. I need a paper trail.

What I don't say is the dismissal is permanent. Right now, I need to focus on locating the missing money. I need to get home. I need to get out of dodge.

As I finish the email to Martha, my emergency phone rings. It stops me in my tracks.

Only two people know this number, and one of them is dead. I open the drawer and fish the cell phone out. Caller ID says it's June. But that's impossible.

I swipe to take the call. I don't have a choice.

I don't say hello. This isn't the kind of call that requires pleasantries.

"You'll want to come home," the voice tells me calmly. "To see about your wife."

I glance at the watch on my wrist. I have a lot of work to do here yet. I could say this, but it's of little use. So, I settle on the obvious. "My wife—"

"Yes," he says. "The one who isn't dead yet."

CHAPTER TWENTY-SEVEN

MELANIE

"Melanie, why?" I hear my mother cry. She's pleading with me. I don't understand. "Why didn't you say something?"

"She didn't know," I hear my father say. He tells me to go inside. My nanny waves me in with one hand, the other covers her mouth. My mother wails. It's a guttural scream, one like an animal might make. The kind you never forget.

I watch as my father comforts her. "She's just a girl, darling."

"She could have alerted us." She throws up her hands and then when she can't figure out what else to do with them, she covers her face. I watch as my father rubs her back. He uses small circles. I'm old enough to know my shapes. "She could have done *something,* Charles. You know she could have."

I look on from inside the window that overlooks the backyard. There are men in jackets, men taking photos. Police people are talking to mommy and daddy.

My sister's lifeless body lies beside the pool. She looks like she is sleeping. But I know she is not.

"Watch me jump Melly. Watch me."

"You're not supposed to," I said. "Mommy and Daddy are sleeping."

She climbed higher on the diving board. "You're such a baby," she teased. "Who cares?" She bounced. "I'm a big girl. I can swim," she told me, her knees knocking together. Once. Twice. Three times. Her face lit up with that Cheshire cat-like grin she used on mommy and daddy. "Not like you."

"I'm telling." I meant to run inside. I meant to, but I couldn't look away.

"You're such a tattle-tale."

"Am not." I folded my arms across my chest and looked up at my parent's bedroom window. Tiffany was going to be in so much trouble. Mommy never got mad at Tiffany. Not like she did me. For this, she would. Finally.

"Do you dare me?" My sister held out her arms for balance. She pretended she was walking a tightrope the way we did when our bedroom floor turned into lava. "Come on, you big baby," she laughed. "Jump with me."

I shook my head. "Mommy will be mad."

"Dare me then."

"Fine," I said. "I double-dare you."

Her eyes shifted. "If I do it, what will you give me?"

I thought about it. Tiffany had so much. She was a good girl, mommy said. Not like me. "My donut. I'll save half for you."

I could see the wheels turning in her mind. We were waiting for Daddy to wake up. If we were good girls and watched cartoons so mommy and daddy could get extra sleep, Daddy promised he'd take us for donuts. Mommy didn't like him getting us all sugared up. But sometimes Daddy won.

"The whole thing," Tiffany said. She expected me to say yes, I could see it in her eyes. That was the thing about my sister. She had a way of making you do things.

It would make mommy happy if I wasn't all sugared up. "Okay," I relented. She smiled like she was in on a secret I wasn't privy to. And then she jumped. I waited for her to come up. I watched the water. I stood on the side looking in. It took a long time. And then she was asleep forever.

~

"GET UP, SLEEPING BEAUTY," THE MALE VOICE ORDERS. I WASN'T sleeping which is how I see it's Mark standing over the trunk. I'm exactly what you'd call surprised. I curl into myself. "She's naked," he says. "Why is she naked?"

"I didn't do it," Adam confesses, holding his palms up. "She's pretty hammered. Just started dropping her clothes all over the place."

"You." I blink rapidly peering at Adam. "You did this?"

"Wonderful," Mark says. "Now Beth really is going to kill me."

Adam shrugs. Mark sighs. They both stare at me in my birthday suit. "You know she hates it when I bring work home."

"Tom should be on his way."

"Where are we?" I ask. *Make a note of your surroundings.* My eyes feel like they're matted shut. It's dark out. My mouth is dry. I feel like I've bathed in my own saliva. My head feels like someone has it in their fist and they're squeezing and releasing, squeezing and releasing. It doesn't hurt. But there's pressure. So much pressure. "I need water."

"Shut up," they say in unison.

The two of them chat amongst themselves. I'm not the praying kind, exactly, but I say a silent wish that the video uploaded to Instalook. With my luck, it'll probably get flagged on account of me being topless.

"Come on," Mark says. "Let's get you covered, before my wife kills me."

Adam lifts me from the trunk.

"Am I going to die?" Obviously. The trunk is about as far from first class as it gets. They don't put you there without reason. You have to earn it.

"If you don't shut up," they say, again in unison. Mark finishes. "You might."

Fuck. I reach for the phone. My fingers brush it, but as I'm lifted, they're forced to let go. It's like one of those claw games where you try to win stuffed animals. It just slipped right through my fingertips.

I try to make a break and turn back for it. It's no use. Adam's grip tightens around my forearm. They've closed the trunk.

"I need to get back in there," I tell them. "I forgot something."

"Your shoelaces?" Mark laughs.

I'm not wearing shoes.

It's a humid, cloudy, moonless night. Which is better than the alternative, on account of my nakedness. The further we get up the walk, the more I recognize where we are. Beth's lake house. I've seen the photos on Instalook.

Inside, Mark tosses a robe in my direction. "Beth will be down soon."

I'm sober now. But I could use some alcohol to numb me up, if only to touch the outer edges of my consciousness. I have a bad feeling about being here. I have a feeling I know what this is. They're going to human sacrifice me.

"Sit," Mark orders, once I've dressed in the robe. It's not so hard to get people to do what you want when you're holding a gun. "I hear you've been snooping around..."

"Me?" I motion toward my chest and then shake my head. "No."

"Here," he says, handing Adam the gun. "Just in case she tries to run."

"There's something I need to know," Mark informs me. "Is it you who is the liar, or is that husband of yours in on this too?"

"I don't know what you're talking about."

He makes a clucking sound with his tongue meant to convey his disappointment. "And to think we've given you so much. Look at you, looking like a Barbie doll. And this is how you show your appreciation?"

"I'm flattered at the comparison," I say. "But I have no idea what you're talking about."

Beth comes down the stairs. "Finally." I straighten the robe. "Now things should start making sense."

But then nothing makes sense because Beth crosses the room and backhands me. "After all I did for you." She hits me again. And again. She has a way of making her resentments felt. When my tongue touches my lip, I taste blood.

She's been crying. I can tell by the way her chin quivers.

"Maybe we should talk about this," Adam suggests.

"What's there to talk about?" Beth sniffles. She can't decide whether to be sad or angry. The struggle between her lack of control and her attempt to suppress it is disappointing. I'm embarrassed for her.

"She's a liar," Mark says. "She put the whole project at risk."

"What project? Can someone tell me what's going on?" I pull my lip between my teeth and suck the blood away. It can be dangerous to ask a question when you already know the answer.

"What the fuck?" Beth inhales deeply. She's staring at her phone. Her eyes meet mine for a second, and then she looks over at her husband before finally settling on Adam. "You didn't bother to take her phone?"

Recognition registers on his face.

"She Instalook Live'd from the trunk."

"Fuck." Mark runs his hands through his hair. "Where's the phone?"

"Don't worry," Beth says to him. She exhales loudly. "Her location settings appear to be off and thank God I'm an admin on her account. I deleted it." I watch as she holds up her screen, on it a vague outline of my face. My lips are moving, but nothing is happening. Beth laughs and shakes her head slowly from side to side. "It wouldn't have mattered anyway," Beth laughs. "She had the sound off."

Adam paces. "So what does this mean?"

"It means nothing," Beth assures him.

"Hey," I say. "Twenty-thousand people were in queue to watch that."

"It's basically just her face in the dark," Mark says as he glares at Beth's phone. He shakes his head and then crosses the room. "Twenty-thousand. Unbelievable." I watch as he fishes a magazine from the coffee table. He holds it up to my face. "Recognize this guy?"

I do recognize that guy. "No," I say.

"His name is Richard Fisher. Richard is the head pastor of Divine Life."

"So?"

"So, you slept with him."

I should say nothing. Silence is rarely misunderstood. Instead, I cock my head. "And?"

"And—Richard Fisher just so happens to be one of our biggest competitors."

"You're a church. How can you have competitors?"

This time it's Mark who hits me.

"And this guy, Elliot Walls…" He holds up another photo. "You slept with him too."

"Jesus." Adam rubs his jaw.

"Do you know who Elliot is?"

I shake my head.

"He's the finance manager at All Saints."

I roll my shoulders. It was cramped in that trunk. "Okay?"

"What I think Mark is trying to say," Adam tells me. "Is that you've fucked all the competition."

Beth stands over me. I brace myself for what I know is coming. Out of everyone, girls always fight the dirtiest. "And what I want to know is…why?"

“It’s not personal.” I wait for her to hit me again. It’s coming. I can see it on her face. Now doesn’t seem like the time to bring up the fact I can’t feel any pain. “They’re philanthropists. They donate to my parents charity.”

“How convenient,” Mark says.

“Really, more of a coincidence,” I say.

“I have to run,” Adam says. This gets everyone’s attention. Especially mine. He nods at his phone. “The wife is expecting me home for dinner.”

“That’s fine,” Beth replies, dismissing him. Then to everyone but me she says, “Tom will be here soon. We’ll let him handle the traitor.”

“I’m not a traitor,” I say. “I just really like sex.”

“Shut up,” they all say.

I watch Adam leave. He doesn’t even say goodbye. Fair weather friends. They’ll get you every time. I should have known better. I thought he might help me. I thought my charm would work on him. Clearly, it didn’t. I feel like something very bad is going to happen.

CHAPTER TWENTY-EIGHT

TOM

To go or not to go, that is the question. I could just as easily skip town. Take the money and run. Keep it simple. I'm on the fence about it, to be sure. What would it take to drive in the other direction and not look back? What does it take for a person to betray those they're supposed to love most? Do I have it in me?

People like to think it's the spilt-second decisions that make the difference, do or don't, walk away or stay, and sometimes it is. More often than not, it isn't. Usually, there's momentum behind that decision, a whole set of forces, seen or unseen, leading up to the act. It's important to understand those forces. It's important to understand what momentum can do. You let things build, brush aside your feelings, delay the conversation, ignore the slight gnaw in your gut. Until one day, it happens. You're sucker-punched. *Jab. Uppercut. Right hook.*

How could I have missed the signs, you'll ask yourself.

You didn't miss them. You just weren't looking hard enough.

June insisted we take the family to Cabo San Lucas one summer. It was against my better judgment to travel to a country where the odds of kidnapping are quite high. But June insisted, so I took a class on counterterrorism and negotiation tactics. Just in case. I'd hoped not to have to put them to good use, but as they say, every dog has his day.

First, I can tell you this. In any negotiation, there's always leverage. Negotiation is never a linear formula: add A to B to get C. Everyone has blind spots. Mark is no different. He's irrational, yes, but like anyone, he has hidden needs, a universe of variables that can be leveraged to change his ideas and expectations.

Now that he has something of mine in his possession, the goal is to shape his reality so it conforms to what I ultimately want to give him, not what he initially thinks he deserves.

And if this doesn't work, I can always throw a bit of jujitsu in the mix.

"I told you," Mark warned. "I gave you time. I was patient. You should have moved on your first target by this point."

"How?"

"I don't know—you're a smart man. Figure it out."

"But how could I do that? I've been dealing with the quarterly reports… I've been up to my eyeballs in work." Already, I feel my training kicking in. It's like a bicycle. Once you learn, you can't forget.

As I expected, his tone grew more agitated during our second phone call. "I told you to handle it or I'd handle her."

I want to ask why he's doing this. Why now, when I was so close to getting away from here. But that's not the question to ask. "How am I supposed to do that?" I demand with a loud exhale. *Never ask questions that start with "why." "Why" is always an accusation, in any language.*

"Like I said. You're a smart guy. I trust that you'll figure it out." Mark excels at speaking vaguely. Best not to incriminate himself. But the manipulation, the incessant persuasion, the indirect bullying it's all there just underneath the surface waiting to be unearthed, begging to be misunderstood.

"You had choices," he cautions. Nails on a chalkboard to my ears. When people issue threats, directly or indirectly, they create ambiguities they fully intend to exploit. In this case, it's me. A loss, even a perceived one, is far worse than a gain. He knows this. It could be conscious. It could be subconscious. But he knows. This is why he has my wife.

"I'm sure we'll figure something out."

"Do you want to make this right, Tom? That's what I need to know."

"Yes, but how?" *Yes is nothing without how*. I listen to Mark breathe into the receiver. I let the silence between us linger. The less one says in any negotiation, the better. Listening is one of the most powerful tools a person can have in their arsenal—one which few people utilize for all it's worth.

"You tell me."

The secret to gaining the upper hand in negotiation is giving the other side the illusion of control.

"How about this...how about I come to you and we come up with a plan? You know better than anyone that acting in haste is senseless."

"Okay," he says, as though this was what he'd wanted all along. "That sounds good. We're at the lake house."

"The lake house." It's not meant to be a question. I turn the car around and I drive in the direction of my wife's captors. I've already lost enough. I won't let them make me a coward, too.

"Oh, and Tom..."

"Yes?"

"Don't fuck this up."

~

I VEER LEFT IN THE DIRECTION I'VE BEEN INSTRUCTED TO TAKE. NOT to my house. For this to go as planned, I knew I had to negotiate away from there. I had to come at Mark with a surprise. I call him back.

"This is good," I say. "About the lake house."

He doesn't say anything.

"She can't swim."

"Beth is here."

"Mark," I remind him. "We have to do what we have to do." He doesn't know that I know why he wants those men killed. They're not just men my wife slept with. They're competition. Competition that will be as quick to put the move on his devotees as he would be on theirs. Austin isn't big enough yet for multiple gurus. Mark wants to be the only one. I take a deep breath in. "We can't have people thinking deception among us is okay. No one respects weakness."

"No one," he agrees.

"That's why we have to be smart about this. We must send a message without outing ourselves. We have to subdue the enemy without fighting."

"Maybe I should just kill her now." He's testing me. Melanie is Mark's leverage. Without her, there's only me. If he'd wanted to start there, he would have. Mark does not do busy work.

"Whatever you want," I tell him. "I just want what's best for the church. We need strong leadership. We need someone in control. You're always saying that..."

"Excellence, yes." He doesn't think I'm the guy for the job. He wants to—but he's not sure.

Now that I'd anchored his emotions in a minefield of low expectations, I play on his loss aversion. "She's my wife. Wait and let me handle this like I said I would."

Mark wants me to level with him. He seeks control. He wants me to compromise my own. I refuse. People don't compromise because it's right; they compromise because it is easy. It's safe. I refuse to show some pretend moral good that in essence only exists as weakness. Unlike me, most people in a negotiation are driven by fear or by the desire to avoid pain. Too few are driven by their actual goals.

I can hear Mark breathing. I can hear the wheels turning.

"Yeah, you're right. Sometimes it's good to make an example out of a person." He cackles like the unstable person he is. "Don't you think?"

"Yes," I say. "I do."

"At least this way my wife won't get any ideas." He exhales. "Beth never cared for her anyway."

"Beth was right about her all along," I offer as a concession. It's not a lie. That's why it works.

Mark hangs up. I step on the gas. Sure, I could leave her. I could let her answer for her mistakes. The only problem with that is eventually, everyone has to. And as the saying goes, the best way to ride a horse is in the direction in which it is going.

~

It's pitch black out when I arrive, save for the lights that line the drive. I doubt Mark knows about the missing funds yet. Chances are, with my wife around, he has his hands full. That's my play, if things get too bad. I have something he wants—his money—he has something I want—my wife.

"Speak of the devil," he says, opening the door to greet me. I don't even have to knock. I take in what I've walked into: the shiny metal glint of a gun tucked in his waistband.

I follow him into the great room. I've always liked the windows in this place. It helps that at night they look like mirrors. In the reflection, I can see my wife is seated in an armchair, one wrist cuffed to it.

"You realize she could just drag the chair," I say to Mark. Clearly, he doesn't know Melanie when she's determined about something.

He shrugs. "It's a heavy son of a bitch."

Beth is seated on the couch opposite my wife. She doesn't acknowledge me. She's staring at her phone.

"Glad you could finally join us," Melanie says to me, one

eyebrow cocked. She doesn't like how much I've been working recently. "If you'd come home sooner, you could have saved us both a trip out here. Although I'm sure yours was more comfortable."

I glance at Mark. I should have assumed. "You put her in the trunk?"

"She was naked," Beth answers.

This makes sense. I do not recognize her clothes.

Mark pulls me aside. "You say Melanie can't swim..."

"That's right." When Mark wants to make a point, he enjoys taking the scenic route.

"In that case, I thought the lake would be an appropriate place to do the job. Makes sense, doesn't it? Four friends go out on a boat. They take a moonlight swim. Only three come home..."

"There's no moon," I say.

"Details, my friend."

I glance over my shoulder at my wife. "Devil's always in the detail."

She's dressed in jeans that are too big for her, a navy striped boatneck tee and Sperrys. She has a red bandana tied around waterfall curls. "You look like Boating Barbie," I say to her when we walk back into the great room. I hope she takes the hint.

She presses her lips together. "Always one to play the part."

"I let her play around in my closet," Beth mentions. "While we were waiting on you." This doesn't make any sense. If she wants Melanie dead, why would she let her play dress up? Beth glances at the time. "I don't understand why you have a fast car if you insist on driving the speed limit."

I guess this means we're even. But I don't owe Beth the dignity of an answer, so I don't give one. After several moments, Mark clears his throat. Subtlety has never been his strong suit. "Speaking of speed—you haven't seen the new boat, have you?"

I read his expression. He winks. He hasn't told his wife what we've planned. She doesn't know my wife has been brought here to die.

"No," I say. "I haven't."

"You have to see it."

Beth frowns. But she does not look up from her phone. "It's too late to take the boat out, darling."

"Nah."

"You've been drinking."

"You drive."

She uses her toes to point at the wine glass on the coffee table. "I've had a few glasses myself."

"Tom can drive."

Beth lets out a heavy sigh. "You're relentless."

"I hate boats. I can't swim," Melanie says.

I know what she is thinking. We've had this talk before. Once when we were first together. When our relationship consisted of hotel rooms and time constraints. Her teaching me, me teaching her. *Never let them take you to a second location.* I give her a look that asks her to trust me. I can see she doesn't.

"That's okay," Mark tells her. "We won't be doing much of that."

Mark goes over the boat in great detail, which under normal circumstances I would appreciate. Here and now, it feels like overkill. After he's taken nearly an hour of my time explaining boating terminology at length, all the while he and the rest of the crowd consume another bottle of wine, I am finally allowed to stretch my sea legs. "Stay in the middle," he instructs, and you'd think I'd never been on a boat before. "We'll take her over to the cove."

Beth and Melanie sit up front. I'm in the driver's seat. Mark is to my left.

I start out slow at first. Get my bearings. Then I push faster. *Use barriers. Make them guess wrong.* I want my happy ending. It is a speedboat, after all. I push it to the limit. Mark smiles. He likes his toys. Melanie's hair whips in the wind. It's a lovely night, save for what I'm about to do. She glances back at me. I mouth the word jump. She shakes her head slightly. Mark looks at me. We're going so fast he has to yell. He gives me the thumbs up. "She's really something isn't she?"

"She is," I say. I know he's talking about his plaything. I'm talking about mine.

"Jump," I mouth to Melanie. I slow a bit, and then I push the lever all the way down. She doesn't listen as usual.

I correct my steering, wavering just a little. Beth glances back. Mark holds his palm up. He wants me to slow down.

I overcorrect hard to the left. My gut sets.

"Sorry," I yell in Mark's direction. There's an icy burn in my throat. I didn't have to speak to know it was there.

I realize this is it. It's now or never. I want him to realize what is about to happen. I want him to get a feel for having a dead wife. It's still revenge, no matter how short-lived.

His face is contorted as his mind works to slowly piece together his future.

My eyes dart toward Melanie as though to say, *what choice did I have?*

This is for June, I tell myself as I line up the proper angle. And then, all of a sudden, everything is happening in slow motion. Life is on pause, in rewind, before it is in fast forward. Somehow this does not seem like enough for all he's put me through over the years. I want to dig a hole and put him in it. Alive. I want to set fire to his feet and watch it rise until it engulfs the rest of him. I want to starve a pack of dogs and feed him to them limb by limb. There are a million ways I'd like to kill Mark Jones, and I die a little inside knowing that I have to settle on one that will be quick.

I take a hard left straight into the side of the cliff.

I bail, hitting the water hard. Given my speed, I knew I would. I call for Melanie, hoping she managed to make it off in time. Whoever was still on that boat when it hit is no more.

The boat itself is mostly no more. What's left is a blur of fiberglass and aluminum twisted around itself. It's sure to catch fire.

I swim hard. I call for her, searching the water out in front of me. There's nothing but darkness.

After what feels like an eternity, I feel a tug on my arm. My heart leaps into my throat. "Tom!"

"Melanie?"

"Oh my God," she cries. "What were you thinking?"

"I was thinking I don't want to die."

"I can't see anything."

"We have to swim."

"I can't."

"You're doing fine," I say, slipping one arm under hers. "Hang on to me."

I swim. I kick with everything I've got.

"You have to help," I tell her. I'm panting hard. I can't suck in enough air. I smell gasoline. "It could still blow."

"The trick," I tell her, "Is not to panic."

The smoke from the boat rolls over us.

Suddenly, we're moving faster, and eventually, we find, or rather we hit, a jagged edge. I hoist Melanie up.

"I have to catch my breath," I say. "I think my ribs are broken."

"How are we going to get out of here?" She does exactly what I've advised her not to do. She panics.

"We're going to have to swim up the lake for a bit until we find flat land..."

"You know I can't swim, Tom. I can't."

"I'll help you," I assure her. "We'll do it together."

"It's pitch black out here."

"It's better this way."

I hear Melanie pull herself further onto the ledge. "They're dead. We killed them."

"They had a boating accident," I correct her. "We weren't here."

Eventually, she says, "That's really brilliant, Tom. Really brilliant."

"What are you doing?" I can't see anything. "Is there room up there for me?" I don't know if I have the strength to pull myself up.

"Thank you for coming for me." Her voice is far away.

"My pleasure." My ribs ache. "Come down. You have to get back in the water."

"I can't."

"We have to swim now. We can't stay here. Someone's bound to have heard the crash."

She doesn't respond.

"Melanie?"

"I can't, Tom."

"I'll help you." It hurts to talk. It hurts to move. "Just let me catch my breath."

CHAPTER TWENTY-NINE

MELANIE

I meant to help Tom. But my feet come up with another plan without saying so. I can't see my hand in front of my face, but I do my best to search the small area. I'm like a blind person trying to find the light. Just when I'm about to lose hope, my foot finds it first. A rock big enough to do the job. It's larger than I would have liked, but I guess beggars can't be choosy. It barely fits in the palm of my hand. "Tom?"

"Over here," he says. I can hear him; he's trying to drag himself up onto the ledge. He doesn't yet realize I've gone somewhere too dark for him to follow. It's steep, and he's injured. "Stay there," I call out to him. Everyone knows water washes away sin.

"Let me help you," I offer. My voice reverberates in my ears. It smells like a mixture of death and fuel. It smells like plastic burning. Like faint rotten eggs. If I crane my neck far enough I can just barely see what's left of the boat around the way. It burns bright orange. But not bright enough to provide any real light from where I stand. I cough, trying to clear my throat. The smoke feels thick and heavy in my lungs. It feels like it's everywhere. Tom's labored breathing and the water hitting the rocks has a calming effect.

He grunts. I feel the weight of the rock in my hand. I bring it over my head. With everything I have in me, I bring it down onto my husband's skull. I do not want him to suffer because I am weak. I put my back into it, as they say.

"Say hello to June for me."

I lift again and bring it down. It's like one of those lever things at the carnival when you're trying to win a teddy bear. But I'm only trying to win my freedom.

"You should have loved me."

I bring the rock down again.

I feel it collide with bone.

Tom makes a noise. Like static on the radio. I don't know how long these things take. My arms feel like jelly.

I lift the rock as high as I can.

I bring it down again.

Tom sounds like he is gurgling. Like a fish tank on recycle.

Row, row, row your boat.

I bring the rock down. I don't like that sound.

Gently down the stream.

I bring the rock down. I have to make it stop.

Merrily, merrily, merrily, merrily.

I lift higher.

Life is but a dream.

~

I PUSH TOM'S LIFELESS BODY INTO THE WATER AND THEN I SWIM and I swim. I swim until I find flat land, just like Tom said we would do. Then I walk. I walk and I walk. I let my clothes dry out. I have to get home before someone finds the wreckage. I know that if I walk the road along the lake I will eventually come to Beth and Mark's gate. I just hadn't realized how far I would have to go. It feels like a pilgrimage to my future.

Beth's shoes are slightly too big and wet; I hardly manage to keep them on. Finally, when I'm worried daylight might break before I find their property, I do. I must have walked six miles at least.

All the way, I thanked God, or the devil, or the Easter Bunny, that my live stream was silent. I think about what I will tell my followers. Whatever I come up with, I know it will be good. They say everything happens for a reason.

I kick off Beth's shoes and climb the steps that lead from the dock up to the house. A motion-sensored light flashes on, and I nearly jump out of my skin. I remember Beth saying she'd turned the security cameras off. I plan to double-check that she wasn't wrong. Beth is a liar, or rather, was a liar. Just thinking of it now, thinking of her in past tense makes me smile.

The back door is unlocked, just as it was when we left. That's the funny thing about the wealthy. They never think anything bad is going to happen to them. I'll never be like that. Letting your guard down is a fool's game.

The lights are still on in the living area, but I don't bother turning on more. I can see blood has stained Beth's shoes; I guess water doesn't wash everything away. I can't set them down just yet, so I'm forced to carry them around like the bad reminder they are.

The first thing I do is check the security system, which I am relieved to find has indeed been turned off. So trusting. So stupid.

In the kitchen I roll out a thick layer of paper towels and set the shoes on them. Under the sink, I find a pair of rubber gloves, which I bet Beth never touched in her life. They're coming with me. I scrub the wine glasses, and then, bit-by-bit, I work to erase any trace that I was here. I still feel buzzed to see how everything is coming together. Not exactly how I planned, but better.

I smell like Tom's blood. Musky and metallic. This must be what freedom and money smell like when you put them together. Just an hour ago, I was someone's wife. Just an hour ago, I was nearly a drowning victim. Now, I'm a widow. A soon to be *rich* widow. I'll never know why they didn't drown me on that dock, or more simply, just blow my brains out. I'll never know why they chose a joyride in the dark instead. Tom always said you can't explain illogical acts with reason. I chose well with him. It's funny how things work out in the end. I'm glad he was such a cheapskate. More for me now. The long game, I think it's called. I really shouldn't forget. All that worry, and over what? I make a mental note for next time.

At last, I shower, and then I have to double and triple check everything. I feel like Tom would be proud. I can't take the risk of making even a minor mistake. I am not Goldilocks and these are not the three bears. This is real life, and mistakes will get you caught.

When I'm all fresh and clean, I choose something from Beth's closet. I consider taking something as a memento, something other than the Chanel dress I slip into. But I don't want to be tied in any way to this house or to this night, and as much as I know it will kill me to discard the vintage dress I've selected when the time comes, I know I will be better for it in the end.

It's just a dress. I will have enough money to buy my own Chanel and my own lake house. In fact, I will have something better. I will have things no one can take away. Not my parents, not my husband, no one. I will have the power and the influence I've always wanted. God knows, I've earned it.

When everything is neat and tidy, scoured clean, brushed of evidence—just as they would have wanted it—I walk to the nearest gas station, which is another five miles away. From there I call Adam.

"I can't pick you up," he informs me.

"Well, what do you expect me to do? My phone is in your trunk. I don't have any money. And I wouldn't be in this situation if it weren't for you."

"Yes you would."

"You kidnapped me!"

"I had to," he says.

"I was terrified. I never saw your face. Jesus, I uploaded what I thought were my final moments to Instalook…I had no idea it was you behind this. Your shenanigans—your lack of communication— it could have ruined everything."

There's a long silence neither of us rushes to fill.

"Adam?"

"Hold on," he sighs before another layer of silence blankets the conversation, smothering the words we're both thinking but won't say.

When he comes back on the line, he gives me a credit card number. "You'll have to call a ride-share. I can't leave now."

I don't have anything to write it down. He doesn't hide his annoyance when I mention this. "Four numbers, four times. Surely, you can manage sixteen digits."

I exhale into the receiver.

Adam spits the numbers out once again.

This time, I do remember. Tom would be proud. They will come in handy.

"It's the church card," he tells me. Just in case I get any ideas.

CHAPTER THIRTY

MELANIE

When you rule something out, you limit your focus. Thankfully, I'm smarter than that. But I am disappointed. To say the least. I'm particularly pissed Adam expected me to use that credit card. Surely, he would have known that to do so would have been too close for comfort. He had to have understood it would've linked me to the scene. I guess I shouldn't be too surprised. This wasn't the first time he betrayed me. Nor was it likely to be the last. If only Adam hadn't failed the test. I really wanted to believe in him.

Everyone slips up at some point

Just not me. When the driver delivered me to my house, I simply ran in and grabbed cash. I refuse to have my every movement tracked and traced. I won't be tied to that lake house in any way.

Afterward, I was so tired that I dropped to Tom's side of the bed and fell fast asleep. I dreamed that I woke up and my husband was downstairs making bacon and eggs. Only in my dream, my husband wasn't Tom. Then the doorbell rings and my stomach sinks. In my dream, I realize I am going to live the same day, thousands of times, a lifetime of times, unless something is done.

Unfortunately, sometimes the dream world and real life collide because I am ripped from my dream to find the doorbell really is ringing, and it is because there are cops at my door. This is never a pleasant situation to wake to.

"Are you Melanie Anderson?" they ask when I open the door. Pretty standard stuff.

I fold my arms over my chest. "I am."

"I'm afraid there's been an accident involving your husband."

I blink rapidly. *Once. Twice. Three times.*

"What kind of accident?"

The woman cop leans forward as though she's rehearsed her lines a dozen times. "I'm sorry to tell you your husband didn't make it, Mrs. Anderson."

I drop to my knees. I try to cry, I really give it my best effort. But nothing comes. She's supposed to use the word dead. Or some form of it. I read that once. I blink again, when I look up at them. Maybe if I hear the word, it will stir something. "Is he dead?"

They glance at one another. "Is there someone we can call?"

I don't answer. There is someone, yes. But I can't tell them. It's not wise to start there.

"Mrs. Anderson?"

"Beth."

"Beth?"

"My best friend."

Again, they look at each other.

Then they break the news about the Joneses. They ask me questions. More routine stuff. Did I know them to be drinkers? Did I know they planned to go boating? Did they often take the boat out at night?

"Yes," I say to all of it. *Tom told me he was stopping by after work to pick up some paperwork. He was supposed to come straight home afterward. I fell asleep and didn't realize he hadn't.*

They follow me into the kitchen. Flashes of the way things were come at me from the side, like ambushes. Or at least I want them to. I have to evoke some sort of emotion, otherwise eyebrows might be raised. Tom's mug is there by the coffee pot as though it's waiting to be filled. The ordinary, a reminder, poking at me. The angle just right. A knife in the back. The sight of it knocks the wind out of me. Tears fall, I lie, and in some ways, things haven't changed that much.

The officers explain that they found the wreckage just after daylight, when a fishing boat saw smoke. Is there someone that could identify the body?

I say I want to do it.

They advise this isn't a good idea. Before I know it I am sobbing—wailing, to be exact. I'm just so thankful to be out from under the life sentence I'd agreed to at the altar.

Adam can do it, I tell them finally. Let it be a warning to him. It probably won't serve as a sufficient warning, since Adam still thinks I bailed from the boat prior to the accident. He thinks Beth and Tom hauled me into the water in hopes that I would drown. He doesn't know what I'm capable of. Yet.

Of the three of them, Adam tells me Mark was the most recognizable. Blunt force trauma did the job, but the rest of him was in good shape. He could have been sleeping.

And Beth? I'd asked. Her neck was snapped in two. Her body bloated from the water.

I don't ask about Tom. Adam volunteers. He was bruised a bit. But that's just how dead bodies look, he said. Adam is a liar. And sadly, an almost believable one. It's okay; we all have our secrets, I guess.

~

Secrets do a lot of things. They make you exciting. They make you adventurous. They make you important. But there comes a point where having a secret without anybody knowing loses its fun. And while, maybe you don't necessarily want to let others in on what that secret is, you at least want them to know you have one.

I tell myself no one will ever know I killed Tom.

Soon, someone has to know.

Maybe it will be Adam I confide in. Sometimes saying nothing says too much.

After all, he started this whole thing that night in a hotel bar. If it had not been for him, I'd be back at my parents. I'd be happily married to someone who wasn't Tom. If it weren't for him, I would not be Melanie Anderson. I shouldn't have fallen in love with him. I shouldn't have played his silly, dangerous game.

Agreeing to that dinner was the start of something. It was the start of secrets neither one of us knew the magnitude of. What I did know then was he wanted power. He wanted to lead New Hope, and he had a plan to propel himself to the top. He said that if I wanted in, there was money to be made. Money sounded nice. But what I really wanted was a home. I wanted something of my own. I wanted not to have to go crawling back to my parents, tail tucked neatly between my legs. I wanted someone to love me. In the end, we both got what we wanted, I suppose. You have to pick your enemies carefully because the way those enemies fight is who you become. It's too bad so much damage was done in the process.

~

I GUT THE HOUSE. I DON'T WANT TO STAY HERE, BUT I CAN'T SELL IT too soon. I had half-expected that Tom's adult children might have contested the will, but they don't. It's apparent that they have moved on with their lives and prefer to leave the past in the past. Tom had told me that he gave them their mother's life insurance settlement, and that they were set. The looks on their faces at the funeral tell me they are sadder about what could have been than what they actually lost. I think about my own parents dying someday. I think I can relate.

Your father loved you, I said to them. He talked about you all the time.

I don't know if they knew I was lying because this time I tried really hard.

Truthfully, Tom rarely spoke of his kids. But then, Tom was private about the things he cared about, and in the end this is how I won. It was his arrogance that blinded him. He wanted to take care of everything, his way, and in the end, I guess he did.

The investigation into the accident was simple enough. I wonder if Tom thought that through. That's the only thing that still bothers me, really. That I'll never know.

Three people go out on a boat. Two of them have alcohol levels near or above the legal limit. One is simply an innocent. A byproduct of trusting too much.

The service for Tom was nice. Quiet, contained. Simple. Cheap, like he would have wanted.

Beth and Mark's was the exact opposite of that. It was quite the affair, and as leaders of New Hope this made sense. Their bodies weren't even cold yet before a change of hands took place. Like the presidency, Adam told me. This is how it works. It's that important. Beth wrote it into the agreement herself. I bet she hadn't planned for this kind of ending.

It didn't take long to find the money Tom transferred. He was good, but then, so was his secretary. She had the transfers he'd made reversed within a few days. Maybe he'd intended to cover his tracks better, but never got the chance. More likely, she knew him better than he thought. Who knows? Some questions are better left unanswered.

~

A FEW WEEKS AFTER THINGS SETTLE, ADAM AND CHERYL HOST THE

quarterly dinner for newcomers. The party is bigger and better than anything we've done before, Adam assures me. No one expects me to be here, considering. I've lost so much. But I've gained something too. A church family. I always mention that. It makes people feel good.

Under Adam's leadership, we will take things to new levels. New Hope is going to be better, bigger. We're opening in three cities next month, and two more the month after that. We have a brand new rejuvenation center in the works and are in the process of drawing up plans for a new resort-like community. Thanks to my Instalook game we are doing well. *Sell, sell, sell.* That's what I do. You wouldn't believe the brand deals you can score if you're good and you're willing to deceive people appropriately. Companies practically throw free stuff at me. I have a whole room in the house dedicated to it, and I had to hire an assistant just to manage it all. You wouldn't believe how much work it is with the scheduling. You really have to plan it all out. You can't use competing products back to back, and that doesn't even count the time it takes to photograph yourself using the stuff —or filtering and photoshopping the photos. It's basically more than a full-time job. Kind of like what real advertising companies used to do. Only now anyone can do it. If they have influence, that is. If they're likable, which I totally am. And who cares that half of it is overpriced crap made by children in sweatshops? My followers eat it up, and the direct deposits in my bank account say none of that matters. *Sell. Sell. Sell.* That's what I do these days. Beth would appreciate this.

And thanks to the Women's Alliance I created, the church is raking in just as much cash as I am.

"Hey, you." Someone grabs my wrist. When I turn I see Vanessa.

I smile. "I wasn't sure you were coming."

"Me, miss a good party? Are you kidding?"

"You look great," I tell her, and it's true. She has a bit of light back in her eyes.

"It's the vitamins."

We laugh like it's an inside joke.

We have a new brand of vitamins. I worked with a drug manufacturer personally to come up with something fitting. It's important to keep our men young and healthy. "If we are taking them," I said to the Women's Alliance at our first meeting, "So should they."

"Will it get them to pick up their socks?" a woman asked.

"It will do better than that," I assured her. "Just wait and see."

That was my moment. It was the moment I knew I had them in my pocket. It was the moment I became the heroine of my story. Maybe theirs, too.

"To vitality," I said.

Of course, the men don't take them willingly. The Woman's Alliance came up with a plan for that.

"I hear you're really shaking things up," Vanessa tells me, glancing around the room.

"Not too much. It's more like boiling a frog."

She smiles, and it feels good to see her happy. Of everything, maybe this is what I'm most proud of. I have a real friend. Vanessa needs me. "Do you really think it's okay? What I'm doing?"

"Yes," I reply. "You have to get back in the business of taking what you want, rather than thinking you need to shove it away so it'll find its way back."

"Take what I want?"

"Why not?" I tell her. "Everyone else does."

"You have a point," she says, looking around at all the secondhand opinions in the room. There are too many to count.

"But really though," I offer, changing the subject. "You look great. What are you doing?"

"It's all the treatments." We can both see she is lying.

Across the room, there's an uproar of laughter. My eyes search until they meet Adam's. His arm is draped around his wife. "It's not fair that she gets all the credit," Vanessa says with a nod. "We all know it's you who is doing the work."

"Ah, it's fine…I can't complain."

"No," she tells me. "I suppose you're smarter than that."

~

My options are wide open. I've had three offers of marriage so far. Just not the one I want. Funny, how men are quite peculiar that way. Always varying alliances, vying for self-interests. Whatever. Now that I don't need the money, now that I don't need a home or friends, because I have all those things, I hardly need a man. Plus, I have something better than any of that, something better than money even. I wasn't sure there was such a thing. As it turns out, there is. For the first time in my life, I have power.

People look up to me. Tom's death may have been unexpected. But I have handled it well. That's not to say I don't miss being someone's wife. Having all the boxes mostly checked was nice. That's where Adam comes in.

Later, I sidle up to him. "We should find a dark corner somewhere."

This used to make him smile. These days he's too on edge to entertain such indulgences.

His fingertips brush mine. I've never wanted anything more in my life.

Wanting something and having it is not the same thing.

"Power looks good on you," I say. It's a concession. The largest I can make, considering.

His voice wavers. "You think?"

"I do. How's it feel to have so much control?"

He looks at me then. "Better than I imagined."

"You promised."

"I know," he says. And then, a concession of his own. "Wait three minutes and meet me in the guest bathroom."

"Why?" I ask. "So you can show me how powerful you are now that I've gotten you what you wanted?"

A small smile creeps up, threatening to show itself. He likes it when I remind him of what he already knows. Most people do. He shifts and then shakes his head and with it goes any trace of amusement. "No," he tells me. "So, I can give you what you want."

"About that," I start to say. But he walks away before the rest of the words slip out. I want to tell him he's a liar. I want to cause a scene. I want to raise a glass and make a toast. I want to tell everyone about his broken promises. I want to tell everyone how he said if I did what he wanted, we'd be together. And yet, he is here with his wife, sneaking off with me to the guest bathroom, giving me what's leftover. In this way, I guess not everything has changed.

~

"HAVE YOU ANY INTEREST IN PLAYING A GAME?" HE ASKS, PEELING my dress up my thighs. Only seven percent of any given message is based on the words. Thirty-eight percent comes from the tone of voice, and fifty-five percent from the speaker's body language and face. This feels like déjà vu. His expression is foolish. He has power on his mind, and illusions can blind you if you're not careful.

I want to tell him that I hate this bathroom. I hate myself for loving him. I want him to know I wish I could go back to before. Back to a time when I hadn't yet learned what it meant to love another person. But then his hands find the spots on my body he knows so well, and we speak a different language, and I don't say any of that. "Depends on the game..." I sigh.

He grins. "It's a fun one."

Like always, I believe him.

Adam comes in two minutes flat and once again, I am the one on the losing end. "Sorry," he offers. "It's just that dress. And you in it. "

"It's okay," I lie. "At least we have a minute…there's something I want to discuss with you…"

He's looking for a way out. "I don't have time."

"You owe me."

"Fine," he relents. "What is it now?"

"I want to discuss the Replacement Wife Project with you."

"That was Mark's idea." His eyes narrow. "How'd you know?"

"Tom told me." Adam isn't the only one who gets to lie.

I watch as he washes up. You can learn a lot about a person when you aren't supposed to be looking.

"I think we should see it through."

He shakes his head. "I never thought it was solid."

"Well, what else are we going to do about that wife of yours?"

"Stop," he says, checking himself in the mirror. "We have to be careful."

I stare at his reflection. He fastens his belt. "We will be," I promise, and then I wait for his eyes to find mine. I need to do something drastic. I need to show that I can handle the role of a leader. The church thinks they aren't ready for a woman yet. But then, they haven't seen what I am capable of.

"She'll get what's coming to her," I tell Adam. It makes me think of Tom, and I smile. "Everyone does, eventually."

A NOTE FROM BRITNEY

Dear Reader,

I hope you enjoyed reading *The Replacement Wife*. If you have a moment and you'd like to let me know what you thought, feel free to drop me an email. I enjoy hearing from readers.

Writing a book is an interesting adventure, it's a bit like inviting people into your brain to rummage around. *Look where my imagination took me. These are the kinds stories I like...*

That feeling is often intense and unforgettable. And mostly, a ton of fun.

With that in mind—thank you again for reading my work. I don't have the backing or the advertising dollars of big publishing, but hopefully I have something better... readers who like the same kind of stories I do. If you are one of them, please share with your friends and consider helping out by doing one (or all) of these quick things:

1. Visit my Review Page and write a 30 second review (even short ones make a big difference).

(http://britneyking.com/aint-too-proud-to-beg-for-reviews/)

Many readers don't realize what a difference reviews make but they make ALL the difference.

2. Drop me an email and let me know you left a review. This way I can enter you into my monthly drawing for signed paperback copies.

(britney@britneyking.com)

3. Point your psychological thriller loving friends to their free copies of my work. My favorite friends are those who introduce me to books I might like. **(http://www.britneyking.com)**

4. If you'd like to make sure you don't miss anything, to receive an email whenever I release a new title, sign up for my New Release Newsletter.

(https://britneyking.com/new-release-alerts/)

Thanks for helping, and for reading my work. It means a lot.

Britney King

Austin, Texas

April 2018

ABOUT THE AUTHOR

Britney King lives in Austin, Texas with her husband, children, two dogs, one ridiculous cat, and a partridge in a peach tree.

When she's not wrangling the things mentioned above, she writes psychological, domestic and romantic thrillers set in suburbia.

Without a doubt, she thinks connecting with readers is the best part of this gig. You can find Britney online here:

Email: britney@britneyking.com
Web: https://britneyking.com
Facebook: https://www.facebook.com/BritneyKingAuthor
Instagram: https://www.instagram.com/britneyking_/
Twitter: https://twitter.com/BritneyKing_
Goodreads: https://bit.ly/BritneyKingGoodreads
Pinterest: https://www.pinterest.com/britneyking_/

Happy reading.

ACKNOWLEDGMENTS

Many thanks to my family and friends for the endless ways you provide love and inspiration.

Thank you to all of my friends in the book world. From fellow authors, to the amazing bloggers who put so much effort forth simply for the love of sharing books—naming you all would be a novel in and of itself—but I trust that you know who you are. Thank you. You make this gig a ton of fun.

To my beta readers and my advanced reader team... there aren't enough words to describe the gratitude I feel for you—for being my first readers and biggest cheerleaders. To Jenny Hanson and Samantha Wiley, thank you.

Last, but certainly not least, thank you for reading. Readers are always good people. Thanks for being that.

ALSO BY BRITNEY KING

The Social Affair

The Social Affair is an intense standalone about a timeless couple who find themselves with a secret admirer they hadn't bargained for. For fans of the anti-heroine and stories told in unorthodox ways, the novel explores what can happen when privacy is traded for convenience. It is reminiscent of films such as One Hour Photo and Play Misty For Me. Classics. :)

Water Under The Bridge | Book One

Dead In The Water | Book Two

Come Hell or High Water | Book Three

The Water Series Box Set

The Water Trilogy follows the shady love story of unconventional married couple—he's an assassin—she kills for fun. It has been compared to a crazier book version of Mr. and Mrs. Smith. Also, Dexter.

Bedrock | Book One

Breaking Bedrock | Book Two

Beyond Bedrock | Book Three

The Bedrock Series Box Set

The Bedrock Series features an unlikely heroine who should have known better. Turns out, she didn't. Thus she finds herself tangled in a messy, dangerous, forbidden love story and face-to-face with a madman hell-bent on revenge. The series has been compared to Fatal Attraction, Single White Female, and Basic Instinct.

Around The Bend

Around The Bend, is a heart-pounding standalone which traces the journey of a well-to-do suburban housewife, and her life as it unravels, thanks to the secrets she keeps. If she were the only one with things she wanted to keep hidden, then maybe it wouldn't have turned out so bad. But she wasn't.

Somewhere With You / Book One

Anywhere With You / Book Two

The With You Series Box Set

The With You Series at its core is a deep love story about unlikely friends who travel the world; trying to find themselves, together and apart. Packed with drama and adventure along with a heavy dose of suspense, it has been compared to The Secret Life of Walter Mitty and Love, Rosie.

SNEAK PEEK: BEDROCK

BOOK ONE

Series Praise

"Clever, intense and addictive."

"A surprising debut. Epic storytelling full of edge- of- your- seat suspense."

"Unputdownable."

"Hypnotic and breathtakingly romantic."

"Bold and in your face from the get-go."

"A twisty and edgy page-turner. The perfect psychological thriller."

"I read this novel in one sitting, captivated by the words on the page. The suspense was startling and well-done."

"Dark and complex."

"Exhilarating and suspenseful."

"A fascinating tale of marriage, secrets, and deception."

"Fast-paced and thrilling."

"A cunning tale that won't let go..."

"Totally on the edge of my seat the whole time I was reading it, couldn't put it down!" – Book Addict Mum

"As a sequel this book works extremely well, as a stand alone thriller it is also very good but clearly readers would be left a little lost about the back story (in which case read 'Bedrock' first)." —Paul Little, Little Ebook Reviews

"I haven't felt this many emotions in a book in a very long time." – Saints and Sinners Books

"The writing... goodness... I would have never thought this was the author's first foray into Adult Romance. The writing... Again... Wonderful!! — Gretchen Anderson, Battery Operated Book Blog

In this dark and compulsive series somewhere along the lines of *Fatal Attraction* meets *Unfaithful* comes a thrilling, addictively suspenseful, and haunting story that grabs the reader, and holds them captive until the very end. For fans of psychological thrillers, suspense, and the forbidden, *The Bedrock Series* hands us a deceptively beautiful tale.

Addison Greyer knows better. Or at least she should.

Never in a million years would she have guessed she'd wind up agreeing to the sinister side-gig her tough-as-nails new boss proposes.

Until she does.

Turns out, one bad decision often leads to another.

He's troubled. She's married.

It's a dangerous game, for sure—one in which she stands to lose the most. Soon, she learns desire is not only dangerous but deadly and there's a price to be paid for her mistakes.

A pound of flesh.

Never in a million years would she have guessed how far her picturesque little suburban life would unravel.

Until it does.

She should have known better. Too bad she didn't.

BEDROCK

BRITNEY KING

COPYRIGHT

Hot Banana Press

Front Cover Design by Lisa Wilson

Back Cover Design by Britney King

Cover Image by Sebastian Kullas

Copy Editing by TW Manuscript Services

Proofread by Proofreading by the Page

First Edition: 2013

ISBN: 978-0-9892184-0-5 (Paperback)

ISBN: 978-9892184-1-2 (All E-Books)

britneyking.com

To Nannie
with love.

CHAPTER ONE

Sometimes you have to look back in order to move forward. Sometimes you find yourself in a situation where that is the *only* thing you can do, which is exactly the situation Addison Greyer found herself in when she awoke in a hazy fog with something warm and wet trickling down her face. She tried to shift, to pull herself up, but it was useless. Her body hurt and nothing was right. *This is what dying feels like.* She did her best to recall what happened *before* she was in this predicament, but nothing came and it took so much effort to try and remember. It was almost more than she could manage. She told herself to breathe. But even that hurt. She brought her fingers to her face, or at least she imagined she did. It was hard to tell. She couldn't see, she couldn't feel, not really. It was cold, *so cold.* Addison inhaled carefully. *Where am I?*

Before her brain could grasp the answer, she felt herself slipping backward, back into the darkness, back to sleep. She willed herself to wake up, to open her eyes, but it was of no use. Her brain and her eyes refused to cooperate with one another. She couldn't focus on a single thought and she went in and out of consciousness several times before finally waking to the clanking of chains. Metal on metal. One second she was here and another *there. What were those crazy boys doing now? And why can't I wake up and make them stop?*

Her head throbbed. Her heart raced and she curled further into a ball. It hurt to move, not that she could move much and there was that sound again. *Wake up, damn it. Wake up.* Finally, her eyes fluttered open, though just barely. She could see a blurry figure standing a few feet in front of her but her eyes still refused to focus and she was too dizzy in any case to determine who it was. *Focus, she told herself. What do you see, taste, smell, touch? Use your senses.* The metallic scent of blood overwhelmed her. Aside from a dry mouth, that's all she could taste. *Blood. Is this a dream and if so, how do I wake up?* She felt the chill of the concrete beneath her. Her head was too heavy to lift, but she forced herself to do it anyway. She wiggled her toes. *She wasn't dead.* Again, she heard the clanking of the chains, which made her breath catch and then a male voice. "Wake up," the voice demanded.

Who was he? Did she know that voice? She thought before she felt herself start slipping again. Suddenly she was jolted awake by something slashing her skin. That did it. She opened her eyes just as the leather whip slashed again.

"Wake up, it's time to talk," the booming voice commanded. It was muffled, disguised, it sounded as though she were hearing it from under water.

Oh my God. How did I get here?

Addison forced herself to focus. *Pain tends to help people with that.* She surveyed her surroundings and quickly realized she'd woken up in her very own version of hell. Glancing around the room, she realized it resembled a dungeon, the kind you might see on TV. The only lighting was a single bulb hanging in the far corner of the room. The room itself was cold, dark, and damp. *Basement like.* Thinking it was sweat, she reached up and wiped at the wetness on her forehead. But when she pulled her hand back all she saw was red. *Her hand instinctively went to her neck.* There was a chain around her throat, shackles on both her hands and feet and her clothes had been removed. Addison tried to get a look at the man, at the voice who spoke to her, but he was behind her, beyond her range of sight, somewhere in the dark. Plus, everything was so foggy. *Where are the boys?* She gasped. *Where are my kids? Does he have them, too?* She started to sob.

The whip struck her again. She didn't care. She couldn't make the sobs quit coming. Struck, again and again, she did her best to shield her face and withdrew into herself trying to make her body as small as possible. As she crawled into a ball, she felt a tugging on the chain around her neck. She was choking. She couldn't breathe. If it didn't stop soon, the darkness was going to take her once again and she was powerless to stop it.

The deep voice spoke again. "Look— we can do this the easy way or the hard way. It's your choice. I actually prefer the hard way, so keep it up if you like. Just know…next come the shocks."

I'm going to die here. Oh God. No, not like this, please. Please, not like this. She thought of her children. *What would they tell them?* She shook her head hoping it might help. It didn't. *Just do what he says. It's your job to figure out what he wants.*

It took everything she had to pull herself up to a sitting position but she held her palms out and then she did it. Eventually, she managed to prop herself up against the far wall of the cage. This is when he came into view, at least partially. He was wearing a ski mask with dark glasses over the eyeholes and that's when Addison realized, *he could be anybody.* Still, she knew she needed to put as much distance as she could between them. Addison felt her survival instincts kicking in.

She met his gaze head on. Not that she could see him, not really. But he could see her. He sat in a chair opposite the cage and watched her. Addison didn't speak. She wanted to beg, to plead for her life. She wanted her kids and her clothes, she wanted out of there. Something deep down told her to keep her mouth shut. So instead of saying all the things she wanted to say she simply watched him, refusing to take her eyes away, her mind running a thousand miles a minute. The two of them stayed that way for an eternity, chills ran through her, tears fell involuntarily, but she didn't look away. Until, finally, he got up from the chair and ascended stairs that were just beyond her line of sight.

He was gone. She took a deep breath in and held it before exhaling slowly. *He's gone now. He can't hurt you. Breathe. But he's coming back. Breathe.* Addison felt herself slipping again, back into the fog, and she didn't fight it. She laid herself down on the concrete floor, slowly and so carefully, unable to take the pain of each small movement. She was so tired, so weak, but it was the blood, and the awareness that he would be back that scared her most. He wanted her to suffer; that much was clear. The fog seemed like the only respite she had. It beckoned her. And she welcomed it.

ADDISON DREAMT SHE WAS SITTING ON THE PORCH SWING WATCHING the boys play with Max. They would run the entire length of the yard, and he would chase after them. They were laughing, she was laughing, and it was nice to feel the warm sunshine on her face. She was glad she could feel the breeze blow across her skin. But then the opera music began and nothing seemed right. *Why in the world would the sounds of the opera fill her backyard?* Suddenly, Addison felt her arms and her legs being pulled in opposite directions. Hard. She opened her eyes and she wasn't in her backyard at all, she was back in that cage, back in the dungeon and she was being stretched out from opposite ends. It hurt— although, for some reason the pain was dull—below the surface as though she were barely feeling it. She felt the sting of the whip across her belly, followed shortly by warm blood dripping from where the leather met her skin. She felt that. It wasn't dull. It was sharp and jarring. *But why? She asked herself. Why is he doing this? Why me?*

"Didn't I tell you to wake up?" the man said. His voice wasn't clear, she realized he was trying to disguise it, and this concerned her more than anything. If he'd planned to kill her right away, he wouldn't care whether or not she saw his face or heard him speak. But he did.

"You disobeyed me. I've told you and I've told you and I've told you. It's time to talk. But no. You're lazy. Just like the rest of them. I just hope you're a little smarter." He cocked his head. "Well… are you?" he shouted. "Are you ever going to learn your lesson?"

He walked around her until she could feel his body heat. He placed a blindfold over her eyes. She struggled but it was pointless.

"You aren't allowed to sleep," he said.

"If I find you sleeping again, the punishment is going to be worse than a whipping. Do you understand?"

Addison said nothing. She saw the hand that contained the whip rise. She held her breath just before it struck her across her thighs. It wasn't so much the pain but rather the sound of the leather hitting her skin that made her sick, it made her stomach want to empty its contents.

"So, are we clear Mrs. Greyer?" he asked toying with the whip. "From now on, when I speak to you, you show some respect."

Addison nodded. He addressed her by name, which meant he knew who she was. It also meant this was not random; it was not some sort of mistake.

"That a girl. I always took you for a quick learner."

She thought about her surroundings once again. If she was gagged, that had to mean he was afraid people would hear her. *Didn't it?* She recalled four corners of the room. Even before he'd blindfolded her, it was too dark to make out much, but she could feel that the walls were made of stone. And then, there was that smell. The stench alone overwhelmed her senses. It was pungent, a mixture of urine and alcohol standing out most. *Where am I? His basement? A warehouse?*

She felt herself floating upward. She thought she was passing out again, or perhaps this was really it. Her eyes grew wide and she struggled against her restraints.

"It's the drugs that make you feel like that," he said. "Well, that and fear…"

Suspended in the air, naked, bleeding, and weak, all she could think about was closing her eyes and pretending to be in her backyard with her children, the sun on her face. So, that's what she did. She needed to remain positive, to think of anything that would help her escape this hell. Addison forced herself to count. She was afraid she was going to lose consciousness and she'd heard his warning about sleep. He wanted her awake and now she understood why. She listened as he toyed with his whips and spikes, his tools of the trade. That was the thing about losing your senses. Everything else became more acute. This was a form of intimidation, she knew. *But how? How did she know this?*

"I know you're probably thirsty. Hungry. But since you haven't yet learned to follow the rules, you get nothing."

After a bit of tinkering, she heard him turn and once again walked up the dark stairs without a word. It may have been hours or mere minutes. She couldn't be sure. There was no concept of time. She had no idea what day of the week it was, how long she'd been there, or whether it was even day or night. It was with this thought that the tears came again. Only Addison didn't sob this time. She was too weak. Instead, silent tears ran down her cheeks, falling onto her bare breasts. She tried her best to fight off sleep and when she caught herself dozing off, she'd play games with herself, recalling a memory of her boys, and then she'd replay it over and over in her mind in order to keep herself awake. She knew she had to get through this and to do that she'd have to stay alert, if she wanted to get out alive. But then, she had to get out alive. There was no other option. Her family needed her. Her children needed her.

Throughout the time that the man was away, Addison dozed

off and on despite her best attempts. But it was fitful sleep at best. When she allowed herself to close her eyes, she made sure her sleep was light, not so different from the early days, when her boys were first born and she'd force herself to stay awake to check on them, to make sure they were still breathing.

Eventually, she heard the door creak and her eyes snapped open. Her heart raced as she listened to his footsteps fall on the stairs. Her stomach churned, unsure of what to expect. When he saw that she was awake, he chuckled. As he walked towards her, Addison's pulse raced. The closer he got, the more she squirmed. She didn't want to have this reaction, but it was innate. Her brain screamed for her to be still and to remain calm and yet the rest of her body betrayed her, giving away her fear.

She felt him remove the gag. She trembled at his proximity. "There, there. Easy does it," he whispered, trailing his cold hand down her cheek. "Don't bother screaming. No one will hear you."

Addison tensed as he moved his hand away. When she felt it on her skin again, he was holding a straw to her lips. "If we don't get some water in you, I'll have gone to all this trouble for nothing," he warned. "Now, be a good girl and take a drink."

She did as he said, taking a small sip at first, but then she couldn't stop. She kept drinking until she choked, and he pulled the straw away. "Ok, I think that's enough," he said pulling the glass away and then replacing her gag. She held her breath as he took a step back and walked around the back of her. It made her uneasy when she couldn't get a sense of where he was or what he was doing—but then, she was just as uneasy as when she could. "You look so beautiful," he murmured. "In fact, I don't think I've seen anything more beautiful in my life."

After several moments, he walked back around and stopped just in front of her. He removed the blindfold and then he stood there for a moment as her eyes adjusted, considering her. He tinkered with her chains, and when he seemed satisfied with how she was displayed, he stepped back and closed the door to the cage. She watched as he sat in a metal folding chair just outside the cage. He unbuckled his belt and removed it, laying it at his feet. Her pulse quickened and she couldn't help but look away. "Look at me, damn it," he ordered and she did as she was told. Hot, wet tears fell onto her cheeks as she met his gaze. His eyes tracked south as did hers and she could see that he was erect. "It's my turn to give you a show," he said as he began stroking himself. It took everything she had not to look away. Swallowing hard against the gag, she felt bile rise in her throat and she wondered what would happen if she were to be sick. *He will kill you*. She held her breath. She couldn't help herself. It seemed to go on forever, and she grew dizzy as the man stared a hole through her.

When he was finished, he stood, picked up his belt and unlocked the door to the cage. The hairs on the back of her neck stood as he walked around her, just as he had the time before. He circled slowly a few times and then finally paused behind her, once again out of eyesight. He replaced the blindfold and then the gag. When he'd finished, she heard him raise the belt as she braced herself for the blow she knew was coming. The belt struck across her rear, forcing all the air from her lungs. Addison gasped; she moaned and tried to say her pleas against the gag. He struck her once, twice, three times until she lost count, each blow worse than the last. Eventually, unable to take any more, long after her silent pleas ran out, as did her cries, she hung her head.

"You're a bad girl, watching me like that. You should be ashamed," he told her as he exited the cage. She listened as he placed the lock on the door. Her head felt too heavy to lift and she'd already come to her decision: if he killed her, he killed her. She could hear him dressing. She could hear his footsteps as he walked towards the dark corner. She flinched when she heard the cranking sound. It almost forced her to look up. *Almost.* Her body stiffened which only worsened the pain. She was being lowered and every inch felt like a mile. Slowly, she descended towards the cold concrete beneath her. When her body hit bottom, she'd expected it to hurt. Instead, she sighed at how good it felt against her wounded backside. She wept long after she heard the man turn and walk up the stairs. *He could be anyone, she thought. But he knew her, and he wanted her to suffer.*

As Addison lay there on the cold, hard floor, wounded and bleeding, she began to think back, trying to recall how she could have possibly ended up here. She began drifting, unaware of whether she was dreaming or awake. The images were crystal clear as they came. Piece by piece the inner-workings of her life appeared vividly before her eyes. Everything was there, every bit of it and was so colorful, so vibrant, that she wondered if she was dying. *Isn't that what everyone said happened before you die?* Still, she watched, mesmerized, all the while praying the answers she needed would come— something—*anything* that would set her free and not death, as she feared.

~

Learn more at: britneyking.com

Made in the USA
Middletown, DE
12 July 2018